Outlaw's Kiss:
Grizzlies MC Romance

Nicole Snow

Disclaimer: The following book is a work of fiction. Any resemblance characters in this story may have to real people is only coincidental.

Description

AN OUTLAW'S KISS SEDUCES, CONQUERS, AND NEVER LIES...

MISSY

The dirty little secret dad left in the basement was supposed to be our salvation. Guess nobody told him you don't take cash from killers without savage consequences.

Now, the Grizzlies Motorcycle Club owns my sister and I. We're only alive because the rugged hulk with the piercing eyes who won't stop ordering me around says so. He saved us, but he's also an enigma I don't understand.

Why does he keep calling me his old lady? Is he really the light to our darkness? And why the hell can't I stop thinking nasty, shameful things about ending up underneath his wicked tattoos and crude lips?

BRASS

I claimed her on impulse, and all my brothers laughed. Didn't know I'd end up with a smoking hot spitfire who looks at me like I'm the devil himself.

I expected my reputation to crack, but my damned mind's going with it. She's got me questioning my own club and asking myself every single day how long I can keep my hands off her.

It was only pretend, a way to keep her safe. But I can't ignore the very real brutality, corruption, and danger stalking us. Just like I can't forget the storm in my blood that won't stop howling 'til she's wearing my brand and bracing for my kiss.

Play time's over. Missy's gonna be my old lady – no more faking it – and nothing's standing in my way...

The Outlaw Love books are stand alone romance novels featuring unique lovers and happy endings. No cliffhangers! This is Brass and Missy's story, first in the Grizzlies MC series.

I: Cursed Bones (Missy)

"It won't be long now," the nurse said, checking dad's IV bag. "Breathing getting shallower...pulse is slowing...don't worry, girls. He won't feel a thing. That's what the morphine's for."

I had to squeeze his hand to make sure he wasn't dead yet. Jesus, he was so cold. I swore there was a ten degree difference between dad's fingers in one hand, and my little sister's in the other. I blinked back tears, trying to be brave for Jackie, who watched helplessly, trembling and shaking at my side.

We'd already said our goodbyes. We'd been doing that for the last hour, right before he slipped into unconsciousness for what I guessed was the last time.

I turned to my sister. "It'll be okay. He's going to a better place. No more suffering. The cancer, all the pain...it dies with him. Dad's finally getting better."

"Missy..." Jackie squeaked, ripping her hand away from me and covering her face.

The nurse gave me a sympathetic look. It took so much effort to push down the lump in my throat without cracking up. I choked on my grief, holding it in, cold and sharp as death looming large.

I threw an arm around my sister, pulling her close. Lying like this was a bitch.

I wasn't really sure what I believed anymore, but I had to say something. Jackie was the one who needed all my support now. Dad's long, painful dying days were about to be over.

Not that it made anything easy. But I was grown up, and I could handle it. Losing him at twenty-one was hard, but if I was fourteen, like the small trembling girl next to me?

"Melissa." Thin, weak fingers tightened on my wrist with surprising strength.

I jumped, drawing my arm off Jackie, looking at the sick man in the bed. His eyes were wide open and his lips were moving. The sickly sheen on his forehead glowed, one last light before it burned out forever.

"Daddy? What is it?" I leaned in close, wondering if I'd imagined him saying my name.

"Forgive me," he hissed. "I...I fucked up bad. But I did it for a good reason. I just wish I could've done it different, baby..."

His eyelids fluttered. I squeezed his fingers as tight as I could, moving closer to his gray lips. What the hell was he saying? Was this about Mom again?

She'd been gone for ten years in a car accident, waiting for him on the other side. "Daddy? Hey!"

I grabbed his bony shoulder and gently shook him. He was still there, fighting the black wave pulling him lower, insistent and overpowering.

"It's the only way...I couldn't do it with hard work. Honest work. That never paid shit." He blinked, running his tongue over his lips. "Just look in the basement, baby. There's a palate...roofing tiles. Everything I ever wanted to leave my girls is there. It was worth it...I promised her I'd do anything for you and Jackie...and I did. I did it, Carol. Our girls are set. I'm ready to burn if I need to..."

Hearing him say mom's name, and then talk about burning? I blinked back tears and shook my head.

What the hell was this? Some kinda death fever making him talk nonsense?

Dad started to slump into the mattress, a harsh rattle in his throat, the tiny splash of color left in his face becoming pale ash. I backed away as the machines howled. The nurse looked at me and nodded. She rushed to his free side, intently watching his heartbeat jerk on the monitor.

The machine released an earsplitting wail as the line went flat.

Jackie completely lost it. I grabbed her tight, holding onto her, turning away until the mechanical screaming stopped. I wanted to cover my ears, but I wanted hers closed more.

I held my little sister and rocked her to my chest. We didn't move until the nurse finally touched my shoulder, nudging us into the waiting room outside.

We sat and waited for all the official business of death to finish up. My brain couldn't stop going back to his last words, the best distraction I had to keep my sanity.

What was he talking about? His last words sounded so strange, so sure. So repentant, and that truly frightened me.

I didn't dare get my hopes up, as much as I wanted to believe we wouldn't lose everything and end up living in the car next week. The medical bills snatched up the last few pennies left over from his pension and disability – the same fate waiting for our house as soon as his funeral was done.

Delirious, I thought. *His dying wish was for us, hoping and praying we'd be okay. He went out selflessly, just like a good father should.*

That was it. Had to be.

He was dying, after all...pumped full of drugs, driven crazy in his last moments. But I couldn't let go of what he said about the basement.

We'd have to scour the house anyway before the state kicked us out. If there was anything more to his words besides crazy talk, we'd find out soon enough, right?

I looked at Jackie, biting my lip. I tried not to hope off a dead man's words. But damn it, I did.

If he'd tucked away some spare cash or some silver to pawn, I wouldn't turn it down. Anything would help us live another day without facing the gaping void left by his brutal end.

My sister was tipped back in her chair, one tissue pressed tight to her eyes. I reached for her hand and squeezed, careful not to set her off all over again.

"We're going to figure this out," I promised. "Don't worry about anything except mourning him, Jackie. You're not going anywhere. I'm going to do my damnedest to find us a place and pay the bills while you stay in school."

She straightened up, clearing her throat, shooting me a nasty look. "Stop talking to me like I'm a stupid kid!"

I blinked. Jackie leaned in, showing me her bloodshot eyes. "I'm not as old as you, sis, but I'm not retarded. We're out of money. I get that. I know you won't find a job in this shitty town with half a degree and no experience...we'll end up homeless, and then the state'll get involved. They'll take me away from you, stick me with some freaky foster parents. But I won't forget you, Missy. I'll be okay. I'll survive."

Rage shot through me. Rage against the world, myself, maybe even dad's ghost for putting us in this fucked up position.

I clenched my jaw. "That's *not* going to happen, Jackie. Don't even go there. I won't let–"

"Whatever. It's not like it matters. I just hope there's a way for us to keep in touch when the hammer falls." She was quiet for a couple minutes before she finally looked up, her eyes redder than before. "I heard what he said while I was crying. Daddy didn't have crap after he got sick and left the force – nothing but those measly checks. He didn't earn a dime while he was sick. He died the same way he lived, Missy – sorry, and completely full of shit."

Anger howled through me. I wanted to grab her, shake her, tell her to get a fucking grip and stop obsessing on disaster. But I knew she didn't mean it.

Lashing out wouldn't do any good. Rage was all part of

grief, wasn't it? I kept waiting for mine to bubble to the surface, toxic as the crap they'd pumped into our father to prolong his life by a few weeks towards the end.

I settled back in my chair and closed my eyes. I'd find some way to keep my promise to Jackie, whether there was a lucky break waiting for us in the basement or just more junk, more wreckage from our lives.

Daddy wasn't ready to be a single father when Mom got killed, but he'd managed. He did the best he could before he had to deal with the shit hand dealt to him by this merciless life. I closed my eyes, vowing I'd do the same.

No demons waiting for us on the road ahead would stop me. Making sure neither of us died with dad was my new religion, and I swore I'd never, ever lose my faith.

A week passed. A lonely, bitter week in late winter with a meager funeral. Daddy's estranged brother sent us some money to have him cremated and buried with a bare bones headstone.

I wouldn't ask Uncle Ken for a nickel more, even if he'd been man enough to show his face at the funeral. Thankfully, it wasn't something to worry about. He kept his distance several states away, the same 'ostrich asshole' daddy always said he was since they'd fallen out over my grandparent's miniscule inheritance.

All it did was confirm the whole family was fucked. I had no one now except Jackie, and it was her and I against the world, the last of the Thomas girls against the curse turning our lives to pure hell over the last decade.

A short trip to the attorney's office told me what I already knew about dad's assets. What little he had was going into state hands. Medicare was determined to claw back a tiny fraction of what they'd spent on his care. And because I was now Jackie's legal guardian, his pension and disability was as good as buried with him.

The older lawyer asked me if I'd made arrangements with extended family, almost as an afterthought. Of course I had, I lied. I made sure to straighten up and smile real big when I said it.

I was a responsible adult. I could make money sprout from weeds. What did the truth matter in a world that wasn't wired to give us an ounce of help?

Whatever shit was waiting for us up ahead needed to be fed, nourished with lies if I wanted to keep it from burying us. I was ready for that, ready to throw on as many fake smiles and twisted truths as I needed to keep Jackie safe and happy.

Whatever wiggle room we'd had for innocent mistakes slammed shut the instant daddy's heart stopped in the sharp white room.

I was so busy dealing with sadness and red tape that I'd nearly forgotten about his last words. Finishing up his affairs and making sure Jackie still got some sleep and decent food in her belly took all week, stealing away the meager energy I had left.

It was late one night after she'd gone to bed when I finally remembered. It hit me while I was watching a bad spy movie on late night TV, halfway paying attention to the story as my stomach twisted in knots, steeling itself for the frantic job hunt I had to start tomorrow.

I got up from my chair and padded over to the basement door. Dust teased my nose, dead little flecks suspended in the dim light. The basement stank like mildew, tinged with rubbing alcohol and all the spare medicine we'd stored down here while dad suffered at home.

I held my breath descending the stairs, knowing it would only get worse when I finally had to inhale. Our small basement was dark and creepy as any. I looked around, trying not to fixate on his old work bench. Seeing the old husks of half-finished RC planes he used to build in better times would definitely bring tears.

Roofing tiles, he'd said. Okay, but where?

It took more than a minute just scanning back and forth before I noticed the big blue tarp. It was wedged in the narrow slit between the furnace and the hot water tank.

My heart ticked faster. So, he wasn't totally delusional on his death bed. There really were roofing tiles there – and what else?

It was even stranger because the thing hadn't been here when I was down in the basement last week – and daddy had been in hospice for three weeks. He couldn't have crawled back and hidden the unknown package here. Jackie definitely couldn't have done it and kept her mouth shut.

That left one disturbing possibility – someone had broken into our house and left it here.

Ice ran through my veins. I shook off wild thoughts

about intruders, kneeling down next to the blue plastic and running my hands over it.

Yup, it felt like a roofing palate. Not that I'd handled many to know, but whatever was beneath it was jagged, sandy, and square.

Screw it. Let's see what's really in here, I thought.

Clenching my teeth, I dragged the stack out. It was lighter than I expected, and it didn't take long to find the ropey ties holding it together. One pull and it came off easy. A thick slab of shingles slid out and thudded on the beaten concrete, kicking up more dust lodged in the utilities.

I covered my mouth and coughed. Disappointment settled in my stomach, heavy as the construction crap in front of me. I prepared myself for a big fat nothing hidden in the cracks.

"Damn it," I whispered, shaking my head. My hands dove for the shingles and started to tug, desperate to get this shit over with and say goodbye to the last hope humming in my stomach.

The shingles didn't come up easy. Planting my feet on both sides and tugging didn't pull the stack apart like I expected. Grunting, I pulled harder, taking my rage and frustration out on this joke at my feet.

There was a ripping sound much different than I expected. I tumbled backward and hit the dryer, looking at the square block in my hands. When I turned it over, I saw the back was a mess of glue and cardboard.

Hope beat in my chest again, however faint. This was no

ordinary stack of shingles. My arms were shaking as I dropped the flap and walked back to the pile, looking down at the torn cardboard center hidden by the layer I'd peeled off. Someone went through some serious trouble camouflaging the box underneath.

I walked to dad's old bench for a box cutter, too stunned with the weird discovery to dwell on his mementos. The blade went in and tore through in a neat slice. I quickly carved out an opening, totally unprepared for the thick leafy pile that came falling out.

My jaw dropped along with the box cutter. I hit the ground, resting my knees on the piles of cash, and tore into the rest of the box.

Hundreds – no, thousands – came out in huge piles. I tore through the package and turned it upside down, showering myself in more cash than I'd seen in my life, hundreds bound together in crisp rolls with red rubber bands.

Had to cover my mouth to stifle the insane laughter tearing at my lungs. I couldn't let Jackie hear me and come running downstairs. If I was all alone, I would've laughed like a psycho, mad with the unexpected light streaking to life in our darkness.

Jesus, I barely knew how to handle the mystery fortune myself, let alone involve my little sis. I collapsed on the floor, feeling hot tears running down my cheeks. The stupid grin pulling at my face lingered.

Somehow, someway, he'd done it. Daddy had really done it.

He'd left us everything we'd need to survive. Hell, all we'd need to *thrive*. Feeling the cool million crunching underneath my jeans like leaves proved it.

"Shit!" I swore, realizing I was rolling around in the money like a demented celebrity.

Panicking, I kicked my legs, careful to check every nook around me for anything I'd kicked away in shock. When I saw it was all there, I grabbed an old laundry basket and started piling the stacks in it. I pulled one out and took off the rubber band. Rifling my fingers through several fistfuls of cash told me everything was separated in neat bundles of twenty-five hundred dollars.

I piled them in, feverishly counting. I had to stop around the half million mark. There was at least double that on the floor. Eventually, I'd settle down and inventory it to the dime, but for now I was looking at somewhere between one to two million, easy.

It was magnitudes greater than anything this family had seen in its best years, before everything went to shit. I smoothed my fingers over my face, loving the unmistakable money scent clinging to my hands.

No shock – sweet freedom smelled exactly like cold hard cash.

An hour later, I'd stuffed it into an old black suitcase, something discreet I could keep with me. My stomach gurgled. One burden lifted, and another one landed on my shoulders.

I wasn't stupid. I'd heard plenty about what daddy did for the Redding PD's investigations to know spending too much mystery money at once brought serious consequences. Wherever this money came from, it sure as hell wasn't clean.

I'd have to keep one eye glued to the cash for...months? Years?

Shit. Grim responsibility burned in my brain, and it made my bones hurt like they were locked in quicksand. Dirty money wasn't easy to spend.

I'd have to risk a few bigger chunks up front on groceries, a tune-up for our ancient Ford LTD, and then a down payment on a new place for Jackie and I.

It wouldn't buy us a luxury condo – not if we wanted to save ourselves a Federal investigation. But this cash was plenty to make a greedy landlord's eyes light up and take a few months' worth of rent without any uncomfortable questions. It was more than enough to give us food plus a roof over our heads while I figured out the rest.

Survival was still the name of the game, even if it had gotten unexpectedly easier.

Once our needs were secure, then I could figure out the rest. Maybe I'd find a way to finagle my way back into school so I could finish the accounting program I'd been forced to drop when dad's cancer went terminal.

It felt like hours passed while I finished filling up the suitcase and triple checked the basement for runaway money. When I was finally satisfied I'd secured everything, I grabbed the suitcases and marched upstairs, turning out the light behind me. I switched off the TV and headed straight for bed.

I sighed, knowing I was in for a long, restless night, even with the miracle cash safe beneath my bed. Or maybe because of it.

I couldn't tell if my heart or my head was more drained. They'd both been absolutely ripped out and shot to the moon these past two weeks.

I closed my eyes and tried to sleep. Tomorrow, I'd be hunting for a brand new place instead of a job while Jackie caught up on schoolwork. That happy fact alone should've made it easier to sleep.

But nothing about this was simple or joyful. It wasn't a lottery win.

Dwelling on the gaping canyon left in our lives by both our dead parents was a constant brutal temptation, especially when it was dark, cold, and quiet. So was avoiding the question that kept boiling in my head – how had he gotten it?

What the *fuck* had daddy done to make this much money from nothing? Life insurance payouts and stock dividends didn't get dropped off in mysterious packages downstairs.

He'd asked for forgiveness before his body gave out. My lips trembled and I pinched my eyes shut, praying he hadn't done something terrible – not directly, anyway. He was too sick for too long to kill anyone. He'd been off the force for a few years too.

I lost minutes – maybe hours – thinking about how he'd earned the dirty little secret underneath my bed. Whatever he'd done, it was bad. But at the end of the day, how much did I care?

And no matter how much blood the cash was soaked in, we needed it. I wasn't about to latch onto fantasy ethics and flush his dying legacy down the toilet. Blood money or not, we *needed* it. No fucking way was I going to burn the one thing that would keep us fed, clothed, sheltered, and sane.

Jackie never had to know where our miracle came from. Neither did I. Maybe years from now I'd have time for soul searching, time to worry about what kind of sick sins I'd branded onto my conscience by profiting off this freak inheritance.

Fretting about murder and corruption right now wouldn't keep the state from taking Jackie away when we were homeless. I had to keep my mouth shut and my mind more closed than ever. I had to treat it like a lottery win I could never tell anyone about.

Besides, it was all just temporary. I'd use the fortune to pay the rent and put food in our fridge until I finished school and got myself a job. Then I'd slowly feed the rest into something useful for Jackie's college – something that wouldn't get us busted.

It must've been after three o'clock when I finally fell asleep. If only I had a crystal ball, or stayed awake just an hour or two longer.

I would've seen the hurricane coming, the pitch black storm that always comes in when a girl takes the hand the devil's offered.

An earsplitting scream woke me first, but it was really the door slamming a second later that convinced me I wasn't dreaming.

Jackie!

I threw my blanket off and sat up, reaching for my phone on the nightstand. My hand slid across the smooth wood, and adrenaline dumped in my blood when I realized there was nothing there.

Too dark. I didn't realize the stranger was standing right over me until I tried to bolt up, slamming into his vice-like grip instead. Before I could even scream, his hand was over my mouth. Scratchy stubble prickled my cheek as his lips parted against my ear.

"Don't. You fucking scream, I'll have to put a bullet in your spine." Cold metal pushed up beneath my shirt, a gun barrel, proof he wasn't making an empty threat.

Not that I'd have doubted it. His tight, sinister embrace stayed locked around my waist as he turned me around and nudged his legs against mine, forcing me to move toward the hall.

"Just go where I tell you, and this'll all be over nice and quick. Nobody has to get hurt."

I listened. When we got to the basement door, he flung it open and lightened his grip, knowing it was a one way trip downstairs with no hope for escape.

Jackie was already down there against the wall, and so were four more large, brutal men like the one who'd held me. I blinked when I got to the foot of the stairs and took in the bizarre scene. They all wore matching leather vests with GRIZZLIES MC, CALIFORNIA emblazoned up their sides and on their backs.

I'd seen bikers traveling the roads for years, but never anything like these guys. Their jackets looked a lot like the ones veterans wore when they went out riding, but the symbols were all different. Bloody, strange, and very dangerous looking.

The men themselves matched the snarling bears on their leather. Four of them were younger, tattooed, spanning the spectrum from lean and wiry to pure muscle. The guy who'd walked me down the stairs moved where I could see him. He might've been the youngest, but I wasn't really sure.

Scary didn't begin to describe him. He looked at me with his arms folded, piercing green eyes going right through my soul, set in a stern cold face. He exuded a strength and severity that only came naturally – a born badass. A predator completely fixed on me.

An older man with long gray hair seemed to be in charge. He looked at the man holding my sister, another hard faced man with barbed wire ropes tattooed across his face. Jackie's eyes were bulging, shimmering like wide, frantic pools, pulling me in.

I'm sorry, I hissed in my head, breaking eye contact. One more second and I might've lost it. The only thing worse than being down here at their mercy was showing them I was already weak, broken, helpless.

They had my little sister, my whole world, everything I'd sworn to protect. No, this wasn't the time to freak out and cry. I had to keep it together if we were going to get out of this alive.

"Well? Any sign of the haul upstairs, or do we need to make these bitches sing?" Gray hair reached into his pocket, retrieving a cigarette and a lighter, as casually as if he was at work on a smoke break.

Shit, for all I knew, he probably was.

"Nothing up there, Blackjack." The man who'd taken me downstairs stepped forward, leaving the basement echoing with his smoky voice, older and more commanding than I'd expected. It hadn't just been the rough whisper flowing into my ear.

"Fuck," the psycho holding Jackie growled. "I like it the fun way, but I'm not a fan when these bitches scream. Makes my ears ring for days. Can't we gag these cunts first?"

Nobody answered him. The older man narrowed his eyes, looking at his goon, taking a long pull on the cigarette. My head was spinning, making it feel like the ground had softened up, ready to suck me under and bury me alive.

Oh, God. I knew this had to be about the mystery money the moment those rough hands went around me, but I hadn't really thought we were about to die until he said that.

Gray hair turned to face me, scowling. "You heard the man, love. We can do this the easy way or the hard way. I, for one, don't like spilling blood when there's no good reason, but some of the brothers feel differently. Now, we know your loot's not where it was supposed to be – found this shit all torn up myself."

Blowing his smoke, he pointed at the mess on the ground. I could've choked myself for being too stupid to clean up the mess earlier.

"You've got it somewhere. It couldn't have gotten far," he said, striding forward. "Look we both know me and my boys are gonna find it. Only question left is – are you gonna make this scavenger hunt easy-peasy-punkin-squeezy? Or are you gonna make all our fucking ears ring while we choke it out of you?"

I didn't answer. My eyes floated above his shoulder, fixing on the man across from me, stoic green eyes.

"Well?" The older asshole was getting impatient.

Strange. If Green Eyes wasn't so busy hanging out with these creeps and taking hostages, he would've been handsome. No, downright sexy was a better word.

My weeping, broken brain was still fixed on the stupid idea when Gray Hair grunted, pulled the light out of his mouth, and reached for my throat.

II: A Day in the Life (Brass)

Hours Earlier

Fuck!

Twinkie's mouth on my dick woke me up. Didn't have a clue how long she'd been sucking, but I was ready to blow. Growling, I opened my eyes and shoved one hand behind her ass, reaching for the wet, pink silk I'd fucked and filled before I crashed out around noon.

Soon as she saw I was awake, the slut began to purr. She did this desperate, throaty thing that vibrated through her cheeks, a special twist that always sent hot pulses straight to my balls. No joke – her trademark finish was like having the world's greatest vacuum hooked to my cock.

I found her clit and pinched it 'til she moaned. Bitch never skipped a beat, furiously bobbing her head up and down.

Too much. Too goddamned early.

"You better swallow every fucking drop. Don't want none of that shit leaking where it don't belong when we're done. Ah...shit. Ah – fuck!"

Her tongue went full fan on my dick. I stuffed it as far

as she could take down her throat and let loose, grinding my hand between her legs like a madman, feeling her pussy gush while my load filled her mouth.

Fuck, she was good. But not half as awesome as a hit of the shit that still filled my dreams while I was out.

It took months to get clean, get my head straight, remember there was more to being a full patch member of the Grizzlies Motorcycle Club than easy smack and endless pussy. Thank fuck for Fang and the brothers, especially Blackjack. If it wasn't for our Enforcer taking me under his wing since I got to Redding, it would've been all too easy to fall back into old habits.

My balls pulsed and shot pure sweet fire to my head. The fire lashed through me as it left my dick in waves.

Too bad my fucked up brain hadn't stopped missing the orgasm on steroids good smack used to give me. Now, this was the best I could do, fucking every pussy, ass, and mouth I could find, hoping it'd give me one one-thousandth of the ecstasy I got from pouring that crap in my veins.

"Mmmm," Twinkie purred, wiping her mouth. "Was this the kinda wake up call you were hoping for, baby? I know what you like, old man..."

I blinked, reaching underneath the bed for my pants. "I'm not your baby, Twink, and you're sure as fuck not my old lady. Get yourself a glass of water and get the fuck out."

She pouted. I grunted, throwing on my boxers and wriggling into my jeans as she headed for my cramped bathroom. The slut really wanted to latch herself onto somebody in the club – she'd be back between my sheets tomorrow if I wanted her.

Same old song and dance. One thing was for sure – sucking and fucking took the edge off old addictions. The girl was medicine to me, and nothing more, same as all the easy pussy who swarmed around this clubhouse like moths drawn to big, tattooed, foul mouthed flames.

If the girls realized half the world of shit this club was facing, I didn't think they'd be so bold. Shit was getting serious. I almost dreaded having to throw on my cut and get my ass out there.

Fang's iron fist clenched tighter every day. Hadn't taken me long to figure out how he'd gotten to be national Prez. Brains and brutality were the ticket, but lately, the shit he ordered was beyond the pale. I was damned lucky they'd let me take a ride to Reno a few weeks ago for my sis' wedding.

Technically, the club was on lockdown. We were at war, a savage war we were losing to the Mexican boys pouring across the border, kicking us in the nuts when we least suspected it.

Dunno how I kept it together watching Shelly tie the knot with Blaze, Prez of the Prairie Pussies up in Montana, no less. I would've loved to draw knives and have it out with those assholes. Would've loved to slice the throat of any sneak cartel fuck who came after me too. But I owed sis a hug, a kiss, and my congratulations hissed through clenched teeth.

Celebrating her happiness meant something – even if she found it marrying a total dick from an MC we'd been fighting with not so long ago.

"Brass!" A loud knock at the door followed the booming voice. "Better shake your ass, bro. Crack's rounding up the guys for church and he's gonna be pissed if you're late again."

Fuck. I told Rabid I'd be out in a minute, soon as the slut was finished pissing behind the door.

Twinkie and the rest of the girls weren't just into riding dick, hoping to land an old man. A couple got caught early this year sneaking cash and valuables outta brothers' rooms. Yeah, they had their asses kicked to the curb – sometimes literally – whenever they were caught. But fuck if I was taking the chance leaving this girl alone with my meager belongings.

The little blonde came striding out a second later, straightening her thong. I scooped her clothes together and threw them at her.

"Get your shit on and hurry the fuck up. I need to get outta here, and you better be gone first. Club business."

She nodded. I folded my arms, watching her cover up her tits and ass. My dick stirred, insatiable as ever. Must've been all this stress.

I gave her one more swat on the way out. She giggled, a high whiny sound that made me wanna swing her around, slam her on the bed, and fuck her all over again.

The clubhouse smelled like shit when I got outside, locking the door behind me. Damned prospects were

22

slacking on the fucking job. Too damned distracted with the cartel drama, just like the rest of us. Cans and broken glass crunched underneath my feet, burned joints and bags of chips, needles and used condoms.

Pretty fucking amazing Fang got anything done at all in this dump. But the Prez barely left his office anymore. He was way too busy screaming at our boys in other states and melting down when the latest disaster came through the phone. Otherwise, he was riding our asses like a maniac, demanding results nobody could deliver.

The cartel was kicking our ass in SoCal. The Mexicans were creeping north, slowly and surely. No sooner than I got back from Reno, the place was crawling with rumors about hit men in town, gunning to cut our throats in our sleep and decapitate our whole fucking club by taking out its head.

We'd already surrendered Sacramento, home to the original mother charter. Fang had no choice but to retreat north to Redding with his crew. Regroup, scheme, and hit them back – that had to be the plan – except we hadn't quite gotten to the hitting part.

A big hand slapped my shoulder. "Looks like we're gonna beat Serial and Splitter after all. Let's leave those fucks to get the evil eye."

I grinned at Rabid and followed him into the big meeting room. The officers were all lined up at the head of the table, and more than a dozen brothers milled around at the other end.

Crack, our VP, looked more pissed off than ever when

he was sober, his dark eyes glaring in his bald head. He'd been demoted after wearing the Prez title in Redding for years. Everybody was subordinate to Fang as soon as he came up from Sacramento, including the man who's charter was unlucky enough to host the Grizzlies' biggest bear.

Then there was Blackjack, our Sergeant-at-Arms. His long gray hair sat unevenly on his shoulders, the only other man here except for me and Fang who didn't indulge in anything harder than Jack and old fashioned cigs. He looked like a mean ass wizard and occasionally pulled off black magic like one too. He'd saved my ass more times than I could count when we were outgunned.

Then there was Fang himself. A big, weathered badass with a square head and a drill sergeant's haircut gone gray. The front of his cut had more patches than a four star general.

Rabid and I took the last couple seats and waited for the other brothers to file in. Sure enough, the Prez beamed raw hate at the stragglers, several of our guys plus a few transplants from the defunct Sacramento charter.

Bang! The petrified bear claw he used for a gavel hit the table, putting one more dent in the old cedar wood.

"All right, you lazy fucks, listen up. I don't have the time and motivation to rip your assholes to shreds today for dragging your junkie asses in here ten minutes overdue. I'm feeling generous today. Crack and a couple brothers finally brought us some good news."

Veep nodded. "Caught the little prick heading for the

highway late last night. The sentry patrols we got circulating through town did their job. No mistaking the cartel ink on his brown skin. Can't do more than beg in English neither. We got ourselves a hummingbird from south of the border, and it's up to us to make him sing."

"And I wanna hear him all the way back here before you snap his fucking neck," Fang growled. "This could be the break this club needs. The cartel's been shitting down our throats for months because we got rats on our ship who'll sell out their brothers for a few fuckin' pesos."

Rats. Hearing it sent an icy chill up my spine and everybody else's in the room. Nothing worse than treason in any MC – especially this one.

I'd fallen in with a group of rogues back in Montana a few months ago. The Prez defied a direct order to head south and leave everything past Idaho to the Prairie Pussies. I'd almost fucked my club without knowing it before I turned on their asses for screwing with Shelly and me. The motherfuckers killed our disabled Ma too. She'd been an overbearing bitch to me since I was a kid, but nobody deserved to die like that.

My teeth pinched together, hard enough to break when I thought about it. Ma's death must've gotten back to Fang, same as me turning on the rogues. Only fucking reason he'd spared my ass while locking the rest of the traitors in an old building and burning them alive.

I still heard their screams in my dreams. Always woke my ass up with a smile on my face.

"Brass." Blackjack said my name, pointing a finger at

me.

Shit, what the fuck did I miss? I was about to jump outta my chair when he moved to Rabid next, speaking his name, before moving on to Serial and Splitter.

"Excellent choice, Prez. These boys are good for interrogation duty," Blackjack said. "Blood on their hands won't sour their guts when we need to get down and dirty. You can count on 'em."

Fang nodded, looking right at me. Two dozen more pairs of eyes were on us too. Half were jealous, and the rest were just glad they weren't in the spotlight with such an important job.

I stiffened. Couldn't let Blackjack down. He'd helped me get clean since I came south, and I owed the old man big.

Torture was the one thing I hated the most. Didn't have a lotta experience with it either. Most of the time I took my bike and rode with the crew, quick hit and runs, protecting our shipments flowing south from cartel raiders.

Man up and get used to it, a rough voice growled in my head. *This shit with the cartel's just getting started. It only gets uglier from here.*

"We'll do whatever it takes, Prez," Serial said, flexing his muscles.

His eyes were hungrier than usual, peering out between the barbed wire inked across his face. I tried to keep my distance from his twisted ass. Yeah, he was a brother like any other, but his bloodlust never sat right with me. The giddy spark that lit him up whenever he got orders like this turned him into a total pitbull.

"Well?" Fang said, clenching his bear claw. "What're you fuckers waiting for? You don't need to sit through the rest of this shit. I'm not calling any votes today."

Me, Rabid, Serial, and Splitter were on our feet before he could rap at the wood, right behind Blackjack.

Five minutes later, we were on our bikes, riding out to the old warehouse where they had the Mexican.

"Mercy...mercy...please..."

I couldn't remember the last time I felt sick. Something about staring at the bloodied man standing over the shallow pit got to me.

Maybe the fact that he shouldn't have been standing at all. Not after the way Serial and Splitter whaled on his knees, making his legs crack, the same damned thing they'd done to his arms before. Thank fuck Blackjack didn't give Rabid and I any shit about keeping our distance.

We played watchmen by the door, making sure nobody pulled up in the empty parking lot next to our bikes. Took over an hour for the kid to crack – poor bastard held up surprisingly well while the boys stubbed their smokes out all over his bare skin. Burned away the screaming eagles or hawks or whatever the fuck cartel assholes worshiped that was inked on his chest.

When Serial took the cinder block to his left hand, turning it into a broken mess, he started to talk. Rabid and I just looked at each other. Blackjack was the only brother with us who really listened – good fucking thing he was along to take charge because none of us knew shit for Spanish.

The Mexican spilled his guts for ten or twenty minutes. Whatever the fucker said, it was enough to make Blackjack nod, motioning for us to come over. I carried the old shovel, pushing it into Jose's hands before we led him out back to the old courtyard.

Nobody said shit while he dug like a good boy. Quite a challenge with his busted hands and beat up body. Something else must've broke once he'd gotten a foot or two into the earth. Bastard started to beg, whining the same shit over and over again.

"Mercy...mercy..."

Probably the extent of his English vocabulary.

Serial and Splitter barked in his face. Rabid was getting pissed too, and punched the fucker in the back. I could tell by the look on his face that he just wanted this asshole to shut up like I did.

"Come on, you sonofabitch! Just a few more feet and it's done." Serial rolled his shoulders, ready to lay into him with his fists.

I hated the cartel fucks just as much as anybody, but fuck, breaking his ribs wouldn't make him dig the grave faster. I stepped up, ready to pull the weird hothead off the Mexican, but Blackjack got between us first.

"Don't be a jackass, Serial. Get the fuck back there with the rest," he growled, pointing to Rabid and me.

I froze mid-step, slowly ambling back over to where Rabid was standing before the freak joined us.

Serial sulked over to our place against the wall, lighting a smoke. When he was gone, Blackjack leaned into the man, whispering just loud enough for us to hear.

"You're dead, son. There's no getting around that. Your grave was dug the minute you ended up on the wrong side of Redding after making your delivery. Don't make this any harder than it has to be. Just finish up and I promise I'll make it quick."

Jose stumbled a couple steps backwards, tears in his eyes. Blackjack's gaze was colder than Serial's had been, nothing but ice. He was offering him the only mercy we were allowed to give.

Finally, the dude looked down, shuffling his feet. He grabbed the shovel and started to dig, this time without any complaints. Later, I gave him a hand and a cig while he went down in the pit, lowering a light for him. His eyes were pitch black, understanding, the kinda look an animal gives a hunter before he pulls the trigger.

I stood over the grave for a few more minutes. When the Mexican stumbled, collapsing into the small pile next to him, I waved for Blackjack.

"Get back, son," he told me, drawing his nine millimeter. "He held up his end. I'm gonna hold up mine."

The gunshot echoed through the empty courtyard, even with the silencer on the barrel.

I reached into the pit for the shovel, and then went to work, throwing dirt over the dead body as quickly as I could. The four brothers joined me, covering up his carcass, first with dirt and then using a pile of heavy cinder blocks stacked over the smooth earth.

Nobody suspected shit out here. If this place ever got bought and re-developed, they'd probably find a few more bodies deep in the ground besides the ones the club dumped off.

We here heading for our bikes, eager to hit the road and get the fuck back to the clubhouse, when Blackjack caught up to us. He walked up and put his hand on my bars before I could think about starting up the engine.

"We're not done yet," he said, scanning his eyes at the other brothers. "1212 Hawkeye Street. That's where we'll find the one and a half mil the cartel dropped for a dead guy."

"What the fuck?" I couldn't stop it from flying outta my mouth.

Whatever we'd forced outta Jose, I never expected it to be that.

Blackjack smiled. "Prez is wrong about one thing: the biggest swamp rats aren't in this club. Doesn't matter how much money you pay pigs to keep their mouth shut and look the other way – they always flip and sell your ass out when they get desperate enough."

"So, this is a repo job?" Rabid asked.

Blackjack laughed. "If you wanna put it that way...Charlie Thomas got at least a good half mill from our crew over the years before cancer kicked him off the force. Bastard probably flipped and sold our intel to the cartel to leave a few crumbs for his family. Shame the fucking turncoat knew so much. Hell, his job was blacking out what was already on the books – and now those books with all our dirty secrets, slip ups, and weaknesses are in the Mexican hands."

"Shit!" Splitter spat, pounding his bike.

"Whining about it won't do any good, brother." Blackjack lit a smoke, finally moving away toward his own Harley. "Best we can do now is take that fucking money and use it to pad our asses against the hard fuck that's coming."

We hit the road and ripped through town. My rage was extra hot, a wicked contrast against the cool wind whipping me in the face.

Blackjack's talk just confirmed what I already knew deep in my guts: shit was about to get a whole lot worse. No, the king rat wasn't in our club, but it wasn't gonna work any miracles on Fang's paranoia. Burying Jose was the first real shot fired in Redding, but the cartel war had been going on for months.

And now, instead of turning the tide, those motherfuckers just showed us how fucked we really were.

We cut our engines a couple blocks from the ratty old house. The doorknob was loose. Didn't even have to plant my boot on the wood to break through. I just ripped the knob off and pushed it open, heading into the house while the other guys fanned out through the basement.

Sickness burned my nostrils. No wonder the place wasn't very secure for a cop's house – the man hadn't been whole in a long time. Creeping death and strong medicine rolled off the walls, worse upstairs where I was heading.

Serial pushed past me, heading for the room at the end of the hall. I shot him a dirty look, clenching my fists. I'd settle with that asshole later.

Right now, we had to get whoever the fuck was in this place rounded up. We had to find what we came for and get the fuck out.

I peeked in the dead man's room first. Nobody was on the empty bed, just as I expected. Just as I came out, Serial exited the furthest room, one hand over a little girl's mouth.

Shit.

She couldn't have been any older than fifteen. I moved into the next room, hoping like fuck I didn't find another kid. Dealing with Thomas' wife would be a helluva lot easier.

The sleeping girl in the dark was definitely an adult, but she looked too young to have been married to cancer man. I grabbed her phone first, shoving it in my pocket. First rule of any residential raid was cutting communication. Confiscating phones was usually enough – hardly anyone had a fucking land line anymore.

A second later, a loud scream rang out down the hall. Fuck, Serial must've moved his hand, giving her a chance to howl. The woman next to me popped outta bed, reaching for the phone I'd swiped. She practically flung herself into my arms.

I moved on pure instinct, shoving my lips to her ear while I went for my gun. Hoped I wouldn't have to shoot her. Letting 'em know I had it was usually plenty for intimidation. Fucks only got shot when they tried to run, or whenever a senior brother ordered cleanup.

"Don't. You fucking scream, I'll have to put a bullet in your spine." Brushing my gun along her back, I let it sink in for a few more seconds before I drove it home. "Just go where I tell you, and this'll all be over, nice and quick. Nobody has to get hurt."

Hoped like hell the last part was true. Her father was a piece of shit rat, and rats always suffered, including their associates by blood or brotherhood. But fuck, these girls were young.

The woman in my grip could've been fresh new pussy for the clubhouse if she were a little more worn down, a little more desperate...

I tried to keep my cock under control as I led her downstairs. In the dim light, she was pretty fucking hot. So sexy I didn't give a shit when her bright eyes flashed pure venom my way.

Having my hands on her wasn't helping the situation. It was rare to see a girl who had everything going for her, and this chick had it in fucking spades.

I watched it. I felt it. And then I started losing my mind, eyeing her as we walked, sliding my hands across her body with way more interest than any good captor should have.

Those hips, full and lush, perfect for grabbing onto while I drove my dick all the way to her womb. And those tits, perfectly flanked by loose strands of chestnut hair?

Shit! I had to nudge her downstairs fast just to get my

hands off her. One more second too close to those ripe handfuls and I wouldn't have been able to resist. I'd have copped a feel so tight she'd be screaming, threatening our whole operation, and then my brothers would be beating my ass.

But fuck...just looking at her ass wiggling down the stairs ahead of me, I had to wonder if she was worth an ass kicking or two.

Serial had her little sister in his arms. I took my place on the other side of the room, putting several badly needed feet between us.

The old man started his spiel. Nobody had a clue where they'd hidden the cartel's stash, and we weren't going anywhere 'til we had it. Hopefully, working them over would go a lot more smooth and easy than Jose – they were too pretty and innocent to survive half the shit the brothers gave the Mexican.

Blackjack lit a fresh smoke and paced around her, circling the girl like a shark.

"We can do this the easy way or the hard way. I, for one, don't like spilling blood when there's no good reason, but some of the brothers feel differently. Now, we know your loot's not where it was supposed to be – found this shit all torn up myself." He pointed at the torn up mess of cardboard and shingles on the ground.

Odd fucking combination, but it was what the dead Mexican said he'd hid the cartel cash in.

Her sweet red lips stayed shut. His threats kept coming, tough as leather and cold as the arctic. Still, she didn't move, staring over his shoulder at me instead.

Me. Why fucking me? It was like the girl was reading my mind, x-raying through my skull and seeing all the dirty, nasty, downright degenerate things I wanted to do to her.

"Look we both know me and my boys are gonna find it. Only question left is – are you gonna make this scavenger hunt easy-peasy-punkin-squeezy? Or are you gonna make all our fucking ears ring while we choke it out of you??"

I recognized that prickly tone in Blackjack's voice. Shit, if this beauty didn't spill her guts soon, the Enforcer was gonna go ape and squeeze it outta her, just like he promised.

"Well?"

It was his last warning. And she wouldn't talk, pinching her sweet lips together. I watched 'em turn white, hating how they resembled a corpse's mouth as the life drained away.

Blackjack threw his cig down and stubbed it out with one boot. Then he grabbed her, forcing his fingers around her throat. Little sister screamed into Serial's hand, starting to kick and thrash. He swore, growling as he tightened his hold on her.

So, both these girls were fighters. Sisters, maybe, sharing the same wildcat blood.

I took a step closer, hating Blackjack for throwing her up against the laundry machine, one more pinch away from seriously choking her. The chick gasped for air, sputtering as she clawed at his ruthless hand.

"Okay! Just get off me...let me breathe."

Snarling, Blackjack gave her a little space. When she sat up again, rubbing her neck, her eyes went straight to me. I tensed up. Having those wide perfect eyes glowing so helplessly in front of me just fed the crazy ass protective urge swelling in my chest.

Fuck, *crazy* didn't begin to describe it. Wanting to fight my own brothers for a babe I'd only seen for the first time five minutes ago was certifiably insane.

"It's upstairs. Underneath my bed a suitcase. Pull it out and count everything down to the dollar if you want – it's all there. Go ahead and kill me if I'm lying."

Blackjack ignored her. He pointed at Splitter and nodded. It was the only signal the brother needed to know he'd better get the fuck up there and verify what she'd said.

"We'll wait," Blackjack said. "If you're bullshitting me, girl, then I'll finish what I started. I don't give a fuck if the little girl watches either."

That got another muffled sob in Serial's palm. Poor girl. No bullshit, I honestly felt bad for her. Dragging kids into this shit was always rough.

I wondered who the fuck the kid was – the feisty chick looked too damned young for a daughter. If the girl was hers, then she was officially the hottest MILF I'd ever gawked at in my life.

We waited. After awhile, Splitter came trundling downstairs, a fat duffel bag in hand. He pushed through us, plopped it on the dryer, and flung open the first.

Glorious cash lay inside, stuffed to the seams, rolls upon rolls of crisp hundreds bundled together.

"Must be a full million here, maybe more," he said, looking up at Blackjack. "Don't think she's bullshitting. It's all here."

The Enforcer nodded. He walked over, zipped the suitcase, and then passed it to Rabid.

"Let's get this over with," Serial said, reaching for his gun and stepping in front of the stairs. "Come on, brothers. We'll make this quick and clean for these bitches."

Serial and Splitter had their guns out in a flash, aimed at the girls. Rabid hesitated. Blackjack stared at me, like he was gauging my reaction.

I hurled myself across the room before anyone could pull the trigger, shoving both hands out like a fucking scarecrow. Trying to cover both girls at the same time wasn't easy.

"Brass? What the fuck are you doing, son?" Blackjack sounded pissed, but amusement flickered in his old eyes.

"We don't have to do this! The chick kept her word...she gave us the fucking money! We got what we came for, right? What's the fucking point of this?"

"You gotta be shitting, brother." I hated hearing that word from Serial's fucked up mouth. "What do you want to do with these bitches, then? Leave 'em free to run off to daddy's old friends in the police? Sending every dime to the fight with the cartel's already got us strapped. We can't afford bigger bribes to keep pigs' mouths shut. Tell him, Blackjack."

"Never said they'd get turned loose, asshole," I growled,

trying to make up an alternative on the spot.

If I didn't, these girls were sure as dead, and I'd never find out what those wide soft hips were like naked.

Think, dammit! Alarms blasted in my head. *You've got about five seconds to start talking and stop the guns.*

"Come on, Blackjack. You know this shit's unnecessary. We don't need to start wiping people up like the cartel fucks. They'll keep their mouths shut if we bring 'em with us. The clubhouse is a shithole...we need somebody to clean house. These girls are perfect for that."

Sweet Ass shot me a vicious look. No gratitude whatsoever. Guess I was gonna fuck myself one way or another and end up on somebody's shitlist, but being on hers was better than seeing her and the kid dead.

"You're outta your fucking gourd, Brass," Serial growled, tightening his hold on the young one's shoulders. "I'd love to see you bring these bitches back. Fucking love it! Prez would kick your ass right up your throat. You're damned lucky Blackjack's not that stupid."

I looked over. The older brother wasn't moving. His lips were curled – curiosity or confusion, I couldn't tell which.

Fuck. I wracked my brain at light speed, trying to find something, anything that would save them from ending up underneath the old warehouse like the Mexican and so many more.

Then it hit me. A crazy, stupid idea so outta bounds it just might work. Effective or not, I was about to make myself a fucking laughing stock to every brother in Redding, and maybe beyond.

Whatever. I'd be glad to have the humiliation if it saved these chicks from holes in their heads.

"You can't snuff her out," I said, reaching for Sweet Ass and throwing my arm around her. "This is my old lady. Right here, right now, I'm claiming her."

She flinched when I said the c-word. If those eyes were stormy honey colored oceans before, now they were full of tsunamis, spinning with hate and confusion and disbelief.

I pointed. "Don't touch the little girl neither. She's family. You fuck with my old lady's blood, you fuck with me. I'm dead serious."

Splitter lowered his gun, busting a gut. His nose ring swung as he let it pour out, the only brother laughing at my pure insanity.

Rabid looked at me like I'd lost my fucking mind. Serial snorted, waving his gun at his side. Whatever, at least he'd lowered it – but only for a second.

Next thing I knew, the fucker had it up again, this time pointed at me. "So much for being clean. You must be back on that shit if you're seriously doing this, Brass, you junkie asshole. Just give the order, Blackjack. I'll put this asshole outta his misery so we can –"

"Put the damned gun down," Blackjack growled, taking a heavy step forward. "The brother's right. Crazy and stupid as this is, I'm gonna allow it. We got what we came for, and we've gotten ourselves a good laugh too. There's no need for a massacre. Yeah, sure, that'd be the neat and clean way, but this fucking club's been stuck on that track for too damned long. We're trying something different."

Serial's jaw dropped. Dunno how I held onto mine. My arm squeezed the chick I'd claimed, pulling her closer, burying her face in my chest so she wouldn't have to look at my brothers anymore.

"I'm gonna give you a week to find a place for these girls," Blackjack continued. "They can't stay at the clubhouse forever. Serial's right, Fang'll tear everybody involved to shreds if we pile this kinda shit on his plate with everything else he's dealing with. Now that you claimed them, they're *you're* problem, Brass. If they start to become a problem for the club again, then I won't hesitate to finish the cleanup we started here today. Got it?"

I looked at him and nodded. Guns were holstered.

I couldn't fucking believe it worked. Hell, I couldn't believe how Blackjack just turned into more of a fucking mystery than he already was. And I *really* couldn't get it through my skull that I now had two strange women on my hands, and I didn't know shit about how to handle them.

"Let's move," Blackjack growled, aiming his hard stare at everybody else. "Get the cash loaded so we can get the fuck outta this dump. Smells like the place where my old man died..."

"You got a name, or what?" I said, helping her onto my bike.

"It's Melissa, but everybody calls me Missy." She eyed me warily. "What's happening to us? What does it mean to be claimed?"

I coughed, looking for a spare helmet. Fuck, it'd been too long since I had a passenger on my ride, let alone an hourglass with such a tight sweet body.

"Means you're under my protection now, babe. I'm gonna help you get outta this shit, but you gotta work with me. We'll link up with your girl when we get to the clubhouse. She'll be all right riding with Blackjack."

Convenient answer. No way was I explaining all the honors and obligations of an old lady 'til I had to.

"Him?" She bared her teeth, pointing to the Enforcer securing the kid to his bike. "He almost fucking killed us!"

"Yeah, he did. But he changed his mind, didn't he?" I winked. "Nice to hear a firecracker go off between those teeth. Keep that shit coming. You'll fit in fine with where we're going. Put this on."

I pushed the helmet onto her head, trying to tuck her hair underneath it. She got pissed real fast and batted my fingers away, fixing the strap herself.

"You ever been on one of these before?" I asked, taking my place up front.

"No. I'll figure it out. I'm more worried about Jackie, my sister..."

I tried to hide the big whoosh of relief soaring through my chest. No, not a MILF after all, and thank fuck for that. My cock wouldn't have blinked at her having a kid, but fuck if it didn't make things easier. Dealing with a kid sister as part of the package was a whole lot easier than a daughter.

"She'll be okay. He's not a bad guy all the time. Blackjack always keeps his word. He'll take care of her, same way I'm gonna make sure you get home in one piece. Hold on tight 'cause we're about to roll."

Reaching behind me, I found her hands and pulled them around me. One rough tug. The girl only resisted a little bit. Soon as I started my engine and the bike jerked, I became her whole world, the only thing between her flying off onto the road.

I grinned to myself. Never fucking failed. These rides always brought the lucky gals closer to the brothers. It took me a second to remember she wasn't choosing it, though, because I'd made her choice for her.

All Missy – beautiful fucking name – could do was lock her hands around me and bear it as we ripped down Redding's streets. Fuck if I didn't enjoy it, even if I'd taken her like a total barbarian.

Her hands pressed tighter around my waist each time I followed my brothers around the corners. I kept it together, but my greedy cock didn't. He was making me come apart a little more by the second, shooting lightning to my brain, making me imagine what her pretty fingers would feel like around my dick, or maybe clawing at my shoulders while I got between her legs and throttled her a hundred times harder than anything she'd feel on this easy cruise through town.

By the time we were a couple blocks from the clubhouse, she'd adjusted. Missy found her balance, loosening the death grip she had at first, just holding her hands on me like they were always meant to be there.

Why the hell did it feel so natural? My brothers and I had already done too much evil shit to her and little sis for it to feel this *good*.

Fuck it. I shook my head, keeping my eyes on the road, following Blackjack and Serial to the gate. Worrying about the rights and wrongs constantly was for fuckheads like the Prairie Pussies. In this club, a man took action. If he saw something good for himself or good for the club, then he didn't wait around to ask questions or ponder the ethics. That shit was for civilian eggheads teaching philosophy.

Taking what I wanted when I wanted was the surest way I'd found to set a man free.

I slowed down and stopped while we waited for the gate to open. A few more minutes and we were in, back in the fortress. I killed my engine inside the hanger-sized garage attached to the clubhouse and started to help Missy unload.

"Where's Jackie?" she asked, without so much as a thank you.

I grunted, pointing as I took her helmet. Blackjack already had the kid off the bike and she ran toward us, throwing her skinny arms around Missy's smooth neck. They hugged for what seemed like ages.

Blackjack watched us from a distance before heading inside, shooting me a warning look. *Keep this shit under control, asshole, or I'll finish what we started in the basement. You know I keep my word.*

He didn't need to say it to read him loud and clear.

When the girls were finally done sobbing all over each other, I laid a hand on Missy's shoulder. Predictably, she shook it off right away. Least I'd gotten her attention.

"Let's go inside. I got a room for you ladies. We can figure out something more permanent later, but it'll be place to flop for now."

I waited to make sure they weren't going to fuck me over. After another one of those doe-eyed stares, Missy followed, holding Jackie by the hand.

The teenager wrinkled her nose as soon as we were inside. "Stinks worse than the house in here!"

Missy gave her arm a jerk. I turned around in time to see her uneasy smile.

"She's right. This place isn't always like this. It's been...hectic lately." I left it at that.

Explaining the ins and outs of the cartel swarming us like angry fucking wasps, killing good men, wasn't my job. It wasn't her fucking business anyway. Of course, I knew she'd be asking me why we'd taken her inheritance and made her prisoner in the first place soon.

I unlocked my room and stepped inside, grateful not to run into any brothers. Hoped like fuck Twinkie or some other bitch hadn't found her way back into my place while we were gone. I stepped in ahead of the girls, scanning it over, glad when I saw it was just the way I left it.

"Have a seat. I got some clean sheets somewhere..."

Fuck, I really had to find 'em. These ladies weren't the type who'd enjoy laying in man sweat and a week of fuck residue.

"You hungry?" I decided to change the subject while I dug through my messy closet.

"I'm good. Jackie needs something, though."

I nodded. The clubhouse was balls deep in junk food. I'd grab her something for the night, but it wasn't gonna win any awards from nutritionist bullshitters.

They stood up while I pulled off the old sheets and changed it over. When I was finished, I pulled out my sleeping bag. Only place I'd be staying tonight with these two in my bed.

It was a damned good thing the kid was with her after all. If she was holed up in my room, all alone, sleeping in my bed with that body...

Fuck! I'd spike a hole through the floor with my dick if I didn't lose it and climb in with her first. Then I'd do something we'd both regret. Well, just her, anyway.

I stepped out and slammed the door behind me. It was a big relief just to be away for a second.

I couldn't shut my fucking brain off as I headed to the kitchen. Sex, sex, sex...and sex. Missy woke something real potent and primal deep inside me with her amber eyes and pumpkin hips. She was the first woman in a long time who seriously competed with my jonesing for a hit.

Too bad that meant resisting her would be about as hard as staying off smack. Shit!

I ransacked the cabinet before anybody could give me crap about it. Chips, pretzels, jerky, and a couple candy bars. If Jackie was like any teen, then she wouldn't be too disappointed in the junk food buffet.

Took a quick peek in the fridge too, expecting to find old burgers and expired dips. Total shock when I saw a pack of berry yogurt sitting there, probably left behind by some slut or a brother's old lady.

Snatched that shit without a second thought. If living with my sister Shelly taught me anything, it was that a girl would kick her little brother's ass for stealing it. Compared to all the other shit in the fridge, it was a fucking crown jewel. I grabbed a spoon and some waters before heading back.

Inside, I dropped the food onto the empty space between them. The girls were sitting on the bed, awkward and closed off, like they were chilling in a waiting room before some shitty procedure.

"Dig in. You girls need anything else, just let me know. I'd give you a grand tour, but you can take this fucking place all in just by turning your heads."

I took the chair across from them, checking my phone while they ate. When I reached for my pocket to put it back, I felt an unfamiliar bump. Shit, I'd forgotten I still had Missy's phone with me.

"Don't suppose you're going to return that anytime soon?" She stared at me intently, ripping the plastic top off her yogurt.

Fuck me. I must've looked like an idiot and let my hand linger near my pocket too long. Well, since the goddamned cat was screaming outta the bag...

I stood up, plucked the phone out in front of her, and dropped it on the ground. I stomped that shit harder than

I intended. It cracked and came flying out underneath my boot in a hundred plastic shards.

"You're not making any calls 'til I know I can trust you, babe." Not this time. I looked at her, holding her gaze, steeling myself against those bright brown gems in her head. "I feel for you, whether you believe it or not. Doesn't mean I'm turning my back before we've reached an understanding."

"We have one: you kidnapped us, and you're holding us prisoner. You stole everything my family had to make a new life together." She was breathing heavy, those sweet round tits rising and falling in waves on her chest.

My head was fucking ringing. I took a step closer, holding in the volcanic heat so I wouldn't spook the kid real bad. I got as close I could before I leaned down, never taking my eyes off her.

Surprisingly, the chick didn't flinch. She held steady while over two hundred pounds of rock hard biker leered down at her.

"We did what we had to for reasons that aren't your fucking business. If it wasn't for me, you'd be a dead husk in an unmarked grave right about now. Gratitude? I really don't give a shit. But you'd better close your fucking mouth and show me some respect. Appreciating this patch is all that's between you and some guys who'd like to do a whole lot worse."

I thumped my chest once, then turned around, making damned well sure she could see the roaring grizzly bear on my jacket. In my younger days, this was the point when I would've went storming outta the house, slamming the door off its hinges while Ma or Shelly screamed after me.

But I was a prisoner in this damned room tonight too. My hell was babysitting the kid munching chips on my bed and the grown brat my crew put through the wringer. Shit, couldn't she understand I'd saved both their asses?

I wasn't fucking around when I warned her what would've happened if it wasn't for me keeping my brothers from putting lead in their skulls. I'd sacrificed my fucking club cred to keep her and the kid whole. Yeah, she had every reason in the world to hate me and spit in my face, but no way was I putting up with that shit.

Tomorrow, I didn't have a fucking clue what was gonna happen. We had to play pretend around the brothers, or else somebody else would be jerking her into their room and fucking her like another slut. The *only* thing keeping her safe and sane was pretending to be my old lady.

And right about now, I had some serious fucking doubts that we were gonna be able to pull it off.

"Missy?" Jackie put down the empty Doritos bag and looked at her sis, trying to keep one eye on me.

Those brown eyes pulled away. She threw her arms around the girl, ignoring me.

"It's okay, sis. I know it's scary and it doesn't make sense...but we're going to get out of this. I'll find a way." She paused, rocking the teenager, who was strangely calm, probably too numb to spill more tears today. "I'll do anything I have to."

Had a feeling the last part was aimed at me. Hoped to

hell she was serious, because that was the kinda attitude that might save me from a few ass kickings and keep her alive.

I swept up the broken phone fragments and took their empty packages. A hasty trip outside to throw away the junk brought me face to face with Rabid. He had one arm around some redheaded bitch I'd seen on his dick a couple times before.

"You still alive in there, bro?" he said, grinning through his short brown stubble.

"Don't see too many dead fucks walking around out here." I had to stop and wonder if that was true – some of the men who'd settled in from Sacramento spent enough time drunk and high to look like the living dead.

"How about the girls?" The redhead laughed when he asked, like she was in on some big fucking secret.

I frowned, hoping he wasn't so loose with those bitches he was spilling club secrets along with his jizz. "They're doing fine. Gotta work on getting 'em somewhere else to crash. They're not a good fit for the clubhouse."

Rabid's eyes narrowed as he saw me looking at his girl. "Whatever, bro. Hope you get them some new digs before Fang finds out."

They walked past me to his room, right across the hall from mine, slamming the door behind them. My favorite brother wasn't kidding.

Having the Prez involved with these girls in any way, shape, or form was an express train to hell. I had to get their attitudes checked and work on shuffling them out as soon as I could. Shit was guaranteed to get more heated with the cartel soon, and then there'd be zero tolerance for loose ends.

They were sprawled out on my bed when I got back. The little one must've been knocked out after eating, but Missy was awake, bathing me in that guilty fire spilling out her eyes.

"It's been a long night. Go ahead and get some sleep," I said. "I'll be right here on the floor if you need anything."

She rolled over without saying anything. Should've given myself the same damned advice. It had been a long night, and it was about to get a whole lot longer.

I slept with one eye open the entire time, running my brain through cash flow, consequences, and choices. If I didn't have to worry about them flipping and running to the police, I had enough to stick them up in a hotel 'til I could find something better, maybe a crappy apartment.

Club business was too serious to keep them under lock and key forever. There had to be a balance, somewhere between covering my ass and doing what was best for them. There had to be some way outta this damned quicksand I'd landed in with both feet.

I pushed my face into my sleeping bag, muffling a growl.

One thing, I had no doubts about: if I didn't get Missy outta here soon, I wouldn't be able to keep my dick zipped up while it strained against my jeans every time I looked at her. And if she kept sassing me with those spitfire lips...

Fuck. If that happened, throwing her down, spanking

her ass raw, and fucking some respect into her was as certain as the moon hanging in the sky while I nodded off to sleep.

III: Many Kinds of Ransom (Missy)

The first three days were hell, and they were the ones where we sat in his crappy room by ourselves, alone while he went out and did...I didn't really know what, but it must've been terrible.

This club, this man, this place – they were all so close to hell I could practically smell the sulfur dripping off the walls. I seriously wondered if Jackie and I died with daddy, and now we were all paying for his sins.

Escape? It wasn't even an option.

The first day he was gone, I found out fast the door was locked from the other side. Even if we'd somehow made it out, the place was always swarming with them.

Big, brutal men stomped around outside, as dangerous and foul tempered as the grizzly bears they wore on their leather vests. Sometimes, I heard them fucking their women through the walls. The girls screamed so loud I couldn't tell if they were being ripped apart by pleasure or having the life torn out of them.

Jackie ate, slept, and took long private trips to the bathroom, avoiding me so I wouldn't see her crying. Watching her kill herself to stay strong really hurt.

I was the fuckup. I'd accepted a bundle of miracle money I knew nothing about, and I'd landed us both here.

Jesus, if only I'd taken a fistful of money and woken Jackie up. We could've left that night while we sorted it out. We could've gotten away, stayed in a hotel, avoided all this. If only I'd stopped to think there'd be others after the fortune daddy left behind in vain.

Now, it was gone. Gone forever, just like any shred of hope that we wouldn't just move from one rung of hell to the next. And that was *if* we were lucky enough to get away from these monsters.

I was skeptical Brass had done anything more than delay what those rougher, darker men wanted to do to us in the basement. Why he'd decided to delay our doom, I couldn't figure out.

Did he really have a heart? Or was he just another demon, driven by something different than money and blood, but just as selfish?

The third evening, he came in carrying burgers and fries. I could've killed for something leafy and green, but my stomach was so empty and unsettled it wouldn't let me resist anything I shoved in my face. My stomach rumbled hard when I smelled the greasy, delicious food.

"Dinner," he said, passing me a burger. "Try to finish it up fast because we got shit to do tonight."

I raised an eyebrow, making sure Jackie got into her food first before I began to eat. She hadn't lost her appetite through all this by some miracle, but I wasn't taking any chances.

Little sis had me to look out for her now. Me, the big sister who'd failed to protect her, and nobody else.

"Yeah? What's that? Spraying us down with Febreze while we're rotting away in here?" A little more venom in my blood replaced the fear the big biker originally inspired every day.

He shook his head. "I'm taking you two to your new place. You've been cooped up in my room long enough. If you think it's been fun for me sleeping on the floor, you're a fucking –"

He stopped just short of saying idiot. For some reason, the weird catch brought a sour smile to my lips. He was civil, in his own twisted way. But that wasn't saying much for men who had no manners whatsoever.

"How do we know this isn't another trick?" I said, biting into my cheeseburger.

"I don't play games, babe. If I was really gonna drive you out into the boonies and off you, I wouldn't be wasting money feeding your mouths." He smoothed his face with one hand. "Yeah, on the other hand, I guess you don't know shit. That's the way it's gonna stay. You'll just have to take my word for it and be good while I drive you over."

"We've had plenty of practice, mister," Jackie chimed in, munching on a fry. "Behaving ourselves is all we've been doing here, in case you hadn't noticed."

Brass gave my sister a dark, angry look, but held himself in check. He never lashed out her, even on the few occasions when she'd insulted him to his face. That surprised me.

It was hard to imagine any decency among these men. With the others, I didn't think we'd be so lucky, but Brass...well, he put at least some limits on his explosive testosterone.

"Fucking finish up. We don't got all day. I'd rather get you girls outta here without dealing with the brothers." He turned, removing his food from the bag and digging in.

I watched him chew. There was no way he could've been more than a few years older than me, somewhere in his mid-twenties. The hormones whistling through his veins did far more than make him act like a barbarian.

He dripped sex. He was raw. Masculine. Real in a way I didn't know a man could be.

When he came into the room, he commanded my attention. His gravity tilted my whole narrow world to his barrel chested center, his emerald eyes I feared had x-ray visions to see what I was really thinking.

I hated – no, *loathed* – admitting it, but if he wasn't holding us prisoner here, wearing that ferocious beast on his jacket, he definitely would've turned my head at any bar.

Not that I knew much about that. Taking care of dad and Jackie finished off what little social life I'd had as a young woman. But like any red blooded woman, big muscles and devilish ink drew my eyes, and Brass was all strength and edge, a living sculpture whose rogue looks were just the type to walk up and punch you in the face.

Bastard. I hated the little flash of heat that started low

in my belly whenever I saw him, the fire that would've kept spreading down between my legs if I didn't look away. And I always did.

Avoiding him was all I had. I couldn't let him infect my mind.

We ate in silence until everyone was finished. He collected our trash and tossed it into a wastebin. We stood and followed him out into the smelly hallway. No matter how many times the door opened, my nose hadn't gotten used to the reeking tobacco and old whiskey that seeped out of everything.

My nerves shook when we walked through the bar, passing several tables with dark, savage looking men. They all stopped and eyeballed us. I could handle the ugly, lecherous looks, but my face burned with rage when their eyes ran up and down Jackie's body.

She stayed close to me, and I stayed even closer to Brass. Yeah, it was definitely bad when the devil I knew was a comfort against all these other demons.

As if sensing the unease, a rough hand reached for mine. I looked up in surprise as Brass took my hand. Refusing to fight it off was an even bigger surprise.

He led us past the bar and down another hall on the opposite side of the large building. We headed for an exit at the end that looked like it led into a big garage full of trucks and motorcycles. I could see them through the glass window in the door.

"Hey!" A rough voice hit the backs of our heads like bricks when we were almost at the door.

Brass released my hand and spun, pushed through us, and stepped forward, keeping Jackie and I behind him.

"What the fuck are you doing with these bitches, Brass? Didn't hear we were ready to release any collateral." A big man with a bald head and beefy Popeye forearms folded his arms, waiting patiently for Brass to catch up to him.

"Blackjack said to get them outta the clubhouse, so that's what I'm doing. I'm following orders, Veep." Brass shrugged, cool as the night breeze outside.

"Fucker should've ran it by me or Fang first. I'm not convinced these cunts aren't gonna talk. Roughed 'em up pretty good from what I heard during the debriefing. Girls don't forget that kinda shit." The big man he called VP grunted, showing his teeth.

"We were all there for church. I know you were paying attention, Veep, same as the rest of us. You know the older one's my old lady, right?"

"Yeah."

"You saying I don't know how to control my own woman? Fuck, brother, I've kept 'em under lock and key every damned minute they've been in this clubhouse. I haven't done anything to hurt the club and I never would. Won't let them do it neither."

The older man stepped forward, flexing one fist. Brass closed the distance between them, pushing his chest against the stranger, tipping his head in the air.

"Go ahead and break my jaw if you don't believe me, Crack. Missy's my fucking property now, and I know how to handle what's mine. I know where club biz begins and ends. I'm not telling her shit, and we're leaving so she doesn't stick her ears anywhere they don't belong here. Shit, I'll watch her and the baby girl day and night if I have to, just as soon as my woman's got my brand stamped on her skin." Brass paused, sucking in a hot, angry breath. "Go ahead and knock my fucking teeth out if you got a problem with that. Just know they're gonna be yours if you do."

I held my breath. The man had balls, and he was fighting for us in his own twisted way. I couldn't deny him that.

The older man's fist jerked – down to his side. With an angry swipe of the arm, he gave Brass a hard push. He caught himself against the wall, never taking his eyes off Crack's snarling face.

"Just get 'em the fuck outta my sight!" the VP roared. "You'd better make sure their mouths are sewn shut for your own damned sake. I won't hesitate to take you out back and use the Mauler on you myself if I hear a peep about either of those bitches going to daddy's old friends. The last fucking thing this club needs is cops sniffing around when the cartel's at our throats."

Brass didn't say anything. He nodded once, then turned, leaving the raging volcano behind.

When he caught up to me, he grabbed my hand more fiercely this time, throwing open the door. We headed for a rusted old pickup and he opened the passenger door, waving Jackie and I inside.

I helped my sis get in and climbed in myself while he

took the driver's side.

"Cover your eyes 'til we're through the gate," Brass growled, backing the truck down a small parking strip. "Can't have either of you looking at this place and it's layout. I'll tell you when it's okay to see again."

Jackie gave me an uncertain look. "Do it," I mouthed silently, covering her eyes with one hand.

She struggled against me for a second, but then relented. We rode for about five to ten minutes in pure silence, listening to the truck's engine humming.

Keeping my brain from going to a thousand pitch black places was a constant struggle. I didn't want to believe he was going to hurt us or drop off our lifeless bodies – especially not after he'd put up such a convincing show – but I just didn't know.

I didn't know anything about this man except that he was a slightly smoother cog in the brutal machine called the Grizzlies MC. Trusting him wasn't going to happen – not without knowing we had our lives.

"Okay. You can open your eyes now," he said firmly.

Uncovering Jackie's first, I looked out through the windshield into the night. We were definitely back in town, judging by all the bright lights. Just in time to watch him turn down a narrow residential street I'd seen a few times before.

We pulled up next to an old square three story building and he killed the engine, then reached past Jackie and I for the glove compartment. I watched him pull out a plastic tag and hang it on the rear view mirror.

"What're we doing here?" Jackie asked, beating me to the punch.

"Sleeping, eating, shitting. Looking pretty." I frowned at his crude answer. "Whatever the hell you girls do in your off hours. This is your new home."

I swallowed. It was too good to be true. Well, as 'good' as having a bland new apartment handed to us by a thug like Brass could be.

He got out and slammed his door without saying another word, stopping by the building's glass door to wait for us. I held Jackie's hand until she shook me off.

Whatever, as long as she was following my footsteps.

The place had that eighties feel, and it smelled just as old too. But after three days in the stinking clubhouse, anything was an improvement. Brass led us up a small staircase and stopped at the second door on the right.

"Number 205. That's your new place." He shoved a key in and popped the door, holding it open for us.

We stepped inside. The biggest surprise was seeing the place fully furnished. The couch, chairs, and little dining table next to the kitchen weren't going to win any awards for fashion, but they looked clean and functional. I walked around, eyeing my new home, leaning close to the tacky brown sofa and giving it a sniff.

Thank God. The smoky old stink of the clubhouse wasn't bleeding out the cushions, so he hadn't gotten it from the there.

Jackie walked straight into the little hall. I joined her a second later, wondering why she looked so perked up.

61

"Two bedrooms!" she chirped. "That's a lot better than the crap I thought he'd –"

She stopped, swallowing her words. Brass stood at the other end of the hall, his arms folded, looking seriously scary in the darkness.

I reached for a switch in the bathroom and flipped it on. The light did a lot to take the evil edge off him, but he still looked like he'd leave scorch marks if I got too close. He was all muscle, all fire rippling in his flesh, and he held every last key to our fate in his big calloused hand.

"Catch." He threw me the small bundle of keys and I threw my hands out, wrapping my fingers around it.

"You're paid up through the end of the month, and I'll chip in something for next month too, as needed." He turned.

I followed him into the living room while Jackie lingered in the bigger bedroom. She'd already claimed hers. Not something I was going to fight her about.

"The couch folds down," he said, flopping on it in front of me. His leather cut jumped up his stomach for a second, revealing a tight set of abs I hadn't seen on a man outside underwear ads in magazines.

I quirked an eyebrow. "Does it matter? Something tells me we're not allowed to have any guests."

"Fuck, yes, it matters. This is where I'm gonna crash while I keep an eye on you two."

My heart sank. Of course. Just because he'd moved us to a better prison, didn't mean we were home and free.

And why not? My first instinct alone would've been to

grab Jackie, head for a hotel, and spill my guts about this nightmare to the first cop I saw.

"It's been a long fucking time since I lived in an apartment," he said, stretching his huge body out on the cushions. "You'll have the place to yourselves most of the time. Club business keeps me busy during the day, you know."

Duh. We'd been left alone for days, never knowing when he'd blow in, or what he'd do with us. His 'business' only fed the hellish uncertainty filling our lives.

I cautiously planted my butt in the wicker rocking chair next to him. "Fine. What about school for Jackie? She's been out all week dealing with my father's death, but she's supposed to be back on Monday..."

He shrugged. "Tell 'em she's sick. I fucked off in school all the time and turned out fine. Guess I'm lucky nobody asked any questions in those days."

I wanted to burst out laughing. Was he fucking serious? Whatever he'd been when he was young, he was an outlaw biker now!

A killer. A thief. A brute.

All the evil things it was hard to visualize when he was right in front of me, looking sexier than any criminal should.

Somehow, I held the crazed, panicky laugh in my chest. Good thing too because if it got started, I knew it wouldn't stop until I was paralyzed on the floor in tears.

"Brass, she's fourteen years old. Her father just died from cancer and her older sister led her right into a pack of –"

Devils. Fuckers. Assholes.

No words were adequate for how the Grizzlies treated us. And I still got angry and sad every time I thought about daddy too.

Leaving us with nothing would've been better than what he'd dropped in my lap – why the fuck did he think I'd have any idea how to handle this? Why did he die painting a target on his daughters' backs?

Because the cancer rotted his brain. Or maybe desperation did. I didn't like that answer. It filled my skull with cruel cement.

Brass threw his feet on the floor and straightened up. "What were you gonna say? You don't have to self-censor here, babe. I've heard it all. You think calling me a rude name's gonna hurt my widdle feelings?"

Bastard. He made a puppy dog face and grinned. I shrugged, guessing it was better than having him jump on me and throw his hand on my throat for the stifled insult.

"We both know what happened," I snapped. "There's no need to resort to name calling. I don't need to sink to your level."

He laughed. A low, rich, smoky baritone sound, older sounding than his face suggested.

"Sure wish you would. Might help you blow off some fucking steam. Christ, I know I need to. If you think I like having to deal with this shit – hostages – you're wrong. Deadly fucking wrong. I'm doing the best I can to make my brothers happy and keep you alive."

He had me there. After bringing us here, I was starting

to believe his bullshit, and that made me hate him even more. I shot daggers out of my eyes as I looked at him, annoyed that his face looked too handsome to cut.

If only he could've been a total gargoyle...feeding the hatred would've been so much easier.

Damn it, why did he look so different from most of the other guys in his club? Rude, savage bikers who acted like demons shouldn't wear the faces of angels.

"You've done enough. I don't like this crap, but I'm not an idiot, Brass. I won't go out. I won't say anything unless I get your permission, *sir*." I practically stuck out my tongue when I said it. "But Jackie...I can't give up on her when she hasn't gotten started yet. She needs an education."

Brass stood up, growling. He moved fast, pacing the room like a frustrated tiger in its cage. I wondered if he was about to kick over the brand new coffee table next to my legs when he stopped next to me and reached for his wallet.

"Here!" Crumpled up bills landed at my feet. "It's all I got 'til the next share comes in from the club. Pull the girl outta school and buy her some fucking lessons. Five hundred's gotta get something. I can't fucking risk her breaking down and tattling to teacher. You'll listen to these lessons and make sure she doesn't say anything she shouldn't."

I was frozen in disbelief for at least a solid minute, looking at his dark, angry eyes. Jesus.

He was very, *very* good at making it hard to hate him, especially when the way he'd given me the money should've made it easy. Hell, five hundred dollars didn't make a dent in the two million we'd lost.

It wasn't yours, a sad voice in my head reminded me. *You didn't do anything to deserve it, and whatever your father did was evil.*

Ignoring the sly voice in my head, I scooped up the money, stuffing it into my pocket. Brass took two more long walks through the room, shaking his head. It was like watching a grenade having its pin stuffed in before it went off.

"Look, I'm really fucking sorry all this shit had to come down like this. I know it was your daddy who sold us out and not you. You and your sis got in the way. The guys are so fucked up and stretched to their limits they would've killed you if I hadn't been there...I stopped it. I saved you." He held up a hand as I opened my lips. "I'm not looking for any gratitude, so you can shove that shit right back down your throat. I'm just looking for an understanding, babe. You gotta tell me you get what I'm trying to do here. This little tango is all that's gonna save *all* our lives – including mine – because I'm the lucky fuck who's responsible for you two. You fuck up, hurt the club, and we all die together."

My eyes burned hard, just looking at him, thinking even harder.

Ugh. He'd never stop being a bastard, but right now, he was right.

"I understand, Brass. I hate to admit it, but I do. I'll try to cooperate."

"Try?" He snorted. "You're gonna have to do better than that, babe. If you ever wanna go free, you're gonna have to prove to the club you can be trusted."

No! There's no fucking way...

My head started spinning all over again. "And how the hell am I supposed to do that?"

"You saw the state the clubhouse was in – shit, you *smelled* it." He paused. "You need money, right? I talked to Blackjack, and he's willing to have you around to clean shit up. We'll pay you two or three times what some maid would get because you've got extra incentive to keep your pretty pink mouth shut."

I was shaking my head before he finished. Started shaking it even harder when he added that last part.

I couldn't go to that stinking, filthy, evil place again. And I definitely didn't need this sick attraction going both ways.

"No." Brass blinked in surprise after I said it. "I'll wait this out. I'll find a different job. I can't go back there again...I just –"

"You can, and you will," he growled. "Babe, much as I wish I was offering you a real choice, it's a fucking illusion. You're gonna do this for me, and you're gonna do it right. If we're lucky, we'll be too busy focusing on our war to get in your hair. If the guys believe you're really my old lady, they won't give a shit if you fade into the background, and neither will I."

Old lady? He'd said that word before. It was strange – crude like everything else that came from his wicked lips.

"Okay, you need to tell me what that means. You talked

about me with that man, Crack, like I was your..." The word stuck in my throat. I had to force it out. "Property. Does old lady mean slave, Brass?"

"Slave to the heart, maybe. Being claimed is the best damned thing a girl can hope for hanging around men like us. You become an old lady, you get special privileges. You're not like the rest of the whores and sluts." He grunted, struggling to explain, his face turning red as he eyed the confusion on mine. "I didn't marry you or nothing, babe. But if you still don't get it, taking a wife's the closest equivalent in your world."

My heart skipped a beat. Shit, maybe ten.

I started to slump back in the chair, feeling the tremor rising in my body. Horror, rage, and hate shot to my throat. I coughed once to push it down. No use.

"You can't be serious! And you waited until now to tell me this?" I shook my head for the hundredth time that night, feeling blood rattle in my temples. "You're sick. This whole fucking thing is. God, I'm starting to wish you'd let the rest of those animals pull the trigger."

Brass moved like lightning. The rocking chair was tipped back and he was face to face with me, all rage, a rough glint in his dark green eyes that turned my skin into goosebumps.

"Shut the fuck up. I know you don't mean that shit, but I'll be a goddamned devil before I let you say that fucking bullshit to my face again. You'd better learn to control your tongue, babe, or someone a whole lot shorter fused than me's gonna cut it right off."

I stopped thinking. My hand went up and grazed his face, slapping him across the cheek.

I didn't care what happened anymore. This hot and cold, good cop-bad cop act had to die, or else I would first. I flew out of my chair before he could grab me and hit the couch.

Rolling, I wondered why he wasn't holding me down, laying into me with words or worse.

What the hell? Brass wasn't even looking at me.

He was staring at Jackie, who'd just come into the room and stood staring at us, one hand clenched on the corner of the wall.

"It's okay!" I spat, twisting my feet to take a normal sitting position. "We were just talking about work...a job opportunity..."

I looked at Brass, hoping he'd give me a little support. His face was completely cold, if it wasn't just pure fire.

"We're done talking. I'm heading out 'til later." His eyes drilled deeper into mine. "I gave you some shit to think about and said everything I needed to. You're gonna mull it over and find a tutor for your sis while I take care of business."

He turned, heading straight for the door, and slammed it behind him without another word.

I hated him even when he was gone. He'd just forced me into this hell's tightest corner: trying to convince my sister everything was all right when I didn't believe it for a second.

I didn't hear him come in that night. When I woke up and padded to the bathroom in the morning, I saw the lumpy blanket thrown across the couch, but he wasn't there either.

It wasn't until I went into the kitchen to check and see if we had any food that I finally saw him. He was leaning on the counter, shoveling a bowl of food into his mouth with a spoon.

"Eggs, hash, and sausage. There's more underneath those lids on the stove if you want it. You find a tutor for your sis, or what?"

"Just barely started looking," I said. "Had other things on my mind."

It had taken an hour just to calm down and convince Jackie everything was okay. By the time I got on the crappy old computer he'd left us and started to look, my brain was overwhelmed with my own selfish problems.

Rock met hard place the instant I held Brass' dirty money in my hands. The bastard made me realize there was no way out unless I did exactly what he said. I hated it, and hated even it more that I couldn't deny it.

Brass finished his last bite and dropped his bowl in the sink. It landed with a clatter that made me jump. Annoyed, I straightened my long pajama shirt and looked at him.

"Listen, I thought about what you said last night..." I waited until he looked up. "Your club's full of the most disgusting pigs I've ever seen. But that doesn't mean I want to live like this forever. I can't be a prisoner, and neither can Jackie. If I have to clean up their messes to get away from this and get on with my life...I'll do it."

He cocked his head. Red shame flooded my cheeks. Jesus, who was actually saying these words? I felt disembodied.

"Good. Had a feeling you'd come to your senses eventually. Go clean up, babe. You're heading in with me today."

Panic clogged my throat. "But...Jackie doesn't have a tutor yet..."

"So? You said you're working on that," he said, taking a step closer. "I trust you're not shitting me about the girl talking, right?"

Part of me wished she would. If it wouldn't mean changing our names and hiding like rats for the rest of our lives, I wanted Jackie to freak out, run to the police. Anything to get this apartment and their clubhouse raided. My heart swelled with grim satisfaction when I imagined all the Grizzlies clapped in irons and loaded into a SWAT team's van.

Everybody except the bastard standing in front of me. For some unholy reason, imagining him in handcuffs tugged at my heart, filled me with a thick, sickly guilt.

Stepping up to him, I closed the distance between us, standing on my tip-toes until we were eyeball-to-eyeball. "I keep my promises. Neither of us will say anything to anyone. She can stay here...just let me talk to her before we leave."

I turned before he could say anything and headed for her room. Knocking several times on her door gave no response. I grabbed the doorknob and pushed it open, finding her halfway awake, sprawled out on the narrow double bed.

"What's going on?" My sister sat up, her eyes wide. There'd been too much bad news lately not to panic when these unexpected visits happened.

"I'm going out for awhile. I need you to stay here. There's games and reading to do on the computer. I'd really appreciate it if you can do some math or history while I'm trying to get you the teacher we talked about."

She wrinkled her nose and sat up, throwing off the covers. "You're working for him, aren't you? Are they even paying you, Missy, or are we just total slaves now?"

My lips tingled, ready to throw sisterly venom back at her. God damn it. It would've been so much easier if the question didn't strike so deep.

"We're working off daddy's debt. Think of it that way," I said, sitting on the bed next to her. I reached out to touch her shoulder, but she pulled away, looking at me like I was covered in stinking motor oil.

"Is that why they took all the money and threatened to kill us? Was it all about the cash in that bag?" She leaned forward, clawing at the blanket. "You're treating me like shit! I'm not a little kid. I can handle the truth, Missy. Why won't you give it to me?"

Because some truths are so fucking brutal it's blinding to look at them head on, I thought. I had to think fast, scramble to find my words, something to shut down the battle brewing.

"I already told you. Before he died, dad made some big

mistakes. Terrible mistakes. The cancer really screwed up his head. He took some things from people he really shouldn't have. I don't like them either – they're bastards. But they've got their reasons for being pissed..."

Jackie closed her eyes and shook her head, annoyed with all my half-answers. If only she knew the half-assed answers really were the best ones I had. I didn't have a clue what was going on with Brass' MC, the cartel, and the money, not to mention all those phantom whispers about a war. A big part of me didn't even want to know *why* we were in this shit storm.

What did it matter? Knowledge wasn't power here. Right now, all I cared about was clawing my way out, and dragging Jackie with me to the safe, distant shore.

"Reasons?" Jackie repeated, rolling the word sarcastically on her tongue. "They must be pretty fucking good to go along with this and live here with this asshole like nothing happened."

My face tightened. "Knock it off. Daddy wouldn't approve of that language, and neither do I. You've still got some growing up to do, sis. I know this doesn't make sense right now. One day, it will. I'm trying to do what's best and it's *really* fucking hard."

I ran a hand over my face. So much for leading by example.

Jackie turned away from me, pulling her feet up to her chest. It was over. When she went fetal, I knew we were done talking.

Damn. Not at all the way I wanted this to go, but staying

73

here trying to reason with the most flawed logic in the world wasn't going to help us get away from the Grizzlies' claws faster.

I got up and padded to the door, stopping one more time on my way out. "Stay here. Be good. I promise I'll keep working on the tutor thing so you'll have something to pass the time without thinking about this crap."

No response. I pulled the door shut behind me and headed for the bathroom. It was a quick shower, cranked up as high as the building's water heater could manage. I let the hot droplets steam off my skin, ignoring the tears mingling with the shower near the end.

When I cleaned up and changed, Brass was waiting for me near the door.

We got on his bike and headed for the clubhouse. It was getting easier to keep my small hands around him, secretly admiring his taut muscles beneath my fingertips. Of course, I hated myself for loving anything at all about this asshole taking me to a job I never asked for.

Just before we hit the highway, he told me to cover my eyes. The man still didn't trust me to see where his clubhouse was. I did what he asked, tucking my face deep into his back. Hot, angry breaths steamed up around his neck, and I knew he could feel them when his skin rippled, the stubble on his face brushing my cheek several times.

Monsters shouldn't feel this good.

When we pulled into the massive garage, I got off and followed him inside. Brass led me to a small closet in the smelly hallway. I found a bunch of long neglected cleaning crap inside, but at least it contained all the gear I needed to make a dent in this place's filth.

"You know how to use this shit?" he asked.

"I'm not a moron. I mopped floors and wiped toilets part-time for my college before I quit. I don't think cleaning up after bikers is worse than a man with terminal cancer either..."

Brass nodded. "Got you. Well, start on the floors and then hit the bar. Fucking thing hasn't been wiped down since well before I got here. If anybody gives you any shit, tell 'em you're Brass' old lady."

We shared an awkward look. Brass looked like he was about to say something else, but then he turned and left just as mysteriously.

The day went about as well as I expected. By afternoon, my shoulders were aching, but the entire clubhouse had gotten fresh Pine Sol swept over its floors. Everything except the rooms where the men smoked, slept, and fucked. I looked at Brass' room and cringed, amazed we'd stayed there for three days.

I couldn't help but wonder what else went on in there when we weren't around.

The men weren't shy about sex. Doors opened and closed at odd hours, releasing men with sweat still shining on their foreheads, or half-dressed girls barely older than me.

They all headed to the bar to pick up whiskey and water, hauling it back to their rooms to resume the insatiable passions happening inside. Some of them looked like they were drugged out of their minds. It was late when I finally started on the bar counter.

I cleared off the bottles, gingerly wiping them down, when I heard footsteps behind me. I would've preferred just about anything standing behind me except for the nasty freak with the barbed wire tattooed on his face.

"Whiskey, bitch," Serial barked.

I held up my hands. "I'm not a bartender. Brass didn't tell me to touch any of this stuff –"

His arms twitched, and then his palms slapped the counter like lightning. "You fucking heard me. Don't make me ask again. I want a bottle of Jack to go, and I want it right fucking now."

His eyes were stranger than the pitch black pools I'd seen on the night he wanted to kill us. They were brighter, but still so vacant, like light reflecting off a marionette's marble eyes.

His sleeve was pushed up. Several patches of skin were gray, discolored, dull red holes along their edges. Unmistakable bruises left behind by a junkie shooting up. I'd seen it plenty of times on ride alongs with daddy as a little girl.

This wasn't a man to reason with sober, let alone tripping out of his mind. I reached for the nearest whiskey bottle I could find and shoved it across the counter.

He popped the cap and took a long swig, pouring the crap down his throat like it was cream soda. "You remember who you're working for. I would've blown your girl's brains out if Brass and Blackjack hadn't pussied out.

You're here at our mercy. This club doesn't need any parasites when it's fighting for its life. We fucking own you, and your little girl. We can stomp you both like a fucking flea any time we choose."

He winked, and pointed his free hand at me like a gun. "BANG BANG! You're dead, cunt. Think I'd start on little sissy first, though." he growled.

Pretty sure my heart stopped then. My fingers trembled as I heard his death threat echoing in my head, the cold, calm closeness to murder. I was still pinching the rag in my burning fingers when he was finally gone.

"Missy."

I nearly hit the ceiling. I threw the rag on the counter and spun. Angry, shaken, and ready to face trouble. Brass was there on the other side of the bar, one hand braced against the granite.

"How'd it go?" he asked, smooth as an assistant manager checking in on me at some bullshit job.

"Your friend with the thorns on his face just told me how much he'd like to kill Jackie. How the hell do you think?"

Anger roiled his face, a more violent, masculine mirror of mine. "Fuck. Don't listen to that shithead. He's always been a twisted little fuck since the minute I got to Redding. Come on. Let's fucking go."

He grabbed the rag and cleaner off the counter and held them for me while I quickly pushed dusty bottles back into place. I'd have to pick up on this nightmare job tomorrow.

When our stuff was put away, we left, riding along the

bluish fading horizon on his Harley. This time, I practically jabbed my nails into his stomach, trying to hurt him whenever he made a turn.

I never asked for any of this shit. And I definitely wasn't cut out for it – not for dealing with these animals.

It was just my first day on the 'job' – and calling it that was being painfully generous – and I was totally ready to lose it.

Jackie's words stabbed deep in my mind over and over. Slaves. That's exactly what we were, shackled to work with these brutes until we were dead or they finally got tired of us.

And what then? I thought about Serial.

BANG BANG!

I pressed my hands tight around Brass' waist. Rage churned in my veins, so potent I refused to recognize how seductive his stupid sexy abs were beneath my hands.

What if we never came back? Jackie would eventually break, leave the apartment, and run, wouldn't she?

I chewed my lip, seriously considering hurling my fingernails into Brass' eyes, making him wreck the bike before we got off the highway. But killing him and snapping my own neck wouldn't get us out of this. Not without giving my sister more hellish memories that would haunt her for the rest of her life.

I wanted it to be easy with him. Just *once*. I wanted to treat him like one of them, an easy target for my hatred, my pain, my will to survive.

Brass parked the Harley next to the apartment and

switched it off. Quickly climbing off, he faced me, ripping off my helmet before I could work off the strap myself.

"Fucking shit, babe. I thought you were gonna tear a hole in my guts the whole ride here. What's eating you?"

I turned away. The painful lump in my throat made it impossible to speak – not without crying, anyway.

"Don't do this, Missy," he growled, throwing one strong hand on my shoulder. "I need you to either keep it together or let me know what the fuck's going on so I can fix it. If you're upset about Serial, I'll break his fucking nose next time I see him. Brother or no, I'm not gonna let that psycho fuckwit shit all over my old –"

"Don't say it!" I snapped.

He tried to hold on, but I was too quick and his grip too tentative. I ripped myself away, climbing off the bike, throwing my hands into my pockets for the apartment's keys.

He knew better than to follow me inside when I was this upset. Jackie was locked in her room, refusing to respond every time I knocked. I left her a thick sandwich I threw together and a tall water bottle outside her door.

Then I cleaned up and turned in. The stink of cleaner and old smoke came off easy enough, but the putrid reek of bad luck didn't. Practically scrubbed my skin raw, wishing I could wipe away every trace of evil.

But it wasn't all on the outside, was it? Of course not, because that would be too convenient.

The real problem was the corruption inside me, the way Brass had gotten underneath my skin. I had my chance to kill him for Jackie's sake, and I knew there'd be more. Maybe there'd be a dozen chances, and I'd pass them all up, wouldn't I?

All because I didn't have a clue how to relate to this *asshole* who should've disgusted me just as much as Serial.

It was fucking sick. And so was I. My pussy betrayed me every time I got close to him, tingling while my nipples hardened, begging to be fucked by King Asshole.

Unfortunately, this asshole saved us. He'd delayed our doom while he continued to drag me back to his sick brothers every fucking day. He was the last little thread that held me together, kept me from lashing out, doing something stupid and getting us all killed.

I shouldn't care. Much less about him. Nothing should've mattered except freeing my sister, even if it cost me my own life.

And I shouldn't have the kinda thoughts I did while riding this bike, imagining what it would be like to run my hands on his stomach without leather and denim between his skin and mine. I shouldn't sweat and shake when his green eyes bathed me in his teal fire, wondering what his glare would look like only inches apart, watching me as I lost my mind on his cock.

Stockholm Syndrome. Wasn't that what they called it when a woman starts admiring her captor? What the hell did they call it when she was way past admiring, aching to run her tongue down his chest, and then even lower?

I wasn't sure, but I sank a little more into its one-way grasp every minute I was around him, and that scared the *shit* out of me.

God, I had a better idea how to handle my slave work with the Grizzlies and the dead eyed killers milling around the clubhouse. Serial's evil words hurt, but they didn't leave me confused, wrecked, disembodied. The hatred between us was a clear wall, keeping him away from my world, and me out of his as long as I watched my step.

I didn't have that luxury in my own fucking home, if I wanted to call this apartment that. I didn't have anything – much less my sanity – while I was forced to live here with *him*.

No protection. No safety. Not even the comfort black and white hate provided.

I never heard him come home, as usual. Whenever he finally dragged himself in and crashed on the sofa, I was already long asleep, my red eyes spinning in their nightmares after crying me to sleep.

IV: Cruel Charade (Brass)

I ripped circles through Redding half the fucking night on my bike, feeling the spots on my stomach where her nails almost tore through my clothes.

Why couldn't anything be easy with this girl? Why the fuck couldn't I catch a goddamned break just one time?

I thought my ship was sliding into happy harbor that morning, when she'd settled the hell down, agreeing to work on the one and only path that might set us all free. Then Serial had to stick his fucked up nose into it.

Shit! I should've rode straight to the clubhouse, kicked down the door, and pummeled his ugly face 'til it shattered. Too bad the asshole was the best shot this club had, and the Prez made it crystal fucking clear we'd need a good sniper on the roof if the cartel ever got the balls to attack our clubhouse.

Didn't stop me from wanting to beat him raw. It'd be satisfying for the first sixty seconds, before all the brothers descended on me, beating my ass to death before they dragged the girls away to the warehouse to be slaughtered like animals.

I hadn't been so frustrated since sitting through sis'

wedding reception, surrounded by Prairie Pussies. I'd kept it together in Reno without taking a hit. But fuck, my whole body ached for one right now.

At least shooting smack up my veins would've cut my fuming body a break. I couldn't lose the hard-on turning my cock to steel no matter how many miles I rode, fighting to push Missy outta my mind like a madman stuck on OCD.

How fucked up was I for wanting her to scratch through my clothes on that tense ride home? If she would've gone at it a little harder, a little lower, I would've parked the bike on the side of the road and thrown her to the ground.

Tossing her to the earth and ripping off her pants sounded better than a shot of pure fucking heaven right about now. What I wouldn't give to feel her, fuck her, mark her with my teeth...I hadn't even given her a proper brand yet.

No, she wasn't really my old lady, but damn if I didn't want to make her fuck like one.

Just the thought of claiming that pussy as mine, stuffing her up to the hilt with my big dick, was the match that lit me on fire. I raced down the highway like an asshole who'd had one too many, weaving in and out the empty lanes, pushing my engine to its limits.

The cold wind couldn't do shit to calm me down. Nothing would. Nothing except ripping her panties off with my bare hands and sinking into that hot, pink, arrogant slit, fisting her hair and grinding my teeth while I fucked her to the earth's core.

Didn't she understand her life and death was in my fucking hands? Christ, I wanted to drive it home, drive it *deep*, drive it hard and rough 'til she lost control and gushed all over my dick.

If she was gonna keep screaming and snarling in my face, then I wanted to give her a damned good reason to.

My balls were still on fire on the way back, hoping enough time had passed to put her down for the night so I could collapse on the couch like a zombie. I was afraid for what I'd do if I saw her again in this state.

My hands and my cock were done listening to my head for the night. They wanted to send a message one way or another, something she'd never forget, something to tell her this old lady shit wasn't a fucking game.

I stopped off at the liquor store for a six pack and barreled back to the apartment. Place was mercifully empty when I got inside. I chugged the brews fast, letting cheap carbonation and alcohol burn my throat, waiting 'til the booze punched me in the stomach and put me down for the night.

I never asked for any of this shit. I was coming apart a little more day by day, caught between my club and this beautiful chick with the bratty sister, without any room for mistakes that would end in us being buried together.

At some point, I passed out, wondering if I'd wake up and find out it was all a bad dream. But then, I would've had to wake up about five years earlier, about the time my life went to shit.

Missy wouldn't even talk to me the next day. We rode to the clubhouse in stone cold silence for another fun filled day ahead. I'd be hearing about the latest cartel raids while she worked her ass off trying to clean this shithole up and earn the brothers' trust.

I kept an eye out for her in between checking in with Blackjack and Crack. It was no small relief to have them riding my ass about cartel business instead of the girls.

Blackjack was in the garage, probably on his tenth smoke that morning. "Three shipments hit last night on the run to San Diego. Fucked beyond all recognition. That's it, boys. The club won't be making any more hops too close to the border 'til we're confident we own the roads south again."

"Fuck!" Crack smashed his fists together. "Did you tell the Prez yet?"

"Nope." Blackjack winked. "That's your job, VP. Don't need to tell you morale's in the shitter too. If Fang finds out, he'll blow the fucking roof off and cancel Lipstick Night tomorrow. And that's if he doesn't send our asses charging into Mexico to get cut to pieces."

The VP growled, giving me the evil eye. "This is all your bitch's dead daddy's fault, Brass. I fucked up letting you haul those cunts outta here, I swear to fucking God..."

He stepped up. Crack was a total hothead, always waving his dick, remembering the days when he used to be the Prez in Redding before Fang spoiled his fun. I didn't move a muscle, bowing up 'til I was at least a good inch taller than the VP.

"It's not their fault," I said coldly. "Cancer man was the rat. You've got nothing to the contrary because it doesn't fucking exist. With all due respect, you gotta let this go, Veep. I'll keep them outta our hair, make sure they never talk. Shit, if anybody could bring the dead man back to life and put a bullet in his skull for the shit he's done to this club, I'd be the first in line."

An obvious lie. I didn't know what the hell to do with anything involving Missy anymore. She made my dick throb in my pants so fucking hard it sucked the blood outta my head. Too hard to think. Maybe so damned hard it pulled the blinders off too, because I was really starting to wonder about the moves my brothers were making.

And doubting my own fucking club was never a good thing.

Crack eased back a single step. He still looked like he was ready to wheel around and send his fist into my jaw anytime. I scraped my boot on the concrete, looking at Rabid next to me.

"The boy's right," Blackjack said, pushing his big beefy body between the Veep and I. "You wanna punch someone in the mouth, I'm right here. It was my call to give the girls a chance instead of burying them. I don't regret making it – especially not when he made such a convincing show out of claiming the older one. Tell me, Brass. Was it worth it, son? You managed to fuck some respect into that pussy yet, or is she still icing down your nuts?"

Rabid coughed, suppressing a laugh. I looked at the

ground and refused to answer the old man. Blackjack was a fuck, but he stuck up for me in his own way, diffusing a situation that easily could've gone sour with the Veep.

Crack was halfway across the garage and almost in the clubhouse when he spun around, pointing at the three of us. "Don't breathe a word about the raid for a couple days. I'll tell the Prez then. No fucking way am I gonna be the asshole who spills his guts and gets Lipstick Night canceled."

The door slammed behind him. I waited a few seconds, ready to go in after him, but Blackjack reached out and stopped me with a tight squeeze to my forearm.

"Easy, boy. You've been on edge since the night we brought those strays in. Don't let her get to you unless you really mean to make an old lady out of her." He held my gaze, looking more wizardly than ever with his hair flapping on his cut. "Your choice. If you're not gonna take this thing all the way, then drop the fucking show and have some fun tomorrow. Fuck. Drink. Be merry. Life's shorter than we know."

What the fuck was I supposed to say to that? It was like he'd given a voice to the whirlwind inside me, beating everything I thought I knew before Missy to tatters. Blackjack tightened his grip – hard enough to pinch my muscles – and then let go all at once.

Rabid followed me inside and we hit the bar together. Suzy the bartender was standing there, a cigarette in her mouth and a blank expression on her face as she watched the TV. The woman was in her late forties, an old lady transplant from Sacramento, property of a dude named Toss. She'd taken on the bartender roll out of boredom, with nothing better to do since Fang ordered everybody and their families north.

Rabid asked for his usual and got a tall glass of whiskey mixed with ginger ale. I never figured out how many shots were in that fucker, but he definitely wouldn't be riding anytime soon.

"What about you?" Suzy asked, her thin lips pulled in a smile.

I shook my head. "Gotta leave with my girl soon. We got family business to take care of with her little sis."

Rabid laughed and hit the counter. "You gotta be shitting me. You, Brass, a family man? Since fucking when?"

"Since I decided I didn't want to end up in the shed with the Mauler if these girls fucked us over. I gotta keep 'em happy and outta trouble too."

"Come on, man. One fucking beer. Shit, when you showed up here, you went on runs with something a lot more potent than Jack flowing in your veins."

Ignoring the grim reminder, I looked at Suzy and ordered a tall one, then took my seat next to Rabid. Fucker was the only brother in this place except Blackjack who'd get away with talking about my sins without a fist to the face.

"Those days are behind me, and you know it. I'm staying clean for the club. This fucking shit with the cartel's getting serious. We slack off drunk too many nights with our hands on our dicks, we'll all wake up one day burned to a crisp, or else having our heads chopped off."

Rabid laughed, making a goofy ass line across his neck with one finger. Just my luck that I related to this club's lame fucking joker best, while all the more serious brothers were so dark and mercenary they made me want to rip their heads off and do the world a favor.

"It's almost like you care," he said, narrowing his eyes as he sipped his drink. "What's going on, Brass? You trying to undo the shit with your own family looking after these chicks?"

My hand balled in a fist. Okay, I definitely would've laid his ass out if he were anyone but Rabid. I settled for twisting the seat and stabbing my finger into his chest, holding it there while I told him exactly what the fuck was going on.

"I don't owe anybody shit for what happened. The guys I thought were my brothers turned on me. Killed my Ma and almost murdered Shelly too...I blame that shit on the smack. I was too fucked up to know any better 'til it was almost too late." It felt like smoke was hissing through my teeth. "I'll never make that mistake again. Long as I stay clean, I stay clear headed. I'm not trying to undo fuck ups and oversights that happened in Montana. I'm trying my damnedest to make sure they don't go down here, and I'd appreciate it if you'd stop sticking your dick where it doesn't belong. Save that shit for the redhead you've been railing all week."

Until the last part, he'd been flexed, ready to give me a

rough shove if I didn't lay off his ass. Then, he just smiled. Probably thinking about the fire crotch burning up his cock. Typical Rabid.

"Whatever, dude. Blackjack's right. I hope you're not so stuck on bad memories you can't loosen up and have some fun tomorrow. I know I'm gonna do it with Red. All fucking night."

I snorted, pausing to drain half my beer. "Red, huh? Is that really her name?"

"I call 'em like I see 'em. This baby girl was so new I got to her first and gave her something simple. Classy. Sounds a lot better than Vacuum Lips or Twinkie or some shit, right?"

Fuck if that didn't make me smile for a second. I wasn't even offended he'd insulted my old whore. Of course, it also made me think about Missy's lips wrapped around my cock, pretty and perfect, lined up with my lust where they were always mean to be.

Twinkie didn't have shit on her tits, her eyes, her awesome ass.

And Red didn't have a single shade of pink on my girl either. On the other hand, Rabid didn't have his slut turning his balls ocean blue every goddamned day with her prancing around him, lashing him with a tongue he wanted to hold down and bite, never putting out.

No, that was all down to my shit luck. My stupidity. Didn't doubt that I was the only biker in the world who'd been dumb enough to take an old lady he hadn't even fucked.

"Brass? I'm all done."

I heard her voice just as I was draining my beer. Rabid spun with me, tilting his head, wearing amusement on his face as he gawked like a fool.

"Then let's go home. My business here is done today." I threw my leather coat on over my cut and walked her out.

"Don't forget the party, brother!" Rabid yelled after me. "Gonna take a whole lotta cleaning to sweep that dirty night under the rug."

If I'd have turned around, I was a hundred percent sure I would've seen his shitty grin again. It was easy to be all smiles when all you had to do between getting your dick sucked and fucked was watching out for a cartel hit.

She didn't say much the second evening either. We got to the apartment just as the young redhead with glasses was finishing up with Jackie at the computer. She'd put my money to good use hiring this chick named Christa to tutor the kid.

I eyeballed the woman. *This* hipster girl was who she'd picked? Teachers were supposed to be older and wiser, but fuck if I was gonna make a fuss over it.

Missy walked her into the kitchen and they settled on their fees before the chick with the sexy librarian look left. I fucking hated myself for thinking anything at all. She was really Rabid's type more than mine, but that my balls were so blue by now it was no fucking joke.

Sure, I snuck peeks at other chicks, especially when the club sluts batted their eyes at me in the clubhouse halls.

But ever since Missy landed in my lap, an ice sculpture with a hot chick's body, I was losing my mind. Losing my manhood too.

I could look, but there was no fucking way my cock would be satisfied with anything less than her.

Rabid's Red and the equally fire haired teacher got my heart going, but they were tepid hags compared to the brunette slaving away under my watch. Night time was the worst. Thinking about how the hell I was gonna pass out on the sofa without marching to her room and shoving my dick between Missy's legs already hurt.

When she finally came outta the kitchen, carrying chips and salad for herself, I sank down in the chair next to her. Little sis gave us some badly needed privacy by rushing off to her room. Hoped like fuck the homework or reading or whatever the hell the teach handed out would keep her occupied for a little while.

"You're gonna need to pay that tutor extra to stay late or get Jackie a babysitter tomorrow."

She looked up, crunching on a chip, cold and annoyed with me at once. God damn. How the hell did she stay on edge all the time without going off like dynamite?

"Why's that? Something to do with this lipstick crap I've been hearing about?"

Fuck. Just my luck she would've heard whores and brothers talking about it. Those fucking parties were usually the biggest every quarter. Before shit got bad with the cartel, brothers came north voluntarily, eager to get their dicks sucked, ringed with every shade of lipstick the

NICOLE SNOW

sluts wore before fucking them to the wall.

It was pure debauchery. The last one was when I started fucking Twinkie, fisting her blonde locks as she got my load down her throat. Bitch added her deep ruby stamp to the lighter shit left by the two girls before her.

My cock jerked just thinking about it. And then it jerked a whole lot harder when I imagined Missy dolled up like a whore, her tongue all over my dick. Having her sweet lips full of me would sure go a long way to giving her some damned humility.

"Well?" she asked again, working through a few more bites.

"Yeah. I want you there to clean like usual. Trust me, you'll wanna do it too. Less work the next day. This bash'll undo some of your hard work after a buncha brothers and their girls crash through the clubhouse like a drunken fucking whirlwind."

She shrugged. "Isn't that every day? I hear them through the walls..."

I shook my head. "You haven't seen shit. Tomorrow's gonna be worse because we're all on edge. Best way for most guys to blow off some steam is getting their dicks wet."

"Nice. I'm glad us old ladies have such an important place in your world." She looked disgusted.

I was starting to get pissed. No matter how many times I kept my cool and took her bites as they came, she always managed to get underneath my skin.

"It's the way things are. I don't make the rules in the

Grizzlies MC. I just follow them, same as all our traditions." I tried not to growl. "Look, you've got the wrong idea if you think old ladies are running around screwing every brother in sight. That's the sluts' job."

"Whatever. I'm just glad you're not pimping me out. I doubt the rest of your buddies would be so kind."

My eyes fixed on her harder, wondering if that was a compliment. One thing was certain: no matter what the fuck I did, she loathed every minute with me and the club. And that made me want to strangle my dick every time it pulsed for her, as if this was just another tease I could claim by throwing her on my bike and carrying her to my room.

If this was playing hard to get, then it was the most fucked up chase I'd ever seen in my life.

"It won't be bad. All you gotta do tomorrow is collect trash and serve drinks. Suzy'll mix the shit at the bar, so you don't have to worry about that end of it. I'll be there the whole time. Shit, you can have a few drinks yourself and drive us both home when it wears off. I'll take my truck instead of the Harley."

"Joy!" The wicked smile beaming on her face almost had me fooled. Then it melted into the same lifeless frown dragging on her face since I'd pulled her into my life.

"You don't have to love this, babe," I said. "But you do have to get through it. These little outings are the *only* way you're ever gonna convince Blackjack and the others to let you go. They gotta know you're one of us, trustworthy and absolutely —"

I stopped just short of saying it. Calling her *mine* when she damned well wasn't was the dumbest fucking thing I could've pushed through my lips.

Hell, it wasn't even a good act. It never was. Blackjack saw right through it. He proved as much when he gave me shit about it this morning, and I saw the warning written between the lines.

If I couldn't pull her further into my orbit, and at least make her *act* like a good old lady, then all bets were off. They threatened to collapse at any time with the Mexicans lighting fires in our backyard.

I was about to remind her what the fuck we were doing in this crazy arrangement before she held up her palm.

"Don't say it," Missy snapped. "I've heard it all before, and I'm going to follow through. I promised you that much. Even if I hate it – and I will, Brass, every fucking second – I'll get through it. I'll do anything to make sure Jackie and I get out of this alive."

I stood, looking her over, trying to hide the lust in my eyes with pure dark menace. Showing mercy hadn't done shit for that bad attitude. Maybe a little intimidation would.

Just standing over her wasn't gonna cut it. My hands reached out before I knew what I was doing. I reached down and pulled her up, grabbing her, slamming her to my chest.

Fuck, those full tits felt so good pressed against me. One inch closer and she would've felt the hard-on ballooning in my jeans, raging for her, making my heart beat me deaf, dumb, and blind. My dick hummed with enough fury for my heart and soul.

"Make sure you do," I said in the most glacial killer tone I had. "We're all depending on you playing your part. Any fuck up, and we're dead."

I didn't say another word. Neither did she. I let go and took off. Missy didn't yell after me as I stepped out and slammed the door behind me, heading for another long ride through Redding to clear my head.

Bitter satisfaction flowed through me when I realized I'd gotten the last word.

We went in later that day, after she'd made sure the tutor was lined up 'til midnight. The bash started about five, a couple dozen tanked up brothers and just as many women stuffed into the clubhouse.

Everybody was there from our crew, Sacramento, and even a few visitors from Nomads running up and down the west coast. The Prez was conspicuously absent, but it only seemed to liven things up. Having Fang there eyeballing us wasn't anybody's idea of fun.

No brother needed to dig deep to see the darkness ticking away in his eyes, the single-minded obsession with moving us around on the chess board 'til the club or the cartel broke.

Rabid disappeared early in the evening with Red and another girl, some dark haired slut I'd never seen before. I was left alone with a bottle of Jack and molten lava hitting my dick in waves. Girls halfway undressed passed by me with brothers holding their hands.

Some were on the floor, hands between their legs, grunting as they teased their clits and warmed up for the men. Others were still fully unclothed, their ruby red and royal purple lips wrapped around every dick they could find, sucking brother's off in the hallways and underneath the tables. But it wasn't that shit turning me to steel.

It was the little flashes of Missy I caught moving through the crowd, bending over to give brothers their drinks and pick up the shit they'd left on the floor. Christ. Her ripe, round ass did more to feed my furnace than all these other bitches would've buck naked, all of 'em wrapped around me, eager and ready at the same damned time.

The *only* chick I wanted was out there, doing her job like a robot, and she'd been programmed to spit pure fire my way. Especially if I wandered up to her in this state.

Shit. My brain turned to mush an hour ago, sprouting the happy fuzz I always got when I marinated my guts in too much booze. I stayed well away from the assholes flopped on the floor with their girls, pushing nasty shit into their veins.

More guys were drugged and fucking in their rooms, their doors left wide open. I walked down the hallway, dick straining when I saw all the hot, sweaty bodies pumping. The thought of having mine between one special pair of legs got me harder than granite, my dick and nobody else's going in her sweet pussy, claiming what should've been mine by rights for throwing the old lady label on her.

If I ever got a piece of her naked, it wouldn't be slow,

sweaty, or loving. It was going to be a raw, ruthless, mind-bending fuck, a fuck that would leave her shaking long after I erupted in her pussy, splitting her whole fucking world apart and filling it with me. Really, truly making her *mine*.

Fuck, my dick ached like it was recovering from a lightning strike. Guess it was – thinking about Missy's warm pussy without having it hurt just as bad.

I tipped my bottle to my lips and poured more napalm down the hatch, stopping in front of Rabid's half-cracked door to watch him empty his nuts in Red. His bare ass bobbed between her legs, twitching with pleasure as he cursed and tweaked her nipples, blowing his load deep in her cunt.

Shit, shit, shit...

The flap of my boxers was soaked. I'd lost so much pre-come thinking about her, wandering around like the drunken fuck I was, that I was starting to figure out how strippers felt after dancing in their thongs all night.

Halfway down the hall, a hand reached out and jerked my cut. I couldn't resist the pull, growling as I spun and hit the wall. Whoever the fuck did it put their hand way too close to my name patch. Nothing pissed a brother off more than having his colors messed with, front or back. I was just as ready to fight for 'em with my life as anybody here.

"Hey! You better have a damned good reason for fucking with me like –"

Before I could get another word out, a small flash of

curves smashed against me, and lukewarm heat covered my lips. Twinkie's kiss was all tongue and teeth, so warm and wet my dick jerked in recognition.

Fuck me if my arms didn't fold right over the small of her back. Big mistake. The slut took that as a signal to grind right into me, pushing her pussy against my jeans, nothing between her slick little slit except a pair of lacy black panties with GRIZZLIES MC stamped in red on the ass.

I knew those panties well. I'd ripped them off and pushed them in her mouth while we'd fucked a dozen times before.

Her tongue was darting in and out my lips, urging me to tongue-fuck her back, when I finally opened my drunken eyes. The door was still open. Somebody was standing out there watching us, and my vision narrowed on *her* standing there, mouth hanging open and eyes wide in shock.

Missy looked like she'd seen a fucking ghost. Her fist wrapped around the broom so tight her knuckles were like ivory.

The raging bull in my pants collapsed and started to go soft. I tore my mouth away from Twinkie's and gave her a rough push. Bitch had a powerful hold with her fingernails. She spun around and was still hanging on me when I was halfway into the hall, her bare legs sliding seductively on mine.

Enough.

I bucked my hips hard, shoving her to the wall. I'd never hurt a woman, but I wanted her the fuck off me. I used one hand to steady her, making sure she wasn't gonna fall, and then ripped myself away.

"Baby? What the fuck!" Her face wrinkled up in confusion and disappointment.

"I can't do this shit tonight. Find somebody else to suck and ride…"

"This is fucking insane! She's not even your old lady…not really…god damn it, Brass! You're really going to say no for some bitch who won't even get you laid?"

Fuck. Even the slut knew it. I almost turned around and marched back over to her, making her say that shit to my face. But I had to go after Missy, who'd bolted toward the bar like a startled cat.

It was tough going through the club. Too many bodies packed into too small a space. Brothers, bottles, and girls everywhere, standing or else lying on the floor, too fucking easy to stumble on.

A bottle caught me right as I saw her through two big Sacramento dudes gabbing away. I slipped and fell on my fucking ass. My body spun, the whiskey slowing my reflexes. Hit my head on a chair's leg and slumped.

Missy! God dammit.

I tried to call to her, but my lips wouldn't work. The whole world was just spinning, spinning, collapsing in on itself. My vision darkened just as I started to feel the wicked bump by my temple.

My head rolled and I saw the Prez sitting on the old sofa, two sluts on his lap, his hands pinching their thighs so hard they looked like they were in pain. Fang looked right at me and smiled, showing the broken, oversized canine in his mouth. He'd supposedly used it to bite a few men to death in the old days. Same fucked up snaggle tooth that gave him his road name.

Shit, why did he look so fucking evil? His eyes were always dark with anger, and stress pulled his face tight. But he never looked like this...he looked like Satan himself, high and pompous on his throne somewhere in hell.

He lifted a hand. The dim light overhead reflected off the blade in his hand. He pressed it dangerously close to one girl's thigh, sliding higher between her legs, ready to sever a critical vein or shoot up and split her in two if he chose.

Fuck, fuck, fuck...

That's when I knew I was losing my mind. I was fucking hallucinating. Had to be!

Too much Jack and grief on an empty stomach could really twist a man's brain to knots. I blacked out on the floor, right next to two more girls thrashing with pleasure on the ground, drooling the same way I used to when I felt the heroin's coarse purr surging through my veins.

Somebody was crying.

I rolled, threw my hands on the ground, and tried to stand up. The liquor in my veins became a half-faded hangover. The weird near silence in the bar told me I must've lost a couple hours – brothers were long gone with their girls, or else in an even deeper coma than I'd been in a second ago.

I looked at the sofa. The Prez was gone, if he'd ever been there at all with those poor scared bitches.

"Let me go! I'm just here to work. I'm not a whore!" I turned toward the high, feminine distress.

"Heh. Could've fooled me with that fucking mouth, begging to be tamed. He hasn't done shit, has he, girl?" The rough voice paused. "Nobody's buying Brass' bullshit, least of all me. I've seen through that asshole from the very beginning. Fang fucked up failing to burn his junkie ass back in Montana, and now he thinks he's gonna get one over on his brothers, claiming your pussy's his when it really isn't? Shut the fuck up, beautiful, and enjoy yourself. You're nobody's old lady, and that means it's open season on your sweet looking ass."

"Let. Go."

"Not 'til you give it up on top of this bar, baby girl. I'm gonna rip you right open. Show you what a real man wearing these fucking colors can do. You owe me anyway for not pulling the trigger on your little girl..."

"No! No!"

My screwed up brain finally got its shit together. I recognized those voices.

Missy. Serial.

Fuck!

I shot up, ignoring the savage vertigo twisting my brain upside down. Couldn't see anything except pure blood red when I saw him backing my girl against the wall, trying to pull her toward the messy bar top, one of his evil hands pinching her thigh.

I charged him from the side and knocked his ass flat on the ground. Missy screamed. I fell on top of him, hoping like hell I could aim my fists at his face, knock him out before he knew what hit him. I got in two good punches before I felt him moving beneath me, one hand in his pocket.

Motherfucker pulled his switchblade and hurled it at my guts. I barely swerved again, deaf as another one of Missy's screams ripped through my ears. I caught a blur, just her circling around us, shaking and holding an empty beer bottle like a club.

Serial tried to stab my ass again. Too fucking slow. Adrenaline howled through me and I caught his wrist with both hands, forcing the bundle to his throat. It was all down to arm wrestling now, and I wanted to push that knife through his jugular so fucking bad.

"Brothers, no! Get the fuck up! Both you assholes!"

Two hands caught my shoulders and shook. I kicked like mad as they tried to pull me to my feet, throwing my head down one more time. I slapped Serial's forehead so hard with mine the sickening slap echoed in my skull, followed by the dull pain.

More hands landed on me. Dark shapes moved all around us, cutting me off from Missy, taking me away from my target.

I wouldn't stop flipping my shit 'til Blackjack and Rabid had me pressed to the wall, holding me down with everything they had.

"Let me fucking go! That asshole tried to rape my old

lady. I'm gonna put his ass in the ground!"

"You've lost your mind, son!" Blackjack roared in my face. "If you think you're gonna deal justice without running it by your brothers, we'll take you out to meet the Mauler right now. Stop it!"

Rabid's eyes met mine. *Come on, man. I don't wanna fucking hurt you*, they said. *Calm the fuck down.*

Damn it. I started to relax, but I didn't stop kicking 'til I saw Missy behind all the brothers staggering around us. The men were either laughing or giving me the evil eye.

She was safe – for now.

I tried to relax, much as I wanted to break their hold and continue beating the fuckface on the floor. He tried to take her, against her fucking will. He tried to take what's *mine*.

"I'll leave his ass alone. Just let me fucking go," I growled, forcing myself to break eye contact with Serial.

His lip was bloodied and a couple brothers helped him up. He shot me one more vicious look with those dark, merciless eyes. The urge to rip 'em outta his head and blind his evil ass forever was overwhelming.

"Jesus." Blackjack spat contempt in my face. "I can smell the whiskey rolling off you. Drunk as a damned skunk. I'm gonna let this ride, long as I don't find out you hit that other shit."

I shook my head. "You know I wouldn't do that. I'd rather die, brother."

"Nobody's fucking dying here today," he snapped. "In another couple seconds, I'm gonna let you go. Rabid's gonna walk you out to the garages with the girl, and you're heading straight home. Got it? Don't show your fucking face around here again until you sober up and know how to handle everybody in this club – including the brothers you don't like."

I snorted. Blackjack's fingers tightened on my shoulders and he cocked his head, studying me, a stark warning written in his weathered face.

"Really, Brass? You know this kinda shit happens in this club all the time. Brothers get drunk. Some of them let their girls stray. And that baby faced brunette back there isn't even yours. Nobody believes this stage show you're putting on. It's gonna be a long time before we ever turn 'em loose. I'll tell you that much. You don't trust this bitch as far as you can throw her – how do you expect us to?"

My heart sank. Fuck. Saving Missy in the scuffle just brought another consequence that activated pure fire in my chest. My heart slapped my ribs like a heavy pendulum, ready to kill and crush.

He eased up. My cue to turn, rip myself away from him. Rabid still had me by one arm – annoying as fuck.

"I'll go," I said, giving Blackjack one more icy stare. "I'll get my shit together like you want. But, you know, it's a sad fucking day around here when you're admitting defeat and letting rapist lunatics fuck this club over from the inside out. Big surprise we're easy pickings for the cartel. We're rotten to the goddamned core."

Blackjack's mouth twisted in a frown. He was about to lay into me, but my parting shot to Serial set the maniac off. He threw himself at me, too slow for the brothers surrounding him.

"Knock it off, asshole! I'm not gonna tell you again!" Blackjack howled, getting in his face as the brothers held him back, trying to bring some permanent peace for the night.

Rabid kept his grip tight while I circled around and grabbed Missy with my free hand. She followed along limply, matching my steps with Rabid toward the door.

It was a huge relief when the stink of grease and motor oil outside coiled up my nostrils.

I headed for the truck. When we were a few steps away, I let Missy's hand go and reached into my pocket, handing her the keys.

"You drive. I'm too fucked up to get us home."

She blinked, and then nodded. I hated looking into her eyes too long, not when they were all red and shocked to hell after Serial worked his black magic.

At the passenger door, Rabid still hadn't let me go, so I jerked hard. He flew forward, knocked himself into the truck's metal before he released my leather.

"Shit, dude. Take it easy. I'm following orders."

"I know. I just wanna get the fuck outta here." I put my hand on the door handle and felt my knuckles throb where I'd pounded Serial's face.

It hurt like hell, but damn if it didn't feel good too. Just wished my fists had gotten a chance to finish the job before these other fucks broke it up.

"Hey," Rabid threw his hand over mine on the door,

causing me to growl. "I'm hoping you can figure this shit out, brother. You know I would've been right with you, kicking Serial's ass, if everybody knew she was your old lady? I mean, if that's what she really was, and you weren't just doing this for show."

"Yeah? Well, thanks for the support." I stopped just short of adding 'asshole.' There was no point in alienating the last man here who really had my back, even if he half-assed it.

"Brass, you know it's not like that," he said, stepping away. "I'm trying to put the club first, same as Blackjack. You and these girls...it's one more fucked up complication. I want them gone just as quick as you do...but not if there's a tiny chance they're gonna fuck us by blabbing to the police."

"And I'll tell you the same thing I told Blackjack." I paused, pressing my teeth together tight. "This club's fucked up. Rotting, from the inside out, infested with junkies and psycho assholes like Serial. Ask yourself how fucked up it is that you care more about keeping shit together to fight the cartel when we've got guys who are supposed to be our fucking brothers acting just like a buncha thugs from below the border."

His face tightened in anger, but it faded fast. My eyes were fixed on him the whole time as I climbed into the truck and Missy started the engine, slowly putting some distance between us and the hellish scene.

Fuck it. Everybody who still had a soul in this club needed to hear the bitter truth, and I hoped I'd lodged it so deep in Rabid's brain tonight he wouldn't be able to go back to his carefree fucking.

Finally, I looked at her, reaching up over her head to tap the button for the gate clipped to the visor. It opened up and then we took off.

I mouthed a few directions to give her some idea. No blindfold this time, obviously.

I was so tired of fighting, playing this fucking game with her and the club. It hadn't gone down like I wanted, but I was done. So goddamned finished.

If the girl sitting in the driver's seat was gonna screw me over, then there wasn't shit I could do about it. I wasn't gonna drive myself nuts over her knowing where the clubhouse was or pissing off my brothers.

If they came for her again – Serial or anybody else – I wouldn't hesitate to swing my fists 'til I couldn't anymore. I'd die fighting for something. Right now, protecting her was a helluva lot more attractive than fighting for my own club, even if she never gave me a shred of thanks.

She had a good reason for despising everything I'd done. The club was behind all this shit. Stress and siege weren't gonna cut it as excuses neither.

Truth is, my band of brothers turned into a pack of wolves a long time ago. Fuck, they'd been like that since I showed up in Redding, and I was too fucked up to admit it. I couldn't see it 'til now, but when I finally did, it was blinding.

They were gonna kill her. Serial was gonna force her, sure as he would've blown her little sis' head off in the basement that night. Whatever fucked up sins her daddy did for the cartel against my MC, they shouldn't have been paid for this way.

My guts churned, rougher than any other time tonight. Raw, hot bile spasmed in my intestines, rage incarnate, vile as whiskey mixed battery acid.

I reached for her hand on the wheel, gently covering it. "Pull over, babe. Right fucking now."

V: Broken Heartbeat (Missy)

What a night.

Listening to him in the ditch dry heaving was just the cherry on top of my crap sundae. I shook my head, wondering when he'd finally be done. I wondered even more why I didn't just take off, fleeing into the forest that flanked the little strip where we'd pulled over, and not stopping until I touched Mount Shasta looming in the distance.

My brain was still trying to process the evening. Too many bombs exploded in my head too close together.

I was cleaning, trying not to dwell on all the rough brutes all around me enjoying themselves. Then I had to stumble in on him with that blonde bitch's tongue down his throat.

Jealously shouldn't have thundered through my veins. And I definitely shouldn't have taken off running, crazed to get away from him while he pursued me.

Of course, it did, and no reason or wishing was going to make me feel any different.

I didn't want to hear his crap – especially when he didn't owe me any apologies whatsoever.

I couldn't want this man. He was a means to an end, a way to navigate this sector of hell and find my way out of the deep, deep pit daddy dug for Jackie and I.

I was hiding behind the bar, just waiting for him to come out of his stupor on the floor, when Serial attacked. He was so insistent, so fast, his eyes like an guard dog's before it lunges.

I tried to fight. I wanted to believe I could get him off me, get to safety by myself, but the man who threw me against the counter and pressed his nasty hand between my legs was too strong.

That was when I broke. I begged for Brass to wake up and help me. Prayed for it.

The problem with wishes and prayers is that sometimes you actually get what you want.

He fought for me like nobody ever had. When they piled onto him and forced him off the creep, I thought he'd break out like a bull and keep going, even if it meant his own destruction.

More than anything else, he'd put me above his own club, and after I'd treated him like total shit too.

Sure, I could try to ignore these raging uncertainties tearing through me. I'd tried to do that plenty when the liquid heat flowed through me every time I looked at him too long, studying the fierce dark ink scrawled on his hard skin.

But I couldn't ignore the fact that he'd done me right. He'd truly protected me, and not just for his own selfish reasons.

A man fighting for himself wouldn't fight like Brass did. He fought for me, and only me, putting himself against blades and blows without a care for himself.

Didn't that count for something? I shook my head, unwilling to accept the obvious answer in my screwed up brain.

I was still staring at the ground when he rounded the truck, banging on its metal side with one fist. "I'm done. Let's hit the road."

"Are you sure about that?" I reached into the driver's side and grabbed the water he'd left behind, holding it out to him. "Here. Something to rinse away the taste."

He popped the cap and chugged it. Stray water sprayed out the corners of his lips, rolling down his cut, saturating the t-shirt he had on underneath it. The droplets drew my eyes to his body, the muscles I owed a debt to that I tried so hard to forget.

Jesus, he was strong. It was one thing just to see it on him, but to know what those fists could do...

His knuckles were scratched, but his hands were still big, strong, and masculine. Untouched. Unbeaten. My thoughts went rampant, imagining what they'd feel like wrapped around my waist, or hooked around my back, sliding to my ass.

That's it, Missy. This is when you've officially lost your mind.

I couldn't argue with the voice in my head. But the day dreams on the other side wouldn't stop humming. I absentmindedly ran my tongue over my lips, wondering how he'd taste. How would those powerful slabs of meat on his bones twitch and jerk if I put my tongue to them? My lips? My teeth?

A cool breeze blew as he started to walk back to the passenger side and climbed in. It hit me right in the middle, near the waist, pushing against my jeans. I shuddered, realizing how wet these stupid, dangerous thoughts were making me.

I shouldn't have been falling for the good cop. No matter how hard he fought and tried to protect me, I had to remember that's what he was in the end. He was one of them, part of my prison. He was the smooth side of my cage, holding me in rough uncertainty.

And not just me, but Jackie too – the most unforgivable thing of all.

If it were just me...I might've done something really stupid. I might have thrown my hand on his, pulled him close, and kissed him while I thanked him for what he'd done.

But until my sister was free, I wasn't doing anything. These mad, mad fantasies couldn't run amok, couldn't make me do something that would only delay our freedom.

I forced my hands to the wheel and drove when he gave the signal. We didn't talk much on the ride toward Redding proper. When we were nearing the city limits, he turned to me and stared.

"What?" I said, flustered.

"You did good tonight, babe. Shit would've gone off without a hitch if Serial hadn't let his drunken dick get the better of him. I'll do whatever it takes to keep that asshole away from you in the future. No bullshit."

"It was okay up until then," I agreed. "I'm just glad it turned out okay in the end...I mean, assuming those guys aren't going to come after you."

"They'll let it ride," he growled. "Club's got too much on its plate to worry about a little dirty blood between brothers. Long as I can keep it under control on my end and not plant a dagger in that fucker's guts while he's taking a piss."

My chest tightened. Was he serious?

The savage look of satisfaction on his face reminded me once again who and what I was dealing with. These men really killed, and I remembered how close to sudden death they'd brought Jackie and I on the night they came for the money. Brass saved us then too.

I stopped and wondered, new darkness creeping into my head. If he wasn't there...

You wouldn't be here to worry about it, I thought. It was truer than anything else rolling through my head all evening.

"Listen, that other shit earlier..." He bared his teeth.

I knew he was talking about the blonde. Jealousy seethed in my blood, unwelcome as it was surprising.

I waved my hand. "It's none of my business, Brass. It's your life. You're welcome to do whatever you want behind closed doors."

Except this one was wide open. And, of course, I was lying right through my teeth. Thinking about him and the nasty girl with the golden pigtails made me want to claw things to shreds.

"No. You got more than your fill of all the shit the brothers do at these parties tonight. You didn't need to see it from me." He swallowed. "I didn't want it. She tried to stick her pussy where it didn't belong. I've fucked her before, but that shit was in the past. We're done. Something's changed. Thinking about that pussy anymore just makes me sick."

"You can do better. *Seriously.*"

I flushed as soon as the words were out of my mouth. Being rattled so many times in a couple hours killed the brain-to-mouth-filter.

Brass looked me up and down. Then he laughed, filling the truck with his deep baritone. I couldn't help but smile.

"I'm laughing because it's fucking true. Not just with chicks, I mean. Trying to do better's the story of my fucking life since I left Montana. Better's all I got." He paused, as if considering his words. "Thing I hate most about change is how it warps your vision. Some of the shit I see with a clear head, I'd strike down in a heartbeat if I really had a choice."

"The stuff going on with your club?" I asked.

He nodded. "Just when I think we've reached our limit, some new asshole has to make a ruckus, painting everything darker. More bitter. I don't know what's gonna come outta fucking around with the cartel, but I don't want any part of it if. Not if it means my own brothers are gonna keep acting like fucking jackals."

My hands tightened on the wheel. He wouldn't take his eyes off me, tracing my curves. That heat was back, shades of nervous excitement I couldn't quite define, let alone handle.

He was so hard, so intense. No, handling him didn't come natural, but damn if I didn't want to try. This man might be the death of me, a fatal attraction I was destined to follow into the fire. Whether I'd meet heaven or hell there was anyone's guess, and for the first time since all this went down, I was ready to start taking bets.

"You...you never should've been swept up in this shit. I don't care what your father did," he said. "We should've taken the money and let you go. If it wasn't so fucking hard convincing guys to do the right thing anymore, we wouldn't be stuck playing pretend. Fuck, babe, if there was a way I could've saved you and your sis without ever using the words 'old lady...'"

He closed his eyes and didn't finish. I had to keep my eyes fixed on the road, refusing to look over. Hearing him regret claiming me as his hurt.

It defied common sense, but it did, and it shook me to the core too. I leaned in my seat and pushed on, following the narrow streets through Redding toward our apartment. There was nothing left to say. Breathing another word would've only upset somebody, and we'd had enough heartache for one night.

I pulled into a parking space and got out, waiting for him to follow. The whole way upstairs and down the hall, I hoped like hell Jackie would be asleep. When I got inside, one more prayer was answered, and I was left alone to pad off to my room, alone with my fears and forbidden desires.

I woke up sometime before dawn and ran to the bathroom. It was still dark. The water I'd downed before I went to sleep helped kill the hunger pangs nipping at my stomach. I was too upset to eat earlier, worried I'd wake up with my stomach twisted in knots as I slid through my nightmares.

Brass was snoring lightly on the couch, a thin blanket thrown across him, his cut and jeans hanging on the chair next to him. I looked at the coffee table and saw his wallet. There was something else too, thick and shiny, even in the pre-dawn darkness...

I crept up, quiet as a cat, reaching out when I was close. It was the skinny switchblade he'd wrestled away from Serial. My thumb brushed the handle, running over the small bear claw pressed into the handle, one more cruel mark left by the Grizzlies MC.

My finger gently moved along the edge and pushed a small button. The sharp blade jumped out, dangerous as ever in the darkness.

I looked up, studying him in the shadows. He was huge, and right now...completely at my mercy.

The old, frightened, vengeful Missy Thomas inside me stomped her feet, begging me to end this right now. If I killed him here, nobody would ever know. Jackie and I could take off with his vehicle, find our way to Mexico or something.

But the way he'd gotten underneath my skin – God!

Killing him was the last thing I wanted. How could I spill his blood when he'd already given his for me? For Jackie?

He'd sliced into my soul, sure, but he'd ripped his own open and bled ten times more. I wanted to take the easy way. I wanted to be free. But I also wanted *him*, alive and well, and so much more. Primal greed grabbed me by the throat and forced me to look at him, a rugged manly mirror for all my feverish desires.

I wanted him on top of me, hot and throbbing, slamming me into the floor while he worked between my legs. I wanted to smell our sweat mingle when he was deep inside me, claiming me for real, shattering the game of pretend we'd been playing with insatiable lust and twitching flesh.

Honestly, I'd already lost my mind. Now the only question was whether I'd walk into the madness losing him, or else losing myself on his flesh, losing my entire world on him as he filled me, stretched me, clawed at my flesh, and split my mind in two on his dick.

I couldn't kill him. No fucking way. This whole thing was crazy and I didn't know if there even a way out alive anymore, but more bloodshed wasn't the answer.

I turned the knife over in my hand, holding it up. With a heavy sigh, I lowered it, trying to find some way to retract the blade.

I never heard him wake up, much less climb off the sofa. He crashed into me from behind, flattening my hand holding the blade. I jerked once and flipped over, surprised

I hadn't screamed.

We were face to face. He was shirtless and magnificent, pure hellfire in his expression, dark tattoos running up and down his muscular chest. He'd landed between my legs – the last place in the world he should be, especially when I had nothing on underneath my long sleeping shirt except my panties and filthy desires blazing in my belly.

"What the fuck are you doing?" he growled, eyeing the blade in my hand.

It was still tilted up, sturdy, his hand pinning down my wrist. "I don't...I just saw it laying there and wanted to see what it was. I didn't mean to do anything, Brass. Honest."

He stared deep into my eyes and shook his head. Finally, he threw his hand away, but not before pulling my wrist up, aiming the dagger at the tight packed muscles on his abdomen.

"Bullshit. I know a person mulling a kill when I see one." His breaths came heavy, and he spoke slow, soft. "Fucking do it if this is what you want. Put me outta my goddamned misery and leave. Do it!"

My hand shook against his. I tried to release my fingers, drop the knife, get away from him, but he wouldn't let me. He pulled it closer, dragging the very tip of the killer blade to his chest, right above his heart.

"One more fucking push, and you're free. This is what you want, right, babe?"

"No!" I wasn't sure how I managed to keep my voice down without screaming in his face.

It came out sharp, hit him in the face. Brass' hand

squeezed, bending my knuckles in, and then let go. The knife fell onto the carpet next to me. When I looked down to see it, I realized my whole body was shaking underneath him.

"Can't say I never gave you a chance, Missy," he said, peeling back and hovering over me, his hands planted on the floor. "Wake me up when you know what you want."

The smug tension in his voice struck deep, setting off a bomb inside me. Next thing I knew, I jerked up, threw my arms around his neck, and smashed my mouth on his.

Our lips touched like lightning criss-crossing the sky.

Brass' mouth was hard, unmoving for a single second, and then he parted his lips and grunted. His arms slid around me, pulling me up, smashing my breasts against his chest as he pushed my lips apart with his tongue.

God, he was hungry. I'd never been kissed like this. But then, no other man had kissed me after holding a knife to his heart before, baring everything, life and death and lust.

Brass growled, lowering me to the floor, reaching up to my long brown hair. He tangled several strands in one fist and ripped my head back, all the better to access my lips, shoving his tongue deeper into my mouth.

He licked the way I imagined he fucked. Rough, fast, and totally dominant. There was no playful tease in these kisses, no gentle build. His teeth nipped at my bottom lip, holding me open for his tongue. He found mine and led in a fiery dance, licking against my soft, wet tongue until I had to follow him, kissing him the way he wanted.

No mistake: I wanted it hard. I wanted to kiss and feel

and fuck. I was done thinking.

It was the best alternative in the world to screaming and beating at his chest, crying like a broken fool on the floor. He saved me from all that – he saved me. *Again.*

All my blazing emotions shot to my heart, where they were ejected as pure lust, a powerful need to feel him all over me.

For once, Brass and I were on the same wavelength too. Our flesh sang in unison, tense and ready.

After a couple minutes on my lips, his free hand moved, starting at my knee and sliding straight up. His calloused hand kissed my thigh, on its way to the soaked black lace between my legs. He growled through his kiss as he shoved my gusset aside and rubbed two fingers up and down my slit, a short, rhythmic test before he pushed them inside me.

Fuck! Oh. My. God!

I grunted in his mouth as he worked through my folds. My pussy wrapped around his fingers and shifted each time he went a little deeper. His strokes were soft at first, but quickly grew faster and harder, dipping in and out in long jerks until his thumb pressed on my clit.

I broke the kiss, begging for air, feeling my lungs and everything below the waist turning to stone. Brass yanked on my hair and held me up to him as I sucked precious air, face-to-face. Lust incarnate looked back at me, pure desire formed from all the hate and want between us, finally set free.

"Do I need to stuff my hand in your mouth when you

come?" He pushed his face closer, dragging rough stubble across my cheek. My thighs rippled together, locked around his hand, bucking for relief.

I realized he was talking about Jackie, asleep down the hall. *Damn!*

"No...I can't let her hear...I think I can keep it –"

Together? No fucking way. A voice deep in my head laughed.

"Oh!" My lips formed a perfect circle and my vision blurred.

I gasped, sweated, pinched my thighs tight around his palm. Jesus, I needed him, needed him to finish kindling the fire he'd ignited in my core.

Brass' hand went mad, moving like clockwork through my folds, or maybe like a clockmaker who knew exactly how to wind my pussy up until I shattered. It felt so fucking good, but I couldn't scream. I'd never forgive myself if Jackie woke up and came in here to find us like this.

I had to keep it down. I had to stop myself from –

Brass made sure I'd be screaming in his hand, and nowhere else. He moved it out of my hair and covered my mouth as his face moved down. He caught the edge of my shirt and tugged it up with his teeth, stopping the hypnotic circles between my legs just long enough to rip my panties down.

When I realized the only place he was going was *down*, I started to pant. Rough stubble and hard, sucking kisses danced along my cleavage, then rode my stomach, drawing me against his mouth.

His face pushed between my legs and took over where his hand left off. My body jerked against his, grinding into his hot hand. I thought his fingers were good, but his tongue – Christ! – I was finished.

Hot, long, godly licks steamed through my folds. He tongued my wetness eagerly, like my cream was the booze the men sucked constantly at the clubhouse, trailing his licks up to my clit. When he found it, my whole pussy sizzled on his face, ready to come apart.

Muscles tensed up and convulsed, small bundles across my body I didn't even know I had. He must've known I was about to burst because he shoved the edge of his hand into my mouth, forcing me to bite him.

I did. But it wasn't enough. I barely had time to beat my hands on his shoulders before the insistent, tight fireball in my womb exploded. My thighs locked around his head and I came, groaning against his palm, losing total control.

My eyes rolled back, lost in black and white and red. I never came so hard, flailing against him as he held me down, never stopping the wild, rhythmic tongue laps on my clit. He completely smothered it as I rode his face, my pussy convulsing around him, like he was breathing lightning through my nerves with every insatiable lick.

I came. I climaxed the pain and hurt of the last few weeks, the insanity of doing it with him, giving myself over to desires that were sick and taboo on a good day. Having him between my legs was so damned wrong, but my body told me it was right.

There was no doubting it. The saner, rational bitch I became to keep myself safe would've jumped through the roof in horror, but pleasure didn't lie. And pleasure won out in the end, overpowering my regrets, my fears, my doubts.

His tongue fucked me until I couldn't even breathe, buried beneath a couple hundred pounds of huge, hard, tattooed muscle. I barely had time to worry about whether or not his hand stifled the carnal pleas ripping up my throat.

When I looked up, he was hovering over me, the two fingers he'd had inside me near his lips. The fire in his emerald eyes doubled when he stuck them in his mouth, giving them a good, long suck before wiping his chin.

"You taste even fucking better than I imagined. I'd give up whiskey for that sweet little cunt."

I laughed, slapping his shoulders again. Okay, now I knew he'd lost his mind. But Brass acted perfectly sane and determined as he brought his hands to his boxers. My eyes followed, and I noticed the monstrous hard-on straining there, looking like it would punch through the thin fabric any second.

Horny curiosity tingled through me. I swept one hand down below his belly, reaching for his dick. I found it, and squeezed, hissing through my teeth.

God, he was big. Hard. Ready to fuck me through the floor, just like I wanted.

Brass wrapped his hand over mine and gripped, making me squeeze him harder. "That's what you want, babe?

Okay. I would've taken a switchblade in the guts for you. But I sure like satisfying this fucking need a whole lot more..."

I pursed my lips, trying not to drool all over the floor. My pussy wouldn't stop melting as I felt his ridge, running my fingers over it, sensing his pulse in my fingertips.

"Do it." It was my turn to whisper those words.

Brass didn't need any reminders. He hooked his fingers to his boxers and jerked them down. They fell with a snap and he rolled, wriggling out of them, grabbing his jeans off the chair.

My heart did a flip when I saw the small metallic package in his hand. He looked at me, winked, and threw it at me.

"You know how to do this, right? Put it on. I won't pass up any excuse to get your hands on my dick again."

I'd never rolled a condom on a man, but it wasn't like I was going to say no. I eyed the light coming through the blinds nervously, hoping Jackie stayed up late so she'd sleep in. Good thing teenagers were out like the dead most mornings.

I quickly tore the foil, trying not to make too much noise. The latex popped softly in my fingers, and I moved it to him, gnawing my bottom lip when I brought it to his swollen head. Brass grunted, satisfied, watching with new flames in his eyes while I pushed it down his length.

There was something extra sensual about that – almost as good as sinking down on his bare, hard cock. Almost. But of course feeling him skin-to-skin would've been even better.

For now, this would have to do. And when he shifted up, fisting my hair, planting himself between my legs, I knew it'd do *very* nicely.

He kissed me deep, rubbing his length up and down my wet slit, nestling his cock in my folds. I squirmed, wishing he'd just fuck me already. Not that I wasn't enjoying the foreplay, but the fire inside me needed to be fed, needed to be *filled*.

"Fuck, baby girl. You know I wanted this pussy the minute I saw you? *This* pussy, the one I was glad to claim, the one I wanted for real...nobody else's. When I take this beautiful cunt, it's going on a long, hard ride, and it's never coming back. This. Is. *Mine*. Mine!"

That word was like magic. Black, crazy, alien magic, making me tingle all over. The way he rubbed his erection up and down my slit while he whispered his filthy promises in my ear had a lot to do with its power too.

Brass rose up, tilting his hips, ready to sink inside me. I caught one glimpse of the raging bear tattooed to his chest, symbol of the Grizzlies MC, right before he thrust. His cock penetrated deep, opening me, unstopping until his balls rested against my ass.

I was so full, so fast, I started to shake. There was no slowing down, though. Not when he wanted to fuck me this bad, claim me for real. Thrust by thrust, he told me what he wanted to do: twist the crappy lie we'd lived into truth with flesh, sweat, and ecstasy.

Was it possible?

My body didn't say no. His strokes came harder, faster, making my body ripple. He fucked with purpose, taking as much pleasure as he gave. The big, inked claws tattooed on his arms rippled around me, dancing like black flames.

I threw my legs around his waist and locked onto his neck with my hands, all the better to ride out the storm, the tempest we both needed to thrash all the shit we'd suffered to pieces. I felt like I was floating after a minute of taking his dick, but it was just my own hips flying up, desperate to meet his thrusts.

Everything below my waist turned warm and tight, smoky and electric. Soon, I'd be coming again, harder than when he licked me to finish.

As soon as I started to claw at his shoulders, he held one hand to my mouth. My eyes went wide, rolling a little as he pounded his hips to mine, pressing his cock to my limits.

"Don't scream. Let it out in my fucking hand, babe. You sing like a whore with little sis in the other room and we'll never be able to finish." Suddenly, he smiled, a mischievous glint in his eye. "Maybe I ought to finish this faster for both of us? Or do you wanna fuck good and slow, risk everything combusting on my dick?"

I shuddered. Whatever way he fucked me, I was going to come soon, and I moaned into his hand.

It was all he needed. His thrusts slowed, but the pressure increased. He slid back gradually before he threw his hips into mine, hammering me apart, breaking me open for him.

My clit hummed when he dragged his pubic bone

against me. Short, trim hair gave its delicious friction, maddening as it was pleasurable.

I couldn't take it anymore. I smashed my lips straight into his hand and grunted, pushing warm air through my teeth.

He threw the switch. Feeling me tighten up and convulse on his cock turned him into the fuck machine he'd promised. Brass filled my pussy again and again, quicker, shallower strokes, kindling a wicked fire beneath my waist.

I let go, falling so fast and hard I could feel my brain coming out my ears. My hips smashed desperately at his, bucking and writhing, begging for his climax. Brass joined me halfway through the fire licking its way up my whole body, drowning me in its glorious wave.

He grunted, threw his hips forward, and held them there, cock pressed snug against my womb. I felt him swell, even through the condom, and then the heat in his skin became an inferno. His head snapped back and he clenched his teeth, snorting, struggling not to growl or curse so loud it shook the whole building.

If the sex wasn't so amazing, it would've been a total pain holding in our pleasure. Instead, sheer ecstasy muted us, shuddering through our bodies harder in spastic waves, locked together as his cock jerked deep inside me.

He spilled everything. I saw my sweet surrender mirrored in him, the venom leaving his body as he lost his come in the condom, deep inside my pussy.

It felt like we were locked together for an hour before

he finally pulled out. His hand shook as he held the condom to his skin, a satisfied growl leaving his lips.

"Fuck, babe. That was the hottest fuck I've had since –"

He stopped talking and my ears perked up. The only thing that could've ruined the bliss was the creak I heard deep in the apartment.

Jackie!

"Come on!" He grabbed me by the wrist and lifted me up, running for the bathroom as he grabbed half our clothes.

Shit. The door clapped shut. I had my back pressed to the wood, trying not to look too hard at his gorgeous, naked body in front of me. Jackie's soft footsteps moved past us and then stopped when she got into the living room.

I didn't see my bra, or the oversized shirt I'd been wearing...Brass' cut was still somewhere on the floor too.

If my sister saw that mess of clothes out there, we couldn't hide it. She'd have no doubt about the dirty, dirty deed that went down on the floor just a few minutes ago, the wild animal lay I hadn't fully processed myself.

"Brass!" I whispered, hoarse and scared. Panic shot through my eyes.

"It's okay, babe." He gave me a serious look, sliding on his jeans, shirtless and shining with sweat and dark ink. "Let me handle this shit."

I stood there like an idiot as he flung open the door and stepped out. I grabbed the handle, wanting to scream after him, but he strode out as confidently as if he'd just showered.

Watching through the crack in the door, I saw Jackie jump, and turn to face the huge biker standing a couple feet away. Her mouth fell open, and so did mine.

"What'll it be today, darling?" Brass said, his arms folded. "Pancakes, or French toast?"

Jackie looked like she was about to blow up in tears. Oh, God. My heart tightened up and I clutched at my chest with one hand. My nipples were still soft and full from fucking him.

Damn! Why couldn't we have had one more second to grab the rest of our clothes so I wouldn't have to run out there buck naked? And wouldn't doing that make things *worse?*

My legs felt like they were stuck in concrete. Then the silence broke. Jackie opened her mouth and doubled over. Next thing I knew, she was laughing.

High, shrill, girlish giggles I hadn't heard since sometime before dad got really bad. Brass caught her before she fell onto our crumpled clothes, holding her hand and helping her into the recliner. While he was down there, he scooped up the rest of our things, giving her a minute before he stood back up.

"What's so damned funny?"

Jackie took one look at him and burst into laughter all over again. "It's...nothing. You're cool, is all. I think I want the toast."

"Coming right up, soon as I help your sis get dressed." He smiled and padded past her, returning to me.

Jackie spun the chair around to face us. I was still looking at the sassy red sheen on her face before Brass stepped inside and slammed the door behind us, but not before she caught my eyes. I jerked my head away, blushing like I hadn't blushed since...crap, since I was probably her age.

"What...what the hell was that?" I asked, shaking my head.

"A wink and a nod. Don't ask, don't tell. Owning the shit that just happened between you and me without sitting your little sis down on the couch and talking about the birds and the bees. Me and my own sis did this kinda shit when we had dates in the house under Ma's nose. Well, me way more than her...if she'd fucked more guys, maybe she wouldn't have ended up with that Prairie Pussy, Blaze..."

He stepped past me, kicking off his jeans, and reached for the shower handle. I was too stunned to ask what the hell he was talking about with his own family business.

"That's crazy!" I gasped. "She's fourteen, Brass. She knows what we were doing..."

"Exactly." He turned to me and winked. "And she didn't seem real upset by it neither, did she? Best way to deal with it is being open and honest. She doesn't need any dark and dirty details. We'll keep that between us, babe."

He reached behind my back and pulled me in, one hand moving to my ass. Before I could even curse, he had the panties off I'd just thrown on, pushing me against his chest.

I'd never seen his eyes so bright and mischievous. If it

wasn't for the fact Jackie almost stumbled in on us fucking, I would've loved it.

My hands beat his grizzly bear tattoos and I tried to wriggle away. Brass laughed, pulling me closer, pressing his lips to mine.

The shower hissed and filled the bathroom with steam while we kissed. One fast, furious taste and I knew I was in too deep...all the horror and disgust in the world couldn't have stopped my pussy from tingling as he worked his tongue against mine.

Holy shit. So much for shame.

"What are you doing?" I shook my head, breaking the kiss. I shouldn't have bothered asking, because one more squeeze of my ass told me.

"What does it look like? Cleaning up and fucking your brains out before we eat breakfast," Brass said, bringing one hand to my breast, tweaking my bright pink nipple.

I shuddered. My body was completely shameless, and it was quickly overpowering my head.

Oh, shit! This can't be seriously happening, can it?

He looked down at my panties wadded up near my feet.

"I'll stuff those in your mouth if you're worried about sis hearing more than she needs to over the shower, but it's plenty loud with this shit going. Come on."

He brushed the curtain aside and stepped in, pulling me with him. His hands worked fast, picking up where they'd left off, plumping one breast while the other slid between my thighs. He found my clit and worked his fingers, tender trending rough, strokes so filled with need I couldn't have dreamed about saying no.

"Just so you know, this is the last time we're fucking all secret squirrel, babe. Next time, I'm gonna drag your pretty ass somewhere we can fuck good and proper. I wanna hear everything that comes outta your mouth when you come on my cock."

I opened my mouth to answer, but nothing would come out. I barely stopped the moan building in my throat in time, knees shaking, folding my palms tight against the wall. It felt so good having his fingers moving through my folds, swirling against my clit, all while the steady hum of hot water beat against our backs.

My head started to roll back and forth, struggling to hold it all in. Brass slowed the circles around my clit, holding me in suspense. Bastard tease!

Just as I tried to turn, he grabbed my wrists and held me tight, throwing my palms back to the wall.

"Don't. That was just a warm up. No fucking way are you coming on my hands and mouth twice in one morning, Missy. This dick's not halfway done with its workout."

I heard something crinkle up and fall to the floor. He'd snuck a condom out of his pants sometime when I was lost in pure bliss on his fingers. Heat bloomed in my womb and shot up my spine when he rubbed against my ass, hard and sheathed, ready to fuck like never before.

His hand slipped away and found its way over my mouth. I could smell my own scent on him, a wetness against my lips thicker than water.

"Bite this shit when you need to. Taste your cream on my fingers. It's hot as fuck that I did this to you, babe, and now I'm gonna do a whole lot more."

He pushed inside me, and my knees went full jackhammer. His cock slid up more easily this time, probably because I'd never been so wet in my entire life. I sucked my bottom lip and chewed, resisting the urge to bite his hand like he'd invited me to.

I'd need to save that for later. But not much longer – when he started to thrust, I knew I wasn't going to last long.

Fresh lava swelled inside my head, bathing me in creeping pleasure, like someone kindled a fire near my brain stem. My ass lifted up and fell against him, rocking to meet his thrusts, following his lead as he picked up speed.

My lips formed an O against his skin. Brass pounded deeper, harder, faster. My back arched and the firestorm in my belly pinched everything tighter, a vortex that wouldn't let go until every muscle in my body turned to stone.

His hand clamped over my mouth a second before I screamed, pushing it back inside me. The suffocating fire ripping through me made me lose my mind. I couldn't think about the pain or serving the club or what Jackie would think anymore.

All I could think about was how fucking good his dick felt buried in me, swelling as he let go and joined me in ecstasy.

"Fuck! Fuck! Don't. Fucking. Stop." His last words gurgled out before he let go, filling the condom deep inside me, making shallower strokes with his throbbing cock, losing his load.

He fucked right through my pleasure. His balls pulsed against my pussy, hurling seed, stretching our pleasure to its rabid breaking point.

I sweated, clawed, and rasped into his hand all through my climax.

When it finally let up, I slumped down, wriggling my ass against him to milk the last energy out of him. His big chest rose and fell in waves. He cursed as he pulled out, drawing off the condom and shoving aside the shower curtain to toss it toward the waste bin.

I heard it hit the trash next to the toilet. Perfect shot.

"Fuck, baby girl. I'm never gonna get tired of this. I wanna keep fucking you 'til I can't even think. You understand?" He held one hand around my waist and slowly turned me around.

My lips trembled. "Yeah. I think I do."

"Think? Shit, that means I've still got work to do. By the end of the week, I promise I'm gonna find some way to get us both outta this shit for good. I'm done letting anything come between me and this pussy."

I cocked my head, stepping into his warm embrace, listening to the steady slap of the water on our skin. The steamy cloud filling the bathroom was like a second embrace layered over us, a welcome dreamy haze in the post-orgasmic bliss.

"You really think your club's going to trust us? Let me off the hook that fast?"

His face darkened. He leaned in, resting his forehead against mine.

"No." Brass paused, as if he was mulling his words. "I've been wrong about most of my brothers for so long. Everybody except Rabid, Blackjack, maybe a couple other guys...they're all fucked. Fucked up and sick. And it's only gonna get worse."

I shook my head, trying to understand. What was he saying?

"Babe, I'm gonna take you somewhere far away. You and Jackie both. Somewhere you can be safe and live your lives without worrying about a buncha assholes pushing the knife into your throats."

I shuddered. The crude imagery wasn't just an exaggeration. Then I thought about his words, reading between the lines. My heart skipped a beat when I saw it laid out in front of me.

Holy shit.

"You mean you're going to –"

"Leave? Yeah. If that's what it takes to protect you, so be it. We'll head north, all the way through Oregon and Washington. Maybe find some place way up near Canada where nobody's gotta worry about MCs or cartels tearing each other to bloody pieces."

"Brass..." My voice hitched. I started to slide down, but he caught me, laying my cheek on his chest.

"Shhh," he whispered, running his fingers softly through my wet hair. "All we gotta do's go through the motions 'til I figure shit out. One week. That's all it's gonna take to get shit in order and go. I just need to work the logistics and tell a couple guys I can trust what's up. I can't come right away, though. Got some unfinished business with the club, and if I take off permanently, I'd like to leave on good terms."

"Won't they make things worse for all of us when they find out what you're planning?"

"I don't give a shit," he growled. "You're my old lady and I can do whatever the fuck I want with you. If nobody understands that – if I don't have a single fucking brother sticking up for me – then I'll know everything my club represents is a goddamned sham."

He turned, holding my hand, twisting the shower faucet until the steady warm rain stopped. I pulled away, folding my arms over my breasts in the steam, wiping my eyes.

His arm swept the shower curtain aside. He looked at our clothes strewn over the floor, his gaze zeroing in on his cut. I watched his magnificent hard ass as he stepped out, pulling his cut off the ground and letting it fall open in his hands.

"I gave my life and cost some other people theirs trying to do right by this patch." A sad tone darkened his voice. "Maybe one day, I'll be able to. Maybe after the cartel's done thinning out the trash. But not while this club's controlled by a buncha greedy fucking maniacs who think it's okay to kill, rape, and burn the whole world for no good reason."

The leather vest dropped and hit the floor. He turned toward me, naked in the steam, eyes shining brighter than

I'd ever seen them.

"Don't worry. I'm not going back on anything I said while I was wearing these colors, proud and stupid. I'm still a full patch member in the Grizzlies MC. I vote, I fight for the honest brothers, and everything I've said and done since wearing this patch belongs to me." He stepped forward, helping me over the tub's edge to the tile floor. "You're my old lady, babe, come heaven or hell. I don't need any fucking club behind me to back that up. Long as you're willing to have me, I'm gonna have you...every way that's beautiful and dirty and fucking sweet. You and me, Missy. Just us against the whole fucking world, if that's the way it's gotta be."

He took my hand. In the last two hours, everything went crazy. The man I'd thought about killing was staring at me like I was an angel. If it wasn't for the warmth filling my heart, the guilt there would've caused it to sink like a lead weight.

I swallowed the thick lump in my throat and mustered my most serious stare. "I'm ready, Brass. I want you to set things right...and I'm ready to run away if it means we can finally be together, start over, keep my sister safe..."

He tugged me closer, one strong arm around me, pushing a sturdy finger to my lips. "Stop. There's no fucking ifs in what we're gonna do. You, girl, are coming with me no matter what's up ahead. You're *mine*, dammit, and once I lay claim, I don't let go. Not for the club. Not for the cartel. Not for my own fucking mistakes. Not even for the awesome fucking French toast I'm gonna make when we get outta here."

It took me a minute to figure out that last part. Then I remembered Jackie was still outside in the living room, waiting for us and the breakfast he'd promised. Smiling like an idiot, I punched him in the side.

"Jerk. We'll judge how awesome this stuff's going to be."

He grinned. "Dry your hair and get dressed. You'll find out."

We were stuffed around the little breakfast table about thirty minutes later. The entire apartment smelled like warm bread, cinnamon, and syrup, sweet as it was comforting.

Jackie dove into hers with a teenager's appetite, eyeing the big stack of breakfast on the serving plate. He served up eggs to go with the toast and a pitcher of coffee. It looked as good as it smelled.

Brass didn't touch his food. He sat across from me, his Grizzlies MC t-shirt clinging to his chest, waiting for me to have a bite.

I dipped my toast in syrup and brought it to my lips. One crunch, and I was in pure heaven. I think I moaned – dangerously close to the sound I'd made in the shower, when he pushed me over the edge.

"Fuck yeah," he said, reaching for his own bread. "Told you it was good."

Jackie looked at us both, covering her mouth. I rolled my eyes when I finally came out of my sugary high. Whatever, she had every reason to giggle, and it was good to hear her laugh versus all the alternatives weighing on us the last few weeks.

Soon, we'd be heading out for the day while my Christa showed up for lessons. I'd be stuck cleaning up more of the mess from the night before, hoping to god that freak with the barbed wire on his face kept his distance.

One more week. I told myself I could do it. With a few more mornings like this, maybe I could. And maybe – just maybe – being his old lady wasn't half bad.

VI: Escape Plan (Brass)

Fuck. I did it. I really made up my mind, ready to leave behind everything I'd given my life to since I turned eighteen. Ready to turn on the brotherhood that was never anything but a fucking illusion.

Sitting at the table for church the next day was surreal.

Fang came in and took his seat at the head, red as molten steel. When Crack snuck in behind him, moving like an animal with its tail between its legs, I knew he'd broken the news about the cartel hit in SoCal.

The room was stuffy, tense with brothers waiting to hear the Prez go off like fucking dynamite. Instead, he picked up the petrified bear claw, raking its nails just right on the table. Sounded like some asshole teacher scratching chalkboard.

Guys covered their ears and groaned, including me. We only stopped when he slammed the thing so hard on the wood I thought the whole table was gonna go up in splinters.

"All right, you bastards, listen up! Hope you all enjoyed Lipstick Night, 'cause it's gonna be the last time you fuckers got enough free time to get your cocks sucked for a good long while. Half this room was holding out on me about San Diego. You motherfuckers must think I'm stupid or incompetent. Which is it?"

His hard eyes shot to Crack, then Blackjack next to him, slowly moving down the ranks of brothers. When they landed on me, Fang blinked, peeling his lips back in an angry snarl. It was the same ferocious smile I'd seen before I crashed out on the floor, and I remembered those two scared whores with him.

"Well? Clearly, I've lost your fucking faith, or I'd be getting my intel without assholes sealing their lips."

"Fang..." Crack folded his hands and leaned toward him, but froze the instant the Prez shot him the evilest eye I'd ever seen.

"Shut the fuck up. Both you assholes." Fang's head snapped back to Blackjack. "I'm gonna give you one chance to call a no confidence vote for President. Everybody in this room's gonna have their say. If I walk outta here still holding the claw, then I expect to have *everything* flowing to me the instant it happens. And I mean abso-fucking-lutely *everything* – even if it makes me want to tear this place upside down. This club is dysfunctional – fucked – when the head doesn't know the fucking tail's on fire."

Nobody moved. Fang had been the national Prez since...fuck, I didn't even know. Decades.

I wasn't sure what to think. The pale, flat expression on Rabid's face next to me said my brother was just as confused as me. This shit was unprecedented, and now we were gonna see if anybody had the balls to threaten removal the safe and easy way, or if this was some kinda fucking trick.

"Prez, in the interests of full disclosure, I think everybody ought to know about Tacoma –" Blackjack started to speak, but Fang cut him off with another table rocking slam of the bear claw.

"They don't need to know shit 'til they decide if I'm gonna lead, or if some other cocksucker wants to sit on this mountain of shit. Come on, asshole. Be a man." His eyes were dark, intense, drilling into our old Enforcer's.

Finally, Blackjack stood up, his gray hair flopping on his shoulders. "Fine. All right, everybody, we're gonna take a vote on No Confidence for the sitting Prez of the Sacramento charter and acting Prez of Redding. If Fang's deemed to have lost our faith, then we'll have to elect a new man to head the club. Not just our charter, but for the entire Grizzlies MC in the whole twelve state area."

Fang rolled his eyes. "Fucking get on with it. Here, *Sarge*."

The Prez sneered as he passed the bear claw to Blackjack. As Enforcer, it was his job to carry out a vote like this.

My brain was on fucking fire. I couldn't decide if this was a blessing or one helluva curse. If Fang was removed – and that was one big fat *if* – the club would be in so much chaos it'd be a cakewalk moving Missy and her sis north. Shit, even I could slip away in the craziness if I wanted to, assuming the cartel didn't crash the power struggle and

145

burn us all alive.

Blackjack gripped the bear claw. He looked us up and down, letting his eyes linger on Rabid and I.

"Let's do it, brothers. Starting at the head of the table. Every man here gets a vote except the Prez, an aye or a nay. I'll keep count. Crack?"

The VP was the first man up. Thirty pairs of eyes turned toward him. Fuck, the first few votes were bound to set the precedent.

The only way Fang was gonna be removed was if anybody had the balls to effectively spit in his face. And I wasn't sure anybody here had the balls. Dammit. If only the charter allowed these kinda fucking votes to go by secret ballot instead.

My heart stopped. I forgot to breathe. For a second, I thought he was really gonna do it, thought Crack was gonna vote aye for his own selfish ass reasons.

"Nay," the VP choked out.

Adrenaline flooded my head. Rabid let out a little hissing sound, and several brothers next to us looked down, shuffling their boots underneath the long table.

Blackjack moved down the line, cold and efficient, no emotion showing on his face. Nay, nay, nay.

Three more votes to keep Fang. Then six. Then five.

"Nay." Rabid's hoarse, quick vote echoed loud in my ears, like the sound of my own blood running out after getting stabbed.

Fuck. It was my turn, and Blackjack was looking right at me. I didn't have to count everybody else on my right to know they'd all have to vote aye to even make this fucking thing a tie.

I clenched my teeth and waited too many seconds before I let it out. "Aye."

Several brothers cleared their throats loudly. I caught Fang's eyes before he caught mine, holding as firm as I could without shaking, looking right into his devilish eyes.

He'd saved me from being burned alive with the other rebel Grizzlies one fucked up night in Montana. But, fuck, he wasn't good for the club. There were no excuses. We were losing the cartel war, and he was letting desperation eat us alive, turn us into demons no better than the Mexicans.

I had to be honest. The Grizzlies patch on my back felt like lead, and the one on my chest itched something terrible. There was no understanding in the Prez's eyes – not even when the asshole next to me voted nay, followed by Serial and Splitter too.

I tried to do right by the club – the same thing everybody wearing the bear on their cuts was supposed to be about.

Idealistic? Stupid? Probably.

Right? Fuck yes.

It was over long before it swung back around the U-shaped gathering, toward Blackjack. I was the only aye. I seriously wondered if I'd make it outta the room alive when the claw returned to Fang.

I didn't give a fuck what happened to me. All I could think about was getting killed before I had a chance to get

Missy and Jackie out.

Fuck! If there was a God, I really needed a miracle right now, more than I ever needed one in my life. Of course, I was the last asshole in the world who deserved good karma after getting Ma killed and drugging myself blind, but a man could hope.

"Aye."

Fang broke the death stare with me and his jaw fell open. Blackjack stood like stone, his face hard, as if to say, *yeah, asshole. I did it.*

The whole room heard the relief hissing out my nostrils. Now that I wasn't the lone asshole voting aye, I might have a chance to smooth things over, before some brother slit my throat in my sleep.

"The nays have it," Blackjack said, taking his seat. He held the bear claw several seconds longer than he needed to before passing it to Fang.

When he held it out to the Prez, Fang ripped it outta his hand, slamming it down on the table again.

"Okay. It's done. Everybody in this room knows exactly where the fuck everybody else stands." His tone sounded calm, but the tremor in his shoulders said otherwise. "Blackjack, tell them about Tacoma."

"We had another shipment hit by the cartel last night," he said, his voice as icy as Fang's. "Some heavy weapons we picked up from a Chinese drop off. It never made it out of port. The Washington crew found three of their guys dead plus a couple prospects, and all the boxes gone the next day."

"Shit! You mean the cartel's slipped that far north without hitting us in Redding first?" Serial pulled out a cigarette and took a long drag.

"No. Right now, there's no proof it was the Mexicans at all," Fang said, leveling his eyes on me again. "The Devils got a much stronger presence on our northern front. They've been coming through our territory for months, hauling shit to Canada, paying us their toll as agreed. All part of the truce I was a goddamned fool to sign."

My head started to spin. I had to grip the table's edge just to stay focused, before that asshole sucked me into the black hell waiting in his eyes.

Fuck. War with the Devils meant one more thing for me to worry about when it involved my own fucking sister and her Prairie Pussy husband.

"Prez, we owe it to the club to find out what's going on before we do anything," I spoke up. "Seems like the perfect kick in the nuts from the cartel. Hit us somewhere we least expect...make us think it was the Prairie Pussies...fuck everything to pieces up north when we need every guy fighting them in the south."

Fang bared his teeth. The bear claw smacked the table loudly, and then he stood up and roared. "Sit down and shut the fuck up, you little shit!"

The Prez and I both hit our seats at the same time. Rabid looked at me like I was about to get my head chopped off. Hell, for all I knew, maybe I was. Then again, decapitation would've been a whole lot easier than the Mauler, and they'd definitely use that fucking thing if they wanted me dead.

"Nothing's been decided," Fang growled. "But I've got my suspicions. The pussies have been expanding West where they don't belong for too fucking long. They know it's the perfect time to hit us right now. Shit, if I were Throttle up in North Dakota, I'd jam it so hard up our asses we'd scream if I knew about the intel your old lady's dead daddy passed to the cartel, Brass."

I swallowed hard. My throat was bone fucking dry. All the guys in the room looked at me like wolves – everybody except Blackjack and Rabid.

"You know what I think?" Fang said, folding his arms, never taking his eyes off me. "I think we've got more rats biting holes in our ship. Rats on the inside passing shit to the cartel, and possibly our old friends in the Devils too. No, I can't prove anything – yet – but when I do, the Mauler's gonna have a lot of traitor skin to chew on. A hard interrogation and death's the only thing rats deserve. Same fucking thing *any* asshole in this room's gonna get by holding back critical intel from this day forward. New policy. I'll have Crack write it into the club charter later."

Sneering, he turned to Blackjack. "Or would you like me to put that up to vote too?"

"Your call, Prez. You know the charter just as well as I do," Blackjack said, a little hint of sarcasm breaking through. "The national President doesn't need to put all defense decisions up to vote when the club's under imminent threat."

"Damned straight," Fang snapped. "I don't know what's

going on, but I'm gonna find out. When I do, it'll be time to clean house. We can't fight the cartel head on 'til we stomp the vermin in our own midst. And if it means we've gotta fight the Devils too...well, who am I to hold all the boys back who're jonesing for some Prairie Pussy colors hanging on their walls?"

Several of the rougher men grinned, including Serial. Of course that motherfucker wanted blood. What else could anybody expect from a psycho fuck?

The men who lived on senseless war were never my brothers. They never would be. Fuck, I had to get away from this shit, I had to –

The bear claw slapped the table again. Loudly. I blinked, losing my thoughts.

"Business adjourned. Keep your asses on call. I'm gonna need guys back here once I figure out who's been fucking us, and how we're gonna cut the cartel before they bleed us out." Fang looked around the room, casting a wide, wicked gaze. "It's all I fucking do. This club's my life, and I'm its life blood."

He stood up and left first, followed by the Veep. Brothers got up and started to move, more than a couple giving me nasty looks on the way out. I made my way to the door when the room was halfway clear, with Rabid right behind me.

At the bar, Suzy served us some beers, something to take the edge off. I noticed Serial, Splitter, and a couple other ruthless assholes at the other end, and I made damned sure they kept their distance.

How fucked was I? Really? The only thing that hadn't screwed me over today was all the drama keeping their attention on the Prez's vote. Nobody gave me shit yet about Missy not showing up to clean today – or maybe they figured she deserved some slack after what Serial did last night.

"You voted the way I wanted to," Rabid finally said. "You know that, brother? I just couldn't bring myself to do it...the vote was fucked from the beginning. Nobody has the balls to kick him out and take the cartel on. Nobody!"

"It's done," I grunted, staring into my beer. "So's digging my grave deeper. I'm gonna tell you, Rabid, and nobody else. You've been a real brother to me."

Rabid's eyebrows went up. He leaned in close for me to whisper.

"In a week or so, I'm taking the girls north. They're getting the fuck away from this shit in case I can't. I'm not gonna let my old lady and the kid be a slave to this fucked up club."

Rabid peeled away, rocking back. His eyes were wide as he picked up his beer and gulped the last two-thirds, slamming the glass on the counter when he was done.

"Christ, brother. Shit." He shook his head. "You really think that's wise when Fang was practically calling you a rat to you face?"

"Got no choice. I'm a natural target. I tried to vote him out and my sis is married to the pussy Prez in Montana. If Fang's gonna string me up and rip my throat out, I'm not gonna leave my girl defenseless. They've gotta get away from all this."

Rabid cocked his head. "Shit, bro. You're really into this chick, aren't you?"

I nodded. No point in hiding it, and I didn't fucking want to.

"She's warming to me, Rabid. I intend to keep it that way. Sure, I claimed her to keep her alive at first...but now? There's something there. Something real fucking nice. She's becoming the stuff an old lady's made of."

Rabid smiled. He slapped my shoulder in a way that surprised me. The man who likes his girls steady, hot, and plentiful actually understood, and it surprised the shit outta me.

"I got your back, Brass. If you need to get away from all this shit...just get up and go...I'm not gonna stand in your way. Won't help anybody who does neither. You're a true brother."

I didn't say a word. Just finished my beer, turned to him, and gave a manly hug before taking off.

I wasn't sure if I'd be able to walk outta this clubhouse alive in the coming week. But as long as I had one more day, a couple good men, and my girl behind me, I'd die happy. As long as I got them away from this hell, I'd die like a man, working off the junkie fuckups I still deserved to burn for.

I got in late. The apartment was weirdly quiet, and I had to take a stroll through it to see that I wasn't alone.

"Where's Jackie?" I said, stepping into the bedroom.

Missy was curled up beneath a blanket, reading some shit she'd printed off the old computer. "Christa took her out to the museum. I know, you said no trips out of the apartment...but I figured after last night, that might've changed. She won't talk, Brass. She's really grown on you."

My head started pounding. I leaned on the woodwork in the door frame and ran my fingers through my hair.

"Fuck, babe. You gotta tell me when you give the okay for shit like this. We're not free and clear yet."

She sat up, her eyes wide. "Did anybody ask about me today?"

"No. The club was too distracted with other bullshit. I told my number one brother what's coming. He's cool with it."

Missy nodded. She swung her legs over the bed and stood up, dropping the blanket. Did a double take when I saw she was wearing nothing on the bottom, not even panties underneath her long shirt.

"Shit! And you *definitely* gotta start telling me about that," I growled, overwhelmed by the grin creeping across my face.

She stepped right into my embrace. I hugged her close, sweeping my hands down her ass. My cock perked up, ready to fuck both our brains out. Damned if I didn't need it after having Fang's evil eyes all over my mug all evening.

Yeah, baby girl, I thought. *A dude can definitely get used to this if it's what an old man can look forward to.*

I kissed her, rough as the rage and confusion still

swirling around inside me. Fuck, there was a hint of sugar on her lips from this morning. Sugar and spice and everything *very* fucking nice.

I grabbed her hips and squeezed, grinding her bare pussy on my jeans. She gasped when she felt my hard-on.

"Brass..."

"What time does Jackie come home?" I asked, digging my fingers into her round ass. God damn. I'd never, ever get tired of it, and I couldn't wait to take her from every angle while she bounced all over my dick.

"Another hour. Maybe two," she purred, brushing her sweet little lips against mine.

My cock thudded in my pants like a fucking jackhammer. Suddenly, the shitty day was turned on its head, and now I only had one thing to worry about: how many times I was gonna fuck her to the wall before the girl got home.

I was on her like an animal. Picked her up in my arms and flung her down on the bed, tearing off that shirt. Shit, she was missing her bra too, and those pretty pink nipples called to my mouth like sirens.

I fell over her, bracing myself with my hands. She squirmed and giggled as my chin moved down, rough stubble sliding over her throat, not stopping 'til I got her right nip in my mouth.

Holy fucking shit. Every part of her tasted good, and I swore her skin heated a few degrees hotter when I sucked, holding it between my teeth. I had a gift for biting a woman's tits just right, the perfect bite for making them slick and ready for my dick.

When I did it to my Missy, she rolled, hissing rough satisfaction as my tongue flicked her tip. I sucked it 'til it was soft in my mouth, then started on the other one I'd been tweaking with my fingers. When I went in her today, she was gonna be good and ready, wet enough to fuck as many times as I could manage during this precious time alone.

"Brass! Brass..." She slurred my name over and over, starting to go crazy as my stubble and mouth kissed their way down, stopping at the sweet wet V below her trim pussy hair.

It was like a fucking target for my mouth, and I always hit my bullzeye. She started to squirm with the first lick. One day soon I'd drive that self-conscious shit outta her. There was no way – absolutely none – she was getting outta having my mouth on her sweet cunt, lapping deep and long, starving for her taste.

Just let me lick. Listen to my tongue and behave yourself, babe. Don't worry about shit except how hard you're gonna come on my lips.

I couldn't say anything while I had my mouth buried in her sweetness, but I sure as fuck thought it. Couldn't think about anything else while I licked inside her pussy, relishing her taste, her smell, then moving up and making her body jerk when I lashed her clit.

Fuck, she was hot. Hot and responsive enough to make me forget all about the vipers nipping at my heels.

I licked deep. Hard. Loving. I surrounded her clit with

my tongue, sucked it between my teeth, holding it there so I could press her sweetest button again and again, begging her to blow.

She finally did. I knew the minute her legs started trembling in my hands, shaking on both sides of my head. I pressed my fingers into her tender flesh and held her down, circling her clit with fresh licks like a fucking demon.

Her pussy thrashed against my face when she came. Her scream splashed my lips as she tightened up and gushed. Damn if I didn't push my face into her harder. This mess was my pride and joy, a sopping wet symbol of the effect I had on her.

Missy's fingernails pushed through my hair and dragged on my head. Didn't stop me from continuing my assault on her clit 'til she finally stopped bucking on my face. I could practically hear the explosion echoing through her body as she gave it up, coming on my tongue, coming just for me.

Beautiful. Totally fucking beautiful.

In the sweet peace I gave her, coming her pretty brains out, she didn't have to worry about a damned thing. And neither did I when I watched her, felt her, tasted her. If I could've stayed attached to that pussy for the next two days just licking, sucking, and fucking it with my tongue, I would've been a happy man.

But right now I'd be even happier when I let out some of the fire raging in my cock. I stood up while she was still twitching, coming off the high. Tore off my clothes fast and fished out a condom, loving how she was sprawled out and ready for me on the bed.

I rolled the condom on, crawled onto the bed, and pushed between her legs. She opened her eyes and looked seductive as fuck without even trying when I touched her.

"Babe, you better turn over right now. Get on your hands and knees. I'll show you how we make the most of things when our time's scarce."

She moaned and I helped her up, watching her hot ass bob as she got into the perfect position. I reached up, fisting her hair, grinding my cock against her ass cheeks. Fuck, one day I'd take her ass too, but today was all about her pussy. No goddamned way I was gonna let that wet, sweet silk I'd stroked go to waste.

One push and I was in. Missy's whole body jerked, and I held on tight, jerking on her hair like the reigns they were.

We fucked hard. Taking her doggie let me make the deep strokes I loved, gradually picking up speed and tension, shaking her from head to toe. The bed rattled beneath my knees, giving her an extra bounce each time she fell back into me. I loved it.

I watched her tits from the side. Kept the tempo rising 'til they shook like ripe fruits beneath her, bobbing back and forth, pendulums of pure lust swinging each time my dick drove deep.

That fire in my nuts hadn't lessened one bit. Fuck no. It was growing stronger, spilling out my balls and racing up my spine. Hot lava churned beneath my dick and my balls started to tense up after a few breathless minutes of rough fucking.

"Come, babe," I growled, reaching my free hand around her stomach. I found her clit and rubbed hard.

Just what she needed to tense up on my cock and convulse. Missy screamed, and then screamed harder when I jerked her head up, curling her beautiful brown hair around and around my fingers, spooling her to the limit before I joined her.

And I did a second later.

"Fuck! Don't stop shaking that ass. Grind into me, baby girl, hard as you fucking can."

She took orders like a good girl, even balls deep in her climax. My cock pressed against her womb and ballooned when her ass hit my pubic bone. I fucking lost it.

My nut came seething and furious, the kinda release that splinters your brain in half. It was like being lit on fire. Her screams disappeared into a breathless gasp as I shook my dick inside her, feeling the first hot come load blowing into the condom.

I didn't fucking stop. I kept rocking inside her, making shallow spikes deep in her pussy. Marking her, fucking her, loving her every way I could 'til my body gave out.

My heart beat like a fiend against my ribs. Jet after jet of flaming hot sperm shot up my shaft and pulsed heat through my muscles. I felt like I'd grown taller, swelled out, full of total love and lust like a fucking giant.

Shit. That's when it reached up and punched me in the fucking face.

If the club or the cartel didn't kill me, this girl would. She'd drive me absolutely fucking *loco* whether I had her in my arms or my dick buried inside her. Smack didn't have shit on the addiction she ignited in my blood.

I rolled, tugging her in my arms, pulling her to my chest. The big bear on my chest was like a landing pad for her face.

Something natural. Something good. Something worth fighting for no matter how miserable the odds were stacked against us.

"Rest up, babe. Don't go to sleep on me. We're not done here by a long shot." I gave her a playful smack on the ass and she jerked alert.

The annoyed look on her face melted in a smile. "You're the only man who's ever gotten away with that, you know."

I winked. "Fuck, I'd better be, babe. If anybody else has had his hands on this sweet ass, you point me his way and I'll knock his fucking teeth out. You know what this is?"

I reached for both cheeks and squeezed. She whimpered in my hands, then opened her eyes, snuggling into me, staring at the ink on my chest.

"It's my butt," she said, laughing like an angel.

"And it's all fucking *mine*." Why did that word always sound like a saw firing up in my throat when I said it?

Filled me with the same kinda primal fury I felt looking at Fang or Serial or any of the other assholes who'd fucked my club beyond repair. I'd never let anything take this body away from me. *Never.*

"Why do they call you Brass, anyway? Do bikers still have normal names behind all the crazy egos?" She asked.

I grinned. "It happened when I was a prospect.

Everybody's got a different rite when they get in with the club. Some guys just make you do chores and shit – you know, serve them beers, polish their shoes, toss bottles and condoms after the parties. Others are downright fucks who like to see how much pain you can take."

She shook her head sadly. "Sounds like a frat house."

"Yeah, except this is a lot more serious." Or that's what it's *supposed* to be, I thought, my heart darkening when I imagined all the ways our brotherhood went off the rails. "Anyway, there was this one mean fuck in Coeur d'Alene who always punched the prospects in the nuts. Hard as he fucking could, just short of leaving 'em sterile. I knew what was coming that night at the party, when all the boys were drunk and ready to fuck around messing with their new guys. There was an old brass doorknob coming loose in the bathroom. I stuffed it down my pants before it was my turn to serve that fuck a drink. Asshole broke his fucking hand when he nailed me in the balls. I got away a little winded. Nothing worse."

She blinked, then laughed and shook her head. "That's crazy. What stopped him from killing you after that?"

"Prez took a vote to patch me in right on the spot. Said it was the hardest he'd laughed in years. Fuck, I'd give anything if Ox was controlling Redding instead of Fang. He was fucked up in his own way, but fair. Lot like Blackjack."

"So, you're kinda the joker boy, then?" She dragged her fingernails along my chest. My skin sizzled, hair standing on end, crying to fuck her the second I was hard. "You

161

never said what your real name is."

"It's Jordan, babe. Jordan Reagan. Don't wear it out. Best time for me to hear it's when your pussy's exploding on my dick."

"Jordan," she whispered. "It's good. Strong. About what I expected."

"Good. I'd have laughed in your face if you expected me to be called Manny or some shit like that."

"I don't care what they call you. I know what I want, Brass, and it's right here."

Fuck yes, she did.

Missy leaned down, flicking her tongue along my lips. A couple more flicks in quick succession teased me stupid.

Little devil. She knew how to work my ass as well as I knew how to work hers, and I loved it. On the fourth lick, I reached up and fisted her hair, holding her tight to my lips.

I wouldn't let her outta that kiss 'til she reached down and grabbed my cock, hardening against her thigh. She gave it a good squeeze and I grunted. I wanted to pull her thighs open and drive deep inside her, make her ride me for all she was worth, but I needed another condom first.

I saw red, thinking about how I had to get her that shit I had waiting in my jeans. Things would move a lot more natural after I gave her the pills I snatched from the club infirmary.

Not that I was gonna register a single fucking complaint about the filthy deeds going down in this bed all evening. No fucking way. Every day breathing in her sweet scent while I fused my dick to her was a good one.

I just hoped like hell there'd be many more to come, many more perfect days tangled up in my old lady.

"Come on, babe. We gotta get this shit locked in for Friday before you take off."

She pulled on my cut, dazed at all the choices in the rental office. Reserving something to carry her and Jackie north was the best way to get them outta Redding without the brothers being able to track her down. Giving her my truck was way too risky.

"You're sure you can afford this?" she asked, her fingers running over a cherry red hatchback thing in the catalogue.

"Yeah. We'll be good as gold just as soon as my next club stipend comes in. Better to get our pieces together now."

"But we don't even know *where* yet!"

She looked so damned confused, disoriented. I grabbed her hand and pushed my fingers through hers. Raw strength always reassured a woman, and I had no doubt it was gonna work on the one I wanted most.

"I like the look of that car." I pointed at the bright red vehicle. "A little style, and not so much it'll draw attention. Extra space to carry your shit north, and plenty rugged for the mountains and forests we'll be dealing with past NorCal."

She punched me in the arm. I grinned. "Careful, Mister. I just might decide to take that Harley up and have *you* drive Jackie in the hatchback."

I laughed. She knew how to dish it out and take it. My kinda girl, as if it wasn't glaringly fucking obvious by now.

"All right. That one it is. It's even got some fancy USB shit to keep Jackie entertained. I'm gonna get both you girls new phones before we blow town, as soon as we're free and clear."

I left her standing near the counter while I went to arrange the rental. I looked behind me while the skinny fuck with the thin mustache at the counter ran my card. Saw her walking off, probably heading for the restroom or something.

The kid passed me my printout and told me the car would be ready in a couple days. Perfect timing to get the reservation fee off my shit and pay it all in cash, same way I dealt with everything. Before I moved away, I looked him up and down.

The dude wasn't much younger than me, maybe a year or two. He looked like a little boy. I grunted. One thing I'd never regret about this life was that it made me a man, no matter how fucked up it could be sometimes.

If it wasn't for the club...I might've turned into something like that, and then I'd want to blow my fucking brains out. The civilian world wasn't for me. If I really and truly left the patch behind, then I'd have to find something else to do.

There had to be something out there to accommodate men like me. The world still needed a place for roughnecks and road warriors, even if we were an endangered species.

There must've been something better than clacking

keyboards or ringing up pissy, impatient customers at a place like this. Whatever it was, I swore I'd find it. Anything to rake in cash for my girls without lopping off my nuts was fine by me.

A man provides. I should've done it for Ma and Shelly back in Missoula, before my own sis was reduced to shaking her ass at a Prairie Pussy bar for spare cash. But my relationship with the ladies had been...strained, to put it mildly.

A fucked up home was all it took to drive me into the club, and then I found the sick paradise heroin offered. I shook my head, trying to do the math and figure out how many months it had fucked outta my life. Looking down at my arm, I saw the fading impression left by a fat needle. It was the last time those freaks in fake Grizzlies colors forced it into my veins after I betrayed them, trying to make me OD on the one thing I loved.

Blaze and Shelly saved my dumbass that night. I thought Fang did too, but he was just a king, moving his pawns around on the grand board.

You're gonna do better, I vowed. *You fucking have to.*

I waited impatiently by the restroom for Missy. She didn't come out for five minutes. Then ten. Then another five on top of that.

Weird, and seriously fucking suspicious.

A motorcycle growled outside, not far from mine. I spun around, just in time to see a dude with long black hair pulling away. It was quite a distance, but I'd know that damned patch from a hundred yards away.

Shit! The club!

My brain switched onto search, kill, and protect mode. I smashed the door open to the lady's room and called for her.

"Missy? Babe, where the fuck are you?" Nothing. Not even any feet underneath the stalls.

My heart started to beat like it was gonna go nova. I ran, threw myself onto my bike. I started her up and squealed outta the parking lot before I had time to think anything else, heading for the clubhouse.

I knew something was fucked up the instant I stepped into the bar. Half the guys' bikes were parked outside, but nobody was inside. It was a fucking ghost town.

I listened close. Couldn't hear a single brother snoring or fucking like they always did on lazy afternoons.

Shit. I started to back away, toward the door. If Missy was being kept here somewhere, then there had to be a better way to find her...

"Fuck..." I stumbled down the steps leading into the garage, and then felt something behind me that shouldn't have been there.

I whirled, reaching for my gun, and caught a blur right before it crashed into my face. The asshole's metal pipe knocked me flat. Vertigo took over, dragging me down, smearing everything to blood red, the color of rage and confusion.

A fat boot landed on my chest and pressed down hard. My ribs screamed.

"Get this fucking rat off the floor and load him up like Fang wants. We got the girls. If she doesn't make him sing, then maybe the little sister will..."

Serial. If I could've reached up and strangled that sick motherfucker, I'd have done it in a heartbeat. But my brain wouldn't cooperate, spinning into a thick, incomprehensible blackness.

I was out like a light, an early preview of the death they had waiting for my sorry ass.

VII: Under the Blade (Missy)

One Hour Earlier

I never knew how they got in without us noticing. My head was spinning as I walked to the bathroom, wondering how I was going to break the news to Jackie. I wasn't even sure how I'd navigate a road trip this week when I'd never been more than a hundred miles outside Redding my entire life.

I was barely looking for wet floor signs when I pushed open the door, much less three burly men in leather waiting for me. I crashed right into his chest and he had his hand over my mouth before I could scream.

I fought them anyway, kicked and thrashed as they picked me up like a piece of wood, carrying me to the SUV outside. I twisted in the big man's arms and caught a flash of Brass still waiting at the counter. Perfectly normal, and totally twisted.

There were too many blocking the view. God damn it, if only he'd turned around.

Luck was never that kind. As soon as they threw me in the backseat, another man stuffed something fat and rubbery in my mouth. My teeth were struggling with the gag when another rag covered my face, reeking like thick medicine. The smell had a resemblance to all the high powered pain killers daddy was on during his last days.

Ether.

All the horror in my head melted away in one breath. By the second breath, I was falling into a deep black abyss, too lifeless to even think about screaming for help.

"Wake up, bitch." A rough hand caressed my cheek.

I jerked up. Too fast. My head throbbed like a bad hangover, and I struggled to adjust to the bright lamp hanging somewhere overhead. My wrists burned, and so did my shoulders. I realized a second later I was tied to a chair, identical to the girl right across from me.

Jackie! My heart sank and tears pricked at my eyes when I realized it was her, right before the rage set in.

She was still passed out, a tiny shred of mercy, her small face slumped on her shoulder. They must have given her the same crap they'd given me.

"Who are you? Why're you doing this?"

The man who'd touched me from behind stepped into the light. I recognized the fucked up mess of barbed wire on his face right away. Serial, and the other headed bastard named Splitter with the nose ring was right behind him. Several other dark shapes lingered behind Jackie, the light obscuring their faces.

"Let her go, *asshole*," I hissed. "I don't care what you do to me. But my sister doesn't deserve this, she's got nothing to do with anything your club wants. You can't –"

He cut me off with a sharp slap across the face. My cheek burned when I twisted my head back into place. The pain didn't stun me for some weird reason. It only added to the blinding rage tearing through my blood.

"She's got everything to do with helping this club. You and your cute little twin are gonna help us loosen up the rat's tongue before we pour concrete over his fucking carcass."

Jesus! They're really going to kill him.

I started to shake. The animal talked way too easy about killing the man I was just beginning to love. Serial showed no remorse. There was nothing in his dark eyes. Not even pleasure. It was like staring into a machine designed to look and talk like a man, but murder was its sole function.

"Just be a good girl and cooperate, baby," Splitter said behind him, chuckling beneath his breath. "This'll all be over fast if you do. You don't have to die with your old man. Nobody believes that shit about him claiming you."

"He did!" I insisted. Didn't know why I thought it would.

The men just laughed and shook their heads. I realized this was the worst time imaginable to be arguing about what Brass meant to me. But if we were dying here today, then somebody had to know we weren't just playing pretend.

Somebody had to witness what I had in my heart, the only thing I was sure about, other than protecting Jackie on this emotional roller coaster making my heart howl.

"Whatever, princess. Guess fucking a rat's in your blood knowing who your daddy was." Serial walked over to what looked like a small black bag on a nearby table. "You wanna play Romeo and Juliet, I honestly don't give a shit. Those fucks both died in the end, didn't they? Shakespeare was a mean sonofabitch. So am I. Thing is, you don't have to die with him. Neither does the little chick if you stuff that bitch tongue and cooperate."

A zipper opened. The men behind Jackie shifted uncomfortably, their heads turned toward whatever the hell Serial was taking out of the bag.

He spun. The tangle of sharp metal made me want to scream, but then my brain froze, struggling to understand what it was seeing.

Jesus Christ. Was he really wearing that thing on his hand?

It looked like a mess of knives, corkscrews, daggers, and hooks attached to an old baseball glove. Some sicko's fucked up idea of what a Swiss Army knife should look like if it were designed to be worn for flaying skin.

"You like it, cunt?" Serial sniffed, taking a step closer. "We call this nasty fucking thing the Mauler. It's the club's pride and joy, and she only comes out when a bullet to the brain isn't good enough. Sometimes I wish there were a few more rats crawling around. This poor baby goes a long time between her meals, and when she finally gets some blood, she's fucking *hungry*."

His eyes weren't so dark anymore. Now, there was a monstrous pleasure shining in his eyes. Somehow, I held it together, feeling myself leave my body, hovering over all this. I guess it was my natural defense against breaking down in tears or screaming my lungs out in front of this maniac.

No, *maniacs,* plural. Splitter laughed behind me again, low and nasty, and the four shapes behind my sister stood like statues.

One of the silhouettes had long hair hanging down his shoulders. If it was Blackjack – and it probably was – then Brass had been dead wrong him being a decent man.

Jesus, he'd been wrong about how swift they'd move on us too. Well, right or wrong, it was much too late to be upset about it when there was way more horror in front of me.

God. Realizing the only man who could protect us fucked up this bad hurt worse than the demon shaking his murderous glove in my face.

I looked into his dead eyes and cracked. "Don't do this. Please. I'll tell you anything you want to know…"

"You don't know shit, bitch. Neither does your dumb sister. If we wanted you to talk, we'd have stripped you down and mounted both your asses about five minutes ago. You're here to loosen *his* lips. Don't you get it?" He stared into my eyes like a frustrated teacher looking at a dense pupil. "Everything that happens from this point hinges on the fucking rat telling us what we want to know about his involvement with the Mexican cartel or – more likely – the Prairie Devils MC. We'll find out right here how much he loves you. Maybe he'll talk fast, get himself a

173

merciful death, and do the right thing by us. Or, he'll cry and plead, keeping his rat lips shut while we rip you and the baby girl over there to shreds."

He turned away, fixing his eyes on Jackie. I wasn't sure whether I should be happy or horrified she was still out. I sniffed hard, blinking back tears when he stopped behind her, gingerly putting the heavy weapon attached to his hand on her shoulder.

"I think I'll start on the little one first. Just on the off chance you were nothing more than an easy fuck to our boy." Serial turned, sweeping the claw away. Jackie twisted her head and groaned.

Don't wake up...don't wake up...

Please, sis. Don't wake up.

"Rabid!" he barked to one of the men behind him. "Go drag that turd in here. You're used to smelling his shit anyway after all the times you hung around him. Move."

One of the figures hesitated for a good ten seconds, and then finally moved.

I closed my eyes, praying Jackie wouldn't wake up with that asshole's claw next to her. Even if we somehow got out of this alive, she'd be traumatized for life. It was a small miracle watching dad die and being captured by the Grizzlies hadn't made her comatose by now.

But this would be the final straw. I just knew it.

The sound of feet shuffling made me look up. Rabid and another dead eyed man with long hair were carrying Brass in. My heart bled hate and pain all over again when I saw my man.

They'd bruised his face. Scratched it. His wrists and feet were bound by crude cables.

Growling, Serial stepped away from my sister. He walked behind Brass and pushed him out of the other men's arms. He hit the cement floor hard, making an *oomph* sound barely louder than the rattle of his bones.

"Get up, asshole!" Serial kicked him in the ribs. "Don't think you're gonna make this shit any easier playing possum, you fucking rat. I told the wrecking crew out there *not* to beat you senseless. They took it light. I know you're fucking awake. Look up! Look at me, before I make your girls bleed."

Brass grunted, leaned down, and spat a long, sticky trail of blood. My fingers went numb. I rocked in my chair, wanting so bad to look away from all this. But ignoring the grisly sight in front of me was even worse than seeing dead on.

He turned, forcing himself up when the trickle was done running out his mouth. If he saw me at his side, or Jackie at the other, he showed no sign of it.

Brass just turned, looking past my sister, right at the trio against the wall. I realized then his mouth was gagged with a thick handkerchief stuck between his teeth and bound around his head.

"I'm gonna take this shit off so you can talk," Serial said, leaning down and almost pressing his evil lips to Brass' ear. "But first, I'm gonna show you I'm not fucking around here. I'm gonna give you a little preview of what happens when your bitch ass fails to tell me the truth, the whole truth, and nothing but the truth."

The thug snorted. "You think you hurt me after I went after your slut? Huh? Getting the jump on me and cracking my jaw?" Serial shook his head. "Well, I'm gonna hurt you a hundred times worse before I even lay a fucking finger on you."

He stood, heading for Jackie again. I realized what was about to happen before he even raised his arm.

"No! Don't fucking do this!" I rocked in the chair as hard as I could, shaking until it almost broke.

Is this what it feels like when someone's losing their mind? I wondered.

The answer was right in front of me, vicious and blood red: if he put a single scratch on Jackie's innocent skin and woke her up, I'd never be whole again. Every cut, every scratch, every wound on her was a thousand times worse than anything he could do to my own skin.

I couldn't hear myself think. My brain slipped away as he lingered over my sister, taking his sweet time, wiggling his fingers in that fucked up Freddy Krueger thing on his hand.

There was another sound. A harsher, angrier, masculine growl, deep as thunder and just as dangerous.

I realized it was Brass rumbling through his gag. His whole body shook like he had a current running through him. I couldn't see what he was looking at, but it looked like he was gazing through Serial and Jackie, straight to the other men against the wall, grinding his throat like a motorcycle engine running on pure hate, betrayal, sadness.

"Come on, Serial. Get on with it," Blackjack said from his post against the wall. "You're a fucking coward, you know."

Serial stopped. The freak turned his barbed wire tattooed face toward the wall as his superior stepped forward, his gray hair bobbing on his shoulders.

"What did you say to me, old man?" he snorted. "You think you got some big fat balls in your flabby sac just because you pissed in the Prez's face? You're not strong. You're not brave. You're the only fuckhead stupid enough to vote with this rat, and I can't fucking wait 'til Fang lets me take Enforcer and puts your weak ass out to pasture."

Blackjack stepped into the light, and Brass' head followed every move he made. I couldn't see my lover's eyes, but I knew they'd be horrible, like watching a curse starting to wreck havoc.

"I said you're a coward, Serial. You'd rather torture his women instead of face the fist that pounded you in the face. A real man only enjoys spilling blood when he's evenly matched and when it's damned well justified. This shit here..." Blackjack shook his head.

Brass let out another roar through his gag. I could see his hands twitching, tied behind his back, slowly ripping at the cord. His fingers were bloody, but it really looked like he might get it off.

No. This is stupid. You can't get your hopes up.
Brace for the worst, girl. Brace for hell.

I turned my brain off and watched Serial stare at the old man with pure venom. In a blink, he swirled, stepping to

Jackie and jerking her head up by the hair. The big razor-toothed dagger attached to the glove was poised right across her throat.

My eyes wouldn't work anymore. Everything was fading, turning white, like a heavy fog was descending over the room. Of course, I knew it was all in my head, my brain blotting out something it couldn't comprehend and remain sane.

"A coward?" Serial snorted again. "That's the best piss you can come up with, old fart? Would a coward do this?"

His fingers twitched through the glove. *Oh, God.* I knew he was getting ready to cut her throat, maybe kill her on the spot, and I started to squirm, forcing my vision to work again.

"No," Blackjack said coldly. "I expect you to scream like the miserable disgrace to this club you are when you're laid out on the floor. Rabid!"

Two gunshots rang out like thunder bolts. I never knew who drew first and fired. Brass howled through his gag, his body writhing in frustration or relief – I couldn't tell which.

Serial roared, collapsing on the floor, away from Jackie. He screamed and screamed as blood pooled out the hole in his back. His hands twitched and he struggled on the ground, but he couldn't seem to get back up.

Against the wall, the long haired man who'd helped carry Brass in hit the floor, a hole in his head. He was dead before the hit the concrete. Rabid pointed his gun at the other two against the wall.

"Drop your fucking weapons, brothers. I'm not gonna tell you again!"

The two men reached to their waists and the metal clacked on the floor. One kick and they slid it over to Rabid, who caught up with Serial on the floor, standing over him.

Blackjack turned to me and gave a little nod. Then he walked over to Brass. Pulling out a knife and kneeling, he sliced the cords binding his wrists. He cut the gag next, moving to his boots last.

"Jesus, son. It's a good thing I didn't wait a second longer. You'd have rubbed your hands too raw to deal with —"

Brass didn't wait for him to finish. As soon as Blackjack finished with the bindings holding his boots, he bolted up, amazingly fast for a man who'd just taken beating.

He lunged, landed on Serial, snarling like a wild cougar. The psycho couldn't put up much of a fight. Brass ripped the Mauler off his hand and quickly pushed his own fingers into it, holding it over Serial's face for one agonizing second.

"No, Brass! No, brother…"

With his free hand, Brass ripped him up, bashing his forehead on Serial's before letting his head slump again. "Don't you ever fucking call me that again. You were never my brother, and you never will be. Not even in hell…"

I looked away as he tore into the psychopath's face. Serial only shrieked for about a minute before his cries became gurgling rasps. Then there was nothing at all.

I opened my eyes, first checking to make sure Jackie was still out. Thank God for small favors, because she was.

Blackjack stood over my man and extended a hand. Brass ripped off the blood covered Mauler glove and let it fall on Serial's corpse.

"Why, brother?" Brass asked, taking his hand and standing on his feet again.

"Because I'm tired of watching my club turn into a sadistic freak show under Fang. I've made my choice. Let's kick his ass off the throne. We already tried the democratic way, and it didn't work. It never does when brothers are shaking in their boots while they vote. Here."

The older man reached into his pocket and handed Brass something. It must've been a set of keys by the way they jingled.

"Get the fuck out of here," Blackjack growled. "Take the girls somewhere safe. Use my truck. Head north to Oregon – Klamath – and don't do anything 'til you hear more from me. Rabid and I are gonna stay behind and clean this mess up while we figure out who we can trust."

Brass looked back at me, his eyes wide. He was full killer then, his face spattered with dead Serial's blood, and it was all over his cut, his jeans, and his shirt too. He stopped, giving Blackjack a big hug, pounding his back until the old man fought him off.

"Go. We've got surprise on our side. Now we just need time."

Brass ran to me. I shook when he wrapped his arms around me, loosening my restraints with the knife in his hand. As soon as I was free, he passed me the switchblade and I ran to Jackie, getting her untied and then lifting her into my arms.

I checked her pulse and breathing. Normal.

"Brass?" I turned.

He was right behind me, waiting in all his blood flecked glory. "You heard the man. We gotta fucking go. No time to stop at the apartment or anywhere else. You got her?"

I nodded. Brass made one more stop near the door, giving Rabid a manly slap on the shoulder.

"Told you I had your back, brother. Me and Blackjack both, soon as we found out what was coming tonight."

Brass nodded at the lean, muscular man, the way a man can only look at a true brother. I understood then: these guys *were* family after all. And if the last few weeks taught me anything, it's that there's nothing like embracing family when you don't know if you'll see them alive again.

Jackie was a heavy load in my arms. She'd grown since the last time I ever moved her, years ago at this point. When Brass turned, he saw me struggling, and reached out. I passed her into his strong arms, and we were off.

The place they'd been holding us was huge. It looked like an old abandoned factory, or maybe a shipping center. Rusted metal and cracked cement were everywhere.

I saw the truck parked between a gaggle of bikes. We headed right for it, and Brass handed me the keys to open the door. He passed Jackie back to me when I was in my seat. She barely fit on my lap in the truck.

The dream-like coma my brain was in while I was on

that chair started lifting. I looked at him and blinked, feeling the life come back into my tongue.

"Jesus, Brass. Can you believe what just –"

"Don't talk yet, babe. Not 'til we're on the road heading for the state line."

He pushed the key into the ignition. The truck growled to life, and Jackie twitched in my arms as he peeled a tight circle, aiming for an old gate.

Shit. My sister's eyes lit up and she shook her head, trying to comprehend what she was seeing.

"Hold onto her tight!" Brass growled. "We're gonna hit a little bump when we go over."

I backed up in my seat and clutched Jackie tight, burying her face in my chest. Bump was an understatement. The truck bounced in the air as it flattened the chain link fence, bounding over a depression in the ground, then tearing through the tall overgrown grass outside for several feet before we hit the road.

Jackie clawed at me like a scared kitten. "Missy? What the fuck?!"

"Shhh. Easy, sis. We're almost home."

The warehouse – factory? – whatever the hell it was, the place was just a small dot by the time she finally got herself seated between us. My little sister's eyes were bugged out, looking between me and Brass.

"What happened to those men? They knocked out Christa and grabbed me, held something strong to my face so I couldn't breathe..."

I didn't want to say. How was I supposed to explain

away the ruthless bastards who'd punched her tutor out and dragged her to the shitty warehouse, where she'd mercifully slept during the torture and death I'd witnessed? But silence was going to panic her. I swallowed hard, trying to make my brain work.

"You had a bad nightmare, Jackie. There's no men, no –
"

Brass shot me an angry look. "Don't bullshit the girl, babe. Tell her the truth. We're on the road and we're not coming back here 'til it's safe. I'm protecting you both."

He was right. Guilt swelled in my chest, and I grabbed my sister's hand, trying to find the strength I'd had just a day ago. Watching Serial nearly rip her to pieces had sucked it out of me – hopefully not forever.

"We got attacked," I said with a heavy sigh. "It's okay now. Brass and his friends got us out...we're on our way somewhere they can't hurt us anymore. It'll be all right, Jackie. I swear."

Can you really make those promises? Doubt swirled in my brain. I wanted to believe I could, wanted to keep her safe...but if it wasn't for the other men, even Brass wouldn't have been able to save us this time.

"Stop talking to me like I'm a fucking kid!" Jackie screamed, shoving me in the shoulder.

"Jackie!" I grabbed her wrists, trying to hold her down.

She was surprisingly strong for a teen. Brass' knuckles went white as he gripped the steering wheel, trying to ignore the screaming match going on inside the truck.

"I've been through the exact same crap as you, sis. It's

like you've forgotten," Jackie said, tears sliding down her red cheeks. "Daddy died and screwed up big time, leaving us money we never deserved. I get that. I know it's the reason these men captured us. I can put two and two together, Missy. I'm old enough to handle this."

You shouldn't have to, I wanted to say. But she was right – and it hurt for me to see the cold truth. All this hell we'd been through forced my little sister to grow up before her time.

"It's my job to make sure you don't have to," I snapped. "And...and I think I'm fucking failing at it. You want the truth? I don't know what tomorrow's going to bring anymore. I want to find a way out for both of us, and I keep digging, trying to find the light...but there's just more darkness ahead. Even when Brass is in the lead. There's so many things he can't control. No one can."

"Whatever." Jackie covered her face, turning away from me and burrowing into the worn seat.

"You said your piece," Brass said, glancing at me as he drove. "Let her get some rest. We had a close fucking call back there. We'll all feel better by morning."

I looked through the darkness at him, annoyed. I shouldn't have needed any advice about how to handle this...but shit, what did I really know about this life? What did I know about my own sister?

"You told her the truth, babe. That's all you can do, and all I expect. I'm gonna tell you straight too – the next few weeks are gonna be rough. Don't know where it's gonna end. As long as everybody's open and honest, we'll get through it. Right now, my whole focus is keeping you two safe while we get into Oregon. Then I'll figure out the rest, soon as I hear from Blackjack." He turned away, keeping his attention on the road. "I love you, babe."

The words hit me in the chest like an icepick. It was too much to process after everything that just happened. I couldn't speak, so I reached for his hand, gingerly placing my fingers over his on the wheel.

Brass flashed me a knowing smile. For now, that was all I needed.

Jackie slept through the entire trip. Not that I minded one bit. I was feeling pretty drowsy myself by the time we rolled into Klamath Falls after about three hours on the dark, mountainous roads.

We parked the truck and found a hotel with vacancies after a quick stop at a local department store. He sent me in to pick up fresh clothes. He changed before we went into the hotel, doing it in the pickup part, stuffing the bloody clothes in a black bag in the back. Everything except his cut, which would be easier to clean up.

When he was done, we headed inside. Jackie sulked in behind us while Brass got everything set up, then we followed him to the room. He threw me some cash to order a pizza.

We were outside on the main deck, next to a crappy looking pool. I heard him outside talking on his cell. It sounded intense. Jackie was taking a long shower, anything to lengthen her time away from me right now, so I stepped out too.

"Jesus Christ. You've only got half the numbers, Blackjack," he growled into his phone. "Fang's gonna call in other charters to defend his own ass. The cartel war won't matter with the reinforcements he'll bring to Redding."

The other voice on the line was gruff, determined. I couldn't quite make out what he was saying.

"Really? Fucking who? Me and ten other guys aren't nearly enough to stand a chance of dethroning that motherfucker when he'll have double the brothers there in a week."

More rough orders from Blackjack. More tension on my man's face. I leaned in and squeezed his arm.

Suddenly, he tore himself away from me, stumbling to the edge of the pool. "You gotta be fucking shitting me, Blackjack! You're really talking about treason now."

There was a long pause. I could practically see his jaw hanging on the floor before he finally responded.

"Shit. Fuck. It's just...working with the fucking Prairie Pussies?!" He paused, taking a long, slow breath. "Okay. Yeah, I'll call her."

I crept up behind him as he ended the call, moving my hands on his shoulders. "What's wrong? Don't drop the phone in the pool now..."

He turned around and gave me a cynical look. "I'm pissed, but I'm not stupid, babe. Shit's about to get a whole lot more complicated."

"Yeah? Where are we going next?" God, he was tense.

My hands roamed his rock hard muscles, admiring and nervous at the same time. I just wanted to calm him down, let him know that I appreciated everything he'd done.

Against the odds, he'd kept his word. He kept us safe, and now he was taking us away from all this.

He was a rock. My rock. Over six feet of pure masculine granite, inked with an animal that still scared the hell out of me, a beast that only seemed to share his spirit.

I couldn't depend on the world, but I could depend on him.

Brass. Jordan. My old man.

"We gotta head up to Missoula. There's another club up there...the Prairie Devils." He growled the name through his teeth when he said it, giving me the real one instead of the crude slang I'd heard thrown around before. "Blackjack's setting shit up now. If we weren't short on manpower, I'd say he's outta his fucking mind asking for their help. But my sister's got an in with their club. She's married to their Prez, Blaze."

Now, it all came together. I smiled, smoothing my hands on him like he was clay. If only it were so easy to rub away the anger spiking out of his skin in a static aura. I was about to move in for a kiss when the door to our room swung open.

Jackie stuck her head out, wrapped in a towel, and called to us. "Pizza's here!"

"Be right there," Brass said, easing me away.

Before he got two steps further, I reached for his shirt, grabbing a fistful. "Wait."

He spun, staring me up and down.

"I should've said it right away, but I was too damned shocked. What you said on the ride in..." I paused, readying myself to speak the crazy truth out loud. "I love you too. I trust you. I'm here for you, Brass, ready to be your old lady. I mean it for real this time. We're not playing around anymore."

He grabbed me, his rough hands sinking into my hips as he pulled me to his lips. We kissed as long, hard, and hot as the time crunch would allow us, a kiss that said how grateful we were the bastards in the warehouse hadn't taken away everything before I admitted what we had.

It was here. Right here in his marvelous, insatiable lips.

"No we're not, babe. This is all real. I just gotta finish branding you when all this shit's finally done." He grabbed me by the hand and led me forward. "Now, let's go. I'm fucking starving."

Frustration and happiness mingled in his eyes. I recognized the look, praying it would all be over as quickly as he hinted. It needed to be.

Tonight was going to be sheer hell keeping my hands off him while Jackie slept in the other bed.

VIII: Deals With Devils (Brass)

Sleep didn't come easy. It wasn't just club politics weighing heavy on my brain – it was having her pressed up against me in too damned small a room to do anything about it. No fucking way was I gonna make a move and subject the kid sister to hearing us fuck.

But *god damn* my dick ached. Bad. Felt like somebody reached in and filled my balls with lead, heavy and hot, anchoring me to the sheets. Anxious lust hissed through my veins all night. I don't think my hard-on relaxed a second, pressed snug against her ass, taunting me every time Missy twitched in her sleep.

She was obviously having some bullshit nightmares. At one point, I leaned over, kissed her brow, tender as I could without making my cock rage harder.

"It's gonna be okay, baby," I whispered. "All this shit. I'll kill them all myself for dragging you girls into this. Then I'm gonna fuck your brains out, wipe away all the nasty memories with red hot sex. I'm no doctor, but I've got a cure, and I know how to deliver it too."

She stirred, wriggling against me in her sleep. I had to shift my hips. Having my dick on her all night was bound to drive me absolutely nuts by dawn, if I didn't wake up balls deep inside her first.

Truth was, Missy ignited a lunatic inferno in my skull, my blood, and especially below my waist. I'd never told a woman I loved her before the drive up.

Before her, that was the sappiest, most alien shit I ever could've imagined. But having her around let cupid sneak up behind me and drive his arrow deep in my back, and I wasn't gonna pull it out for anything.

It was finally all as clear as a California day.

My life had two stages: before Missy Thomas and after her. The before was complete shit, betrayal and stupidity, my family going to pieces while I was too blasted outta my skull to do anything about it. Shit, I'd helped it along, hadn't I?

What was this after, this new run just waiting for me to follow its jagged path? Remained to be seen. But I swore I'd give it everything to make it the beginning of the rest of my life; a smooth, sweet ride that meshed seamlessly with the future I'd give the babe curled up next to me and her little sis.

I had to. Fucking up again was *not* an option.

The ride was long and hard the next day. Woke up with a nasty bruise on one cheek, plus a few kinks in my shoulders and ribs from all the places those fuck faces hit me at the warehouse.

We all ate a quick breakfast in the hotel, checked out, and then we were on our way, second leg of the two day trip to Missoula. It all hinged on time, getting our ducks in a row back in Redding before Fang had too many of his own to snuff us out. The rest hinged on those Devil assholes cooperating.

Thinking about that shit made me want to rip everything apart. Having Shelly as his wife – or Saffron as he called her, my sis' old stripper name – was the only fucking reason Blaze agreed to talk to me at all. And I still didn't know how I was really gonna sit down with those assholes without punching their teeth out.

I'd barely kept it together during their wedding in Reno. Two Prairie Pussies, Stinger and Tank, nearly beat me to a bloody pulp the minute they saw me. Thank fuck their old ladies were there to talk sense to 'em.

We spent the next night in Coeur d'Alene. I got us all some grub at a sit down restaurant. It was strange to eat in public without my cut on over the tight gray shirt, but the Idaho panhandle was Grizzlies MC territory, and I damned well had to keep a low profile. There was no telling what the charters would do as news about the power struggle in Redding spread.

More than a few Prezes out there had axes to grind with Fang, and there was never a better opportunity. But the bastard also put plenty of loyal thugs in place over the years, far and wide, including pussy fuckers who'd stay with him 'til the bitter end while the cartel had them scared shitless.

Dinner was good. The girls both seemed happier. They chatted and smiled, a welcome thaw in the tension I'd seen between them yesterday. Missy told me about her accounting shit while little Jackie rolled her eyes in boredom. Promised right then she'd be going back to school – shit, both of them – as soon as we were clear and free.

"Brass? This is *it?*" Jackie wrinkled her nose when we pulled up to the only hotel with vacancies.

The kid had good reason to whine. The place was a fucking dump, and I seriously contemplated camping out in the truck for the night over staying here. Too bad a hot shower sounded like it was worth the price of admission alone.

I took a full lap around the place, looking for obvious signs of dangerous deals going down or bitches whoring themselves out. Any one of those things wasn't just bad for the kid – it could indicate a connection to the local MC. The Idaho crew made most of their money off women since the Devils' shipments west started to drain our old business.

I looked high and low, searching for skanks or unassuming bikes parked within a couple blocks. Nothing. Missy was leaning on my shoulder.

Stroking my arm, she whispered in my ear. "It's cheap. It's a warm bed. Let's just take it, Brass. Seriously. We've had worse."

I nodded, parked the truck, and got out ahead of the girls. My ears matched my eyes – the place was eerily quiet.

Yeah, this is the time when most dudes would get in the truck and gun it, or else get gnawed to pieces by some fucked up thing in a bad horror movie. I'd stopped being afraid of anything worse than the murderous freaks I'd run into over the years.

Missy and Jackie hung close while we checked in, right where I wanted them. It took a few rings to rouse the old goat from the back. He spoke in a thick accent – maybe Russian or Polish or some shit – and took my cash without even giving me the stink eye for skipping the card like most decent hotels.

I didn't like the way the fuck's eyes wandered. One of them looked artificial. The other kept skipping me entirely and sinking to the side, staring at Jackie while she messed with a vending machine on the other side of the shitty lobby.

"Something else you need?" I growled, wishing he'd hurry the fuck up.

The jackoff looked down sheepishly and shook his head, reassuring me everything was in order.

Soon as he passed me the keys, I grabbed Missy's hand and walked over to the little girl. "Let's get the fuck inside and rest for a few hours. Don't forget to check for bed bugs."

My girl gave me a worrying look. Jackie just laughed. The room was cramped, a little smoky, but surprisingly not bad.

The women showered, one after another, and then it was my turn. However shitty the place was, it had a working water tank. Feeling the hot jets racing down my muscles felt fucking amazing after two days of pure hell.

Only thing better would've been having Missy there with me, wet and slippery and sexy as the time I took her at the apartment, the first time we fucked.

Fuck, my cock throbbed like mad. Had to fight hard to resist jerking it. No, I wasn't resorting to that teenage shit. Didn't care how many hours were left before I fucked my woman – I wasn't gonna do anything but fucking when the time came.

Truth time: I hadn't jerked my dick in years when there was always pussy waiting for it. But no pussy was more perfect than hers, and the *need* to be inside it almost put me in a straight jacket.

I was practically drooling by the time I stepped out, toweled off, and dried my hair. When I came out, the girls were already crashed out in two beds, exhausted after the day long drive.

I stayed shirtless and climbed in next to my old lady. For a few minutes, I laid there, listening for anything fucked up going on outside the room, any sign I should pass on sleep and meet the Prairie Pussies tomorrow with bloodshot eyes.

My fucking body didn't want to cooperate. The sandman yanked my eyelids like cheap shades. I ended up falling asleep without even realizing it.

I dreamed about anger, violence, and sex. Same shit that always rattled my brain at night. It was more feverish than usual, and at some point I rolled, opening my eyes.

The bed next to us was empty.

Fuck!

I shot up like a lightning bolt and reached for Missy first. She was still there – thank fuck – rolling sharply when she felt my arm sweeping over her. She moaned, rubbing her eyes.

"Brass?" She said, full of grog.

"Stay right there, babe. Don't fucking move. Take this." I reached onto the night stand and took the switchblade, handing it to her.

It was her turn to panic when she sat up and saw what was going on. The covers went flying off the bed and she stood, desperately scanning the room.

"Where's Jackie!?"

"Don't fucking know, but I'm gonna find out."

She called after me, but I was on the move. I'd seen enough shit to know every single nano-second counts in a situation like this. My blood roared like a lion's at his breaking point. Fuck, if anybody took her and plucked a single brown hair outta her head, I'd gut them faster than they could beg for their miserable life.

Outside, it was still pitch dark. Several lights were burned out, and the place was quiet as ever.

No, there was something coming from below. Moaning. A bed creaking. Somebody fucking.

Loud shouts. A woman screamed – this time, not in pleasure.

I didn't bother with the stairs leading down from our second floor room. I hopped right over the fucking rail and fell several feet, hitting the pavement hard. Ignoring the fire in my knees, I headed for the noisy room and threw myself threw the door.

The couple in bed was greasy, disheveled, and ugly as sin. They'd stopped fucking because of the jackass rolling around on the floor, the asshole with the lazy eye who'd checked us in.

He was thrashing around in pain, grabbing his crotch. Jackie was backed into a corner, her clothes messed up, eyes red with tears, shaking. Just like a cornered cat.

Hot air hissed out my lungs. If the fuck managed to do anything, she wouldn't be dressed. I charged like a bull, jumping on the bed, ripping off the covers.

The couple were just as nasty underneath the sheets. They screamed, rolling on the floor, trying to get away. Or that's what I thought at first, before the pudgy asshole who'd been fucking the hag started to laugh.

I looked at the nightstand and saw a familiar arrangement. Smack, ice, several joints half-burned to a crisp, a nine millimeter with its clip laying next to it. Typical junkie shit. I grabbed the drugs in a fistful and threw it on the bitch, who was shaking and moaning, halfway outta her fucking gourd.

These motherfuckers wouldn't say shit. If the motel wasn't deserted, somebody else would've been standing at the door I'd kicked in after all this commotion, but there was no one there except –

"Missy. Take your sis and go. I'll handle this."

My girl looked like she'd seen a fucking ghost. Well, she'd definitely seen some demons. I walked to the corner, took Jackie's hand, and led her out to her big sister.

"I hope you busted his fucking balls, girl. You did the right thing. Don't feel bad for a single goddamned second. I'll do the rest," I whispered in her ear and ran my fingers through her hair before handing her off.

Reaching into my pocket, I handed Missy the keys. "Get the truck warmed up and wait for me. Change of plans. We're heading out early and not stopping 'til we hit Missoula."

I waited 'til I heard the truck's growl to shove the door shut – at least as much as it would close on the busted hinges. Then I walked to the asshole on the floor, reaching for my gun, the lazy eyed fuckface who'd tried to make an innocent girl part of this sick orgy.

He saw me coming, reached into his pocket, and haphazardly flashed a hunting knife. I rolled my eyes, stomping his hand flat with my boot. The knife and his fingers crunched underneath my foot. Didn't let up 'til I had to lean down and silence his screams.

"Lemme go, Mister! I didn't hurt her...ow! Honest, honest – fucking honest! Just wanted to have a little fun...make a little movie..."

I saw the bag behind him on the stand by the bathroom, clearly holding a camera. Good. That would come in handy in a minute.

No, I hadn't gotten an epiphany about peace and forgiveness. The fuck was as good as dead the second I walked in here, but now I had an idea. Skinning his ass was gonna help me out, and maybe my brothers too.

I looked to my side, glancing at the old TV that looked

like it's best days were in the late eighties. "You know, I can handle the peeling paint and the old sheets. But there are some things you really should've upgraded here."

He looked at me like I'd lost my mind. It was the last look the fucked up worm would ever give anyone. I reached down, grabbed his hair, and picked him up, throwing him face first into the TV with all my might.

Funny how broken circuits and glass can drown out a man's screams. He was too shocked to howl or struggle as I picked up his hunting knife and drove it into his back, stabbing him repeatedly 'til he stopped moving. His carcass slumped halfway to the floor and stopped, held up by the TV still attached to his head.

The skank on the floor between the beds was looking at me, trying to process what she'd seen through her druggie brain. I still had a couple little baggies of shit I'd scooped up off the table in my pocket.

Her eyes lit up when I approached, holding the small pack of ice in front of her face the way you tease a dog with a treat. "You want this shit?"

"Yeah! Just give it to *me*. My man's hogged enough for one day..." Over on the other side, the fat man groaned, totally blasted.

"I'd say he has. It's all yours, if you tell the camera who killed this fucker with his head in the screen." I pointed.

It took her a moment to follow my hand. "Who? Who? Who killed you, Joey?"

I let that shit sink in, listening to her mumbling like a demented owl as I picked up the camera, took it outta its case, and gave it a quick look. Everything seemed fine. It was old, still had a tape, but I knew how to use it. Now, I just hoped the piece of shit I'd thrown through the TV wasn't so sloppy it was broke.

"This is a hit ordered by Fang, bitch. Say it. *Fang*, President of the Grizzlies Motorcycle Club, California. You tell 'em I left the fucking message with you, right after I threatened to cut your throat. I came, I saw, I fucked him up for stealing from the club. Drugs, bitch – that ice you're hankering for –

understand?" I used my best interrogator voice while I unscrewed the cap. "Now, repeat that back to me."

Camera on.

"Fang did this. The Grizzlies. Bikers...biker bastards. You...you threatened to cut me open..." She sniffed, eyes more vacant than ever. "This is for drugs...drugs! Shit, where's mine?"

I let the camera pan around the room, focusing on the dead man. Sooner or later, some boys in blue would find this fucking mess, but my junkie "witnesses" would be long gone by then. They wouldn't know what the hell because it wasn't meant for them.

I had it all mapped out in my head. This was Plan B, a backup in case too many charters outside California sided with Fang. Once they saw this sloppy shit, he was one lame fucking duck.

"You killed him! You and your Grizzlies," the junkie screamed, recognition flickering in his eyes. "All over my sweet crystal..."

I teased her, giving the baggie in my free hand a shake. She slapped her fists on the ground, truly upset, rolling her head back and letting tears slide down her cheeks. Perfect.

Switching the camera off, I stuffed it in its case, and then threw the ice in her lap. Turning my head away from her for the last time was a fucking relief. I'd need a couple long, hard nights with Missy to forget those saggy, bruised tits.

"Snort up. Don't use it all in one night."

I heard her laughing behind me as I stepped out and closed the door. By some small miracle, I'd barely gotten Lazy Eye's blood on me when I did him in. Just had his hunting knife with me, and it'd be getting cleaned up and dropped in the trash at the nearest remote place we found on our way to Devils' territory.

Missy got out of the driver's seat and slid over when she saw me coming. I got in the truck and felt her hand on mine.

"How's our girl doing?" I asked, looking across her at Jackie.

"Just fine. He didn't touch her. He never got the chance. He forced her downstairs with a knife...came into our room when we were fucking sleeping." Rage filled her voice.

I nodded, taking the wheel and steering the truck onto the road. "It's all over, babe. We got lucky this time."

"No," Missy snapped. "You did this. You protected us both."

She squeezed my arm something fierce. "God, Brass.

We'd be dead or worse several times over if it wasn't for you."

"You can't sell your sis short, babe. Jackie's strong, just like her big sis. I like hearing how awesome I am, just like anybody else, but fuck me if you're not holding your own. Both of you. And I need you to keep it up."

She leaned into me, resting her head on my shoulder. "We'll try."

"Fuck yeah, you will," I growled, tapping the accelerator to catch some speed on the highway. "You'll stay strong because that's the way I like my woman. If I didn't think you could, I wouldn't have kept you as mine, even with that smoking hot bod."

She smiled, leaned in, and kissed my arm. Over in the darkness, Jackie was glancing our way. I really felt bad for the kid. She'd been through so fucking much. Couldn't catch a break wherever we ended up.

But that little glimmer in her eye said she approved. She understood. She was catching up to Missy, becoming a woman in her own right, forged in the fire no teen should have to face.

And after we got to Montana, I was gonna make sure she never had to again.

The Lazy Eyed fucker I'd killed and greedily recorded had gotten too damned close to wrecking everything. Anger pumped in my veins, and even having sweet Missy's skin on mine wouldn't calm it just now.

There was no pulling back. No letting my guard down. Nothing but red hot rage was gonna serve me 'til I saw

Fang's lifeless eyes and my girls finally had a place to settle the fuck down.

They deserved a home, somewhere to rest without having to worry about who'd be at their throats the next day. God willing, I'd deliver home and a lot more. This shit between us – all three of us – went beyond convenience and love.

They were part of me. They shared my suffering. For that, they'd soon be showered with everything I could give 'em. I'd run my crazy ass ragged so they never had to suffer a damned thing every day they drew breath.

My eyes burned when we got to Missoula, but I wasn't tired. No fucking way was I surrendering to the thing that nearly fucked me over 'til I was good and sure my work was done.

When we got into town, I pulled into a rest stop. Kept a close eye on the girls while I placed a call to Blackjack. Let him know I'd be sending a copy of the video his way in the next day or two.

Back in the truck, Missy was leaning on me a little more with every mile, staring into my eyes.

"You're sure we can trust these men, Brass?"

"No." She looked at me like I'd lost my mind as soon as I said it. "But I do know they don't hurt women and children. The Devils are notorious for picking up strays and nursing 'em back to health. Just in case, I'm not taking any chances..."

She narrowed her pretty eyes, beaming more questions

my way. I refused to answer 'til we were right at their gates. The grinning devil on the building behind their fence leered out, a full blown mural with the guys and their infamous logo painted on it.

The gate didn't open. A tall man with short, spiky hair walked up, and I instantly stifled a growl. It was Blaze, the bastard who'd married my sister. The giant named Tank and the shorter, leaner guy who served as his VP, Stinger, was coming up behind him.

"Stay here!" I heard my girl yell to her kid sis, joining me at the gate.

Fuck, I didn't like her there, right in the open, but I wasn't gonna fight it.

"Hold up," Blaze snapped, throwing up a hand. "Wait here while we open up. Gonna have my Sergeant-at-Arms pat your asses down and make sure you're not fucking with us."

"Nope." Blaze's whole body twitched at my reply. "I'll stand here. You can pat me down, and *me* only. Lay a hand on my old lady or her kid sister in the truck, and I'll turn this fucking thing right around and take my chances alone back in Redding."

Blaze snorted, shaking his head. "You gotta be shitting me. You're the fuck who's come to my doorstep *begging*, remember? My clubhouse, my rules."

Stinger gave a stern nod. Behind him, Tank glowered, flexing his cannon-sized arms. The big fucker still wanted the blows he hadn't gotten back in Reno, when the old ladies held him back from smashing me to mush.

Missy reached over and smoothed her hands over my arm. "Brass..."

One look at her soothed the anger, if only a notch. Fuck. If I was alone, I wouldn't have hesitated to stand here all day and argue with these fucks. But nothing was easy since my old lady and the kid came into my life.

"All right. You're an asshole, Blaze, but I know you're a reasonable man. I know Blackjack talked to you by now about safe harbor for my girls...you give me that up front, right now, and I'm yours. The fucking gorilla behind you doesn't even need to pat me down nicely. You know, unless he's into that."

Tank grunted angrily, taking a step forward. Blaze spun, gave him the evil eye, and then turned back to me, clenching his fists on the iron bars.

"And you're a junkie asshole I don't trust within an inch of my life," he growled. "Too bad you're also my woman's only blood, or we wouldn't be having this talk right now."

His eyes shifted to Missy. Nervous anger and uncertainty showed in her tight face, but she held his gaze.

Blaze let out a long sigh and lowered his face for a second, before bringing it back up. "Fuck. Okay. Here's how it's gonna go. The girls get out, stand off to the side, and I'll have Sting search the truck. If you're not hiding anything fucked up, you hand your chick the keys and she goes on her merry way, straight to the hotel we've got arranged. Nowhere else. I'll keep two guys posted to make sure nobody unexpected shows up."

I didn't like it, but I could live with those terms. I

nodded.

"Tank." Blaze called his name and he stepped forward, punching the code on their side.

The gate slid open. Stinger marched out first, shooting me an uneasy look, heading for the truck. Missy ran ahead of him to collect Jackie.

Goliath stood next to me like a statue. Knew the fucker was waiting to get through searching the vehicle before he had his fun.

Stinger combed everything over thoroughly. Blaze made me grind my teeth and rage on the best day, but I had to admit, the asshole sure knew how to pick his crew. He had more skilled, level headed guys under him right now than Redding had seen for years, despite being a whole lot bigger. Sting's search was all over in a couple minutes, cold and efficient.

"It's clear, Prez. Nothing in there I wouldn't expect to see after a long road trip," the VP said, saluting with a huge smile.

"Okay. Grab Moose and get your bikes to escort this fucking rust bucket home." He turned to me. "Now's a damned good time to hand over the keys. You packing any heat, you hand it over right now."

We locked eyes. I couldn't tell whether or not the fucker was enjoying this, but he was deadly insistent. Growling, I reached into my pocket while Tank eyeballed me, throwing my keys and wallet to Missy first.

"Go, babe. You'll both be fine. I'll get over there as soon as I can later," I said, pulling out my nine millimeter and passing it to Blaze.

She gave me one last, longing look, and then took off. I watched her climb into the driver's seat, waiting for the Prairie Pussies. A couple bikes roared out through the half-open gate a second later, Stinger on one, and a fat bearded dude with an eye patch on the one behind him.

The truck started up and followed the Harleys down the road. Soon as we were alone, the whole world shifted.

Tank picked me up like a measly branch and slammed me into the brick wall next to the gate. My torso hit so fucking hard it sucked the wind outta my lungs. I grinned and tried to laugh, but nothing would come out. Grinning and baring it was all I could do to avoid signing my death warrant, swinging around and throwing my fist into his thick jaw.

His fat hands thumped hard down my back, then rounded my sides. When he got to my boot, I remembered I'd forgot to take out my blade.

Shit!

"Hey, big guy, there's a —"

Tank practically tore my leg off. I hit the ground and he was still pulling on it, growling as he undid the strap with the holster.

He held it up, drawing out the knife, smiling in the faint evening sun. "Figured as much. Looks like it's just this knife, boss. Wouldn't have done us no harm."

Blaze nodded, satisfied. He stared at me on the ground, stepping closer. Finally, he extended a hand.

Shaking his hand like this brought the whole fucked up

reality home. I had to swallow all the bitter rivalry as he helped me up. I was used to venom and bullets from Devils, but fucking handshakes?

"Come on." He gave me a rough shove as soon as I was on my feet. "I'll give you a minute to say hello to your sis, and then you don't step one foot outside the meeting room 'til I say so."

I nodded. There. That felt a lot more like the Devils I knew, and I could relate to it a lot more than that alien nice guy shit.

"Jordan!" Shelly came running toward me before I got two steps into the clubhouse.

She was working at the bar, and she threw herself at me, practically bowling me over on the floor for the second time that day. I couldn't resist locking my arms around her.

Hard to believe so much shit happened in just a couple months since the wedding.

"Hey, sis. It's Brass here around these boys," I reminded her.

She quirked an eyebrow. "Oh? Just like you're gonna suck it up and call me Saffron?"

Damn. Hearing that fucking stripper name was always like a shot in the chest, but right now we had more important things. I hugged her one more time and then stepped back, nodding.

"Whatever you wanna be called, it's damned good to see you again. We'll catch up later when business is done."

"We'll be the judge of that," Blaze growled, slamming a

heavy hand on my shoulder. "Let's go. You've said your piece."

Shelly gave him a disapproving look. Blaze shrugged.

"Club business, baby. You know that." He paused, flashing my sis a knowing smile. "Don't worry. We won't scratch a hair on his head unless he gives us a damned good reason to. All the boys are under orders not to. Even Tank."

She nodded, relief shining in her face. "Make sure you bring him back here when you're finished. We barely got to talk at the wedding."

Great. More drama for later. Didn't have a fucking clue how to tell her I'd picked up an old lady who almost killed my ass at first, plus a little girl.

Being marched into the large Devils' meeting room with Blaze behind me was almost a relief. Everybody was there waiting for me, a buncha guys I'd seen before, sans Stinger and Moose.

Blaze filed in behind me and pointed to a chair in the middle of the table. I sat, watching as he took his place. Typical Prairie Pussy bravado. The other guys looked like they'd suck his dick, all except Tank, who seemed like such a heavy bastard in his own right he didn't need to fawn over anybody.

Still, there was something in their eyes I'd never seen with Fang. True respect. Brotherhood.

They looked at their Prez like a worthy leader, not a man they ran favors for on fear alone.

"All right, bros, let's get this shit started," he said,

picking up a small gavel at the head of the table and slamming it down. "Church is in session, and we have a guest. Never thought I'd see a motherfucking bear at this table."

He shook his head. I snorted. The disbelief was mutual. It was surreal as shit being here, staring at the faces of these men and their devil emblems, everything I'd been trained to destroy.

"Seems there's a power struggle in the Grizzlies MC," Blaze continued. "Worse than the shit we've been hearing about their brush fire war with the cartel. Fang's reached his limit, and that's pretty fucking serious news for our club, seeing as we've always been on edge since Throttle sealed the truce with the bears."

The two national Presidents putting blood aside seemed like eons ago – right here in Montana, no less. But it was really less than a year and a half ago, back when easy pussy and pushing sweet fire in my veins was all I had to worry about.

"Fang's a fucking idiot," I growled. "Traitor to his own club."

A tall, muscular dude around my own age snickered several chairs over. Blaze shot him an angry look. The Devil froze, pivoting his lip ring on his mouth.

"Shut the fuck up, Roller. I'm not gonna disrespect this asshole's colors as long as he doesn't shit on ours." Blaze looked at Tank next to him, and then at me. "Now, Brass, you gonna tell us why the fuck Blackjack sent you racing up to our territory?"

I told them everything. How the fucked up war with the cartel weakened the whole club, fanning tensions that were simmering for years. Told them how they'd tried to kill me, how I shredded that psycho's face who'd tried to kill my girl, how Blackjack believed the club could turn itself around if it just burned away the cancer at the top.

When I was finished, Blaze leaned back in his chair, his jaw clenched thoughtfully. He turned to Tank.

"What do you think?"

"It's a real sad story, boss," Tank said. Not something I ever expected to hear from the giant. "But having this boy here's a real load of bullshit."

There. That's more like the Prairie Pussy badass wannabe I know. I looked at Goliath and grinned.

Blaze folded his hands and leaned forward, all his attention on me again. "I'm inclined to agree. Look, Brass, we appreciate you giving us a head's up about this shit. Mostly so we can stay the fuck out of it. What were you hoping to *do* with this little knock and talk?"

Fuck. Typical selfish Prairie Pussy bastard. I balled fists underneath the table, trying not to let the anger in my eyes flood everything.

"Blackjack and I are trying to save *both* our asses. Can't you fucking see that? I know this club's been through the grinder ever since you started this charter, Blaze. The last thing you wanna do is strap on your knee highs and go wading through our cesspool."

"Damned straight," Blaze said with a smile.

"And you're a fucking idiot if you let the past blind you

to what's coming."

Blaze's smile melted. Tank rose, slow and angry, ready to choke the life outta me for insulting his Prez in their own clubhouse.

"Wait, wait," Blaze said, putting up his arm over Tank. "Let's give him one chance to qualify that before we shut his ass up for saying such stupid shit."

"This shit *will* spill over into your club, Blaze. What I didn't get a chance to tell you is Fang thought I was a rat for the Devils. Not the cartel."

"Fuck!" Tank growled, settling back into his chair.

"I know. We had a major shipment fucked up in Washington last week. He doesn't believe the Mexicans would slip so far north and hit us past Redding. Didn't take him long to draw a target on the Devils, thinking you'd double-crossed us while we've been busy."

"Bastard!" Blaze's fists hit the table. "If that dumb motherfucker wants a war on his northern flank, we'll give him one. We'll ride through Sacramento with this fucking head on our bikes before the Mexicans can get to it."

The Devils Prez was shaking. Hot headed as usual, but for once, I didn't blame him for having such a short fuse.

"Dunno, boss," Tank said, eyeing me warily. "There's only eight of us, maybe double if we put in a call for reinforcements from the Dakota boys. That's enough to take Redding with Brass and his splinter group, but it's not shit if we gotta battle dudes from every other Grizzlies charter too."

Blaze shook his head. "I hate to say it, but you're

fucking right. Having this club on your side isn't gonna mop up every charter from Coeur d'Alene to San Diego. Besides, it sounds like the cartel's got your man on the ropes. Maybe we'd be better off here, beefing up our defenses, waiting for your evil empire to fall."

I laughed. He really didn't see the full picture, and it was like talking to the goddamned wall trying to pry his eyes open.

Don't give up. This is the end of the line, boy. One more try, or settling down with Missy's gonna be the least of your worries.

I couldn't ignore the persistent voice in the back of my mind. I tried to stay calm as I looked at Blaze and stood, hands on the table, not even looking past him when Tank got up and began sizing me up.

"You're totally fucking wrong, Blaze. I wouldn't come here asking you for favors without holding an ace." This time, I looked at Tank, the fiercest skeptic in the room. "He botched a hit a couple weeks ago. Some druggy with an old personal vendetta. When the fucker wouldn't pay up, he sent his boys after the guy. Ended up with a dagger in his back."

"Who the fuck cares?" Tank growled. "Give us something we can chew on or shut the fuck up, bear."

I grinned. "Fang doesn't take trophies like Devils do. He likes to see it all go down on video. Some guys recorded the crime scene. Even got some junkie bitch holed up in the room to squawk about what happened on film. Go ahead and fucking guess who's brought the tape to Big Sky country."

Silence.

Tank and the younger guys eyeballed me like they wanted to drag my ass out back and put a bullet through my head. Blaze drummed his fingers on the table, angrily digesting the bitter pill I'd just forced down his throat. He knew damned well how restless other club Prezes got when shit started to fall apart. One more bombshell that made the head honcho a target for the Feds was one straw too many, one last kick that would bring the whole rotten structure down.

He didn't need to know I'd killed the fuck myself and bribed the junkie to spill what I told her. He didn't need to know the twisted bastard was just a convenient kill I'd made for Jackie, warping the murder into a weapon against Fang.

I swore I'd bring his ass down. Any white lie, any kill, any fucked up stroke of luck was on the table.

Only trouble is, Blaze still didn't look convinced. Shit. I had to head him off before he could open his angry mouth and breathe selfish fear back into all his guys.

"Look, I get it. Calling in your support means a battle, even if there's hardly anyone left standing by Fang's side. But it's a battle that *must* be fought. This shit doesn't end any other way – not even if Fang ends up with his neck on some Mexican's machete. It's not over 'til my club's removed its cancer and starts to heal. Don't you see it? If the Grizzlies fall apart, guess who's next in line for the cartel?"

I gave him a chance to answer. He didn't.

"Those boys from south of the border don't fight like MCs. There's no code, no club charter holding 'em back, no mercy. It's all about green to them. Green money and red blood." I rubbed my fingers together. "My club has a lot of fucking problems, I'm not blind to that. But we didn't fall apart over night either. We were kicking your asses, barely raising a finger, back before the cartel started bombing, shooting, and raping everything in sight. They're taking the Grizzlies down, piece by piece, and we're a helluva lot bigger than your club. What the fuck do you think they're gonna do when we're dead and buried? When there's nobody left to fight them tooth and nail between Mexico and Montana?"

Blaze opened his mouth to give me more hell, but nothing came out. He closed it, his lips twitching angrily, drumming his fingers on the table.

"This is the kinda shit that needs to go up for a vote," he said quietly. "You're not a voting member, Brass. Kindly get the fuck out. I need all the brothers here so we can make our decision."

"You mean I'm free to walk?"

"Wherever you won't trip on our club." He looked past me. "Let's recess, bros. I'll tell Sting and Moose to bring this fucker's girls back around. They can hang out in the bar with him while we make our decision."

Blaze looked at me, and I nodded, exiting the room before his gavel clapped the wood. I headed for the bar to see my sis, wondering if it was really possible we'd just come to some kinda fucked up understanding.

Missy ran to me when they got in. Jackie followed cautiously behind her, taking a seat at the bar.

I dropped the strong man act in my rival's lair just long enough to grab my girl's ass and press her to me. Fuck, her lips tasted good.

There'd been too much drama and too much Jackie around to fuck her like I wanted. Christ, after this vote, I needed to get in her again. Every second my cock wasn't buried in her pussy was a shitty one.

"Did they treat you right?" I asked, shifting my eyes on the two man escort strolling toward the meeting room.

"They were great!" Jackie chimed in before her big sis could answer.

"Yeah." Missy smiled. "Jackie got a kick out of Moose talking like a pirate. He's the one with the –"

"Eye patch," I finished for her. "I know."

I hadn't heard how their Treasurer even lost his fucking eye, but it must've been recent. Still, hearing the good news put me a little bit at ease. The Prairie Pussies were assholes, but I wasn't worried they'd steal my women and cut their throats. It was nice to relax, if only a little bit.

"Who's this?" Saffron said, heading for the table with a pitcher of beer like I asked.

Missy looked at my sister, and I had a weird flashback to me and Blaze sizing each other up. My girl spoke first, studying Shelly's old lady jacket. It had a big PROPERTY OF BLAZE on the back, standard for claimed women in most clubs.

"I'm Missy Thomas, and this is my sister, Jackie. I'm Brass' old lady, and *proud* of it." She stuck out a hand.

"Brass? Holy shit!" Shelly looked at me for a long time before I finally took the pitcher outta her hands and she took my girl's palm, giving it a shake.

Jackie laughed.

Fuck.

Wasn't sure what was worse: waiting to see if the Devils behind the wall voted to save our asses, or trying to explain to my little sis that I finally had something in my life worth living for.

IX: Heart on the Line (Missy)

I had to look close at Shelly Reagan to see the family resemblance. Her eyes were much brighter, and she didn't have that darkness swirling around her like Brass, the same sweet intensity I wanted to tame.

As soon as I said I was his old lady, there was a minute of stunned silence. Then the woman laughed, threw herself at me, and tucked her arms around me in a big, brutal, almost possessive hug. Okay, maybe they had something in common after all.

"Damn it, Jordan. Brass." Shelly – Saffron? – pulled away and stuck her tongue out. "You blather on about being away and all this club intrigue, but don't even tell your own sis you've finally found a girl?"

I watched her do something I thought I'd never see. Saffron reached up and shoved her fingers through his short dark hair, the hair that felt amazing underneath my fingertips. Of course, Brass didn't wait more than a second before he pulled away – something he never would've done with me.

"Whatever," he grunted. "You know there's been some serious shit going on. My mind's been in strange places."

We shared a look. The stern mask on his face broke in a thin smile, and then he grabbed my hand and clutched it to his chest.

"You heard the lady right, sis. This is my old lady, and that's never gonna change no matter what your hubby decides in there." He gestured his head toward the closed meeting room. "I'm gonna fuck up the men who've wrecked my club one way or another. Then I'm gonna give these two everything they seriously deserve."

The hair ruffling fingers must've been infectious. He leaned past me, tossing Jackie's hair, much to my little sister's surprise.

"And where are you staying here in Missoula?" Saffron asked, giving me a good look.

"The Bison. The guys said it'd be the safest place."

She wrinkled her nose. "Come on. We can do better than that. I'll talk to Blaze and see if you can stay at the new lake house we're renting."

"Lake house?" Brass raised an eyebrow. "Fuck me sideways, sis. You've really come a long way in the world after growing up in shitty apartments. Whatever. Long as fucking Blaze is treating you right..."

She smiled. "He is. And you've come a long way too..."

I was about to grab his arm, press it between my breasts, a desperate little preview of all the ways I wanted to show him just how far he'd come. But the door to the meeting room swung open, and all the angry looking Devils came filing out.

Their President, Blaze, marched toward us like he was

running on rocket fuel. Brass instantly tensed up, stepping out of my grasp. Saffron backed up toward the table, and I took a seat with Jackie, trying not to eavesdrop on the serious business unfolding behind me.

Well, good luck doing that. The men were right in front of me, and they looked like dynamite about to explode.

"Well? What's the word?" Brass asked.

"It's an aye. Unanimous. You're a sorry bastard, but you're fucking right. My boys and I can't risk watching the Grizzlies fall apart or become a damned front for the cartel to creep north. We'll help your asses out – on our terms."

The thick tension melted. I turned, even as Saffron looked at me like I was nuts. She looked away, clearly marking the hard border she'd chosen to create between club business and family.

Brass and Blaze shook hands like two long bartering merchants finally making a deal. There was no smiling, none of the manly pats on the back I'd seen among brothers. It was a wartime alliance, a marriage of convenience, plain and simple. Nothing more.

"I'll have my guys bring that fucking video by and get it copied. We'll have it out to every Grizzlies charter as soon as Throttle gives the okay from Dakota," Blaze said. "Better to head off the reinforcements to Redding before we've gotta fight 'em. Hope you're right about this shit making the other charters flip on Fang."

"I am. You read my mind, Blaze."

They shared a grunt, and then Blaze stepped up,

grabbing Saffron and lifting her by the hand. "Come on, baby. Let's get his sidekicks some grub before they head to their rooms for the night."

"Oh, no," Saffron said, standing and shaking her head. "I'm not putting my own brother and his old lady up in that crappy lodge. It's a bad place for a little girl too."

Blaze's eyes bugged out. "What the fuck are you saying, woman? You wanna bring 'em...?"

"The lake house. I knew you'd throw a fit if I said home, so I'm picking the next best thing. Seeing as we're not using it in the off season..."

"Jesus Christ." Blaze pushed a hand through his spiky hair, going red in the face, as if he was trying to hold in a hurricane.

"Fuck. All right!" He turned to Brass. "You're welcome to stay at our favorite vacation spot. Might be safer anyway if any of the fucks from your club come milling around. Just don't —"

"I know how to behave myself, brother-in-law. I'll be a good boy. You don't need to worry about the girls neither. These ladies are always on their best behavior. I wouldn't dream of doing anything that would fuck up the new thing we've got here."

They shared an icy stare. Finally, Blaze shook his head, growling as he threw up his arms and headed for the bar.

"Shit!" Saffron gave Brass an apologetic look and ran after him. "Let's get some fucking food, and then I want them outta my damned sight. There'll be time to play catch up with your bro and his chick after the heavy shit's over."

I could practically hear her rolling her eyes. "Jesus, Blaze. Look, I know it'll be a late night for you, so I'll stay over with them and make sure nothing crazy happens."

Brass looked at me and let out a laugh. I joined him. I wasn't sure how much Jackie followed what was going on, but she must have absorbed something. By the time Saffron returned holding some boxed up dinner for us, my sister was laughing harder than she had in months.

The cabin was beautiful. We ate an early dinner with Saffron and made small talk. Jackie and I weren't the only ones who had our stomachs twisted in knots any time someone mentioned family.

It was obvious Brass and his sister had suffered too. I knew they'd lost their mother to some other Grizzlies killers he'd fallen in with – but the way their eyes fell at the only mention of their mom all evening was all too familiar.

That evening, Saffron turned in early, helping set up a comfy room for Jackie downstairs. Brass and I sat on the porch, feeling the crisp bite of early spring on our faces. He stared out at the darkening lake's waters and the high ridges leading toward Glacier National Park beyond them.

"Damn. Just seeing it makes me want to go hiking, you know?" Speaking above a whisper felt like screaming in the nighttime stillness.

Brass laid a hand over my shoulder, pulled me close, dangerously close to his lap. "Didn't take you for the kinda girl who enjoys getting down and dirty in the woods. That park's got some nasty fucking bears too. Shelly and I used to head up there all the time 'til Ma couldn't make the trips anymore."

I laughed. "I've dealt with more Grizzles than I ever thought I would. What's a few more? Some of them are *really* fucking nice when you get past all the teeth and claws."

My hand slipped into his. I clenched my fingers tight around his. He closed his eyes and puffed dragon smoke into the cool air.

"Fuck, babe. You really wanna play with bears?" His eyes sparkled, drawing me in like they always did. I nodded. "Wrong answer."

In a flash, his hands were on me, lifting me high and plopping me down on his lap. I felt the raging hard-on beneath his jeans instantly. Everything below my waist tingled, and the wetness was instant with my legs spread over his waist, splayed wide for the cool breeze and so much more.

"Brass..." I whispered. "Your sister's not even asleep yet...she's still banging around in the kitchen."

Just past the screen door, a pot clanged, putting a big fat exclamation mark on what I'd said.

"I don't give a shit. Not 'til you choose the words coming outta those sweet fucking lips more carefully, babe. You wanna play with *bears?*" He pushed his forehead against mine. It was warm, pleasant. "Fuck that shit. You better tell me there's only one bear you spread those killer legs for. I'm not the sharing kinda guy. Instinct tells me to rip another dude's dick off if he even looks at what's *mine,* you know that?"

I shuddered. My tongue flicked against my lips, mischievous as the thoughts and desires soaring through my flesh. I wanted him, ached to my core for him, yearned in a way I hadn't known.

"Yeah?" I whispered. "What else does instinct tell you to do?"

His hands spread wider on my ass and then clenched it. His fingers dug in, hard enough to make me wriggle against him, pushing my clit over his dick through our jeans.

Holy shit. He was so fucking hard. Rough and eager as diamond, except diamond didn't feel so warm and smooth, and it sure wouldn't feel as good as him inside me.

Despite all the chaos, I'd remembered my pill. My pussy tingled, swelled, and ached a little more when I thought about pulling him up inside me without a condom.

Deep. Bare. Ready to surrender everything that was quintessentially his.

Fuck it. I couldn't be a good girl anymore, not when he was so close.

How was I seriously supposed to resist *this?* His hips ground against mine, pulling me closer, and resistance wasn't even on the radar when his lips found mine.

His tongue twined with mine and formed slippery, hypnotic, wonderful circles. I moaned into his mouth. It only encouraged him.

Brass grabbed my bottom lip with his teeth, sucking it deep into his mouth, flicking his thick, strong tongue over both our lips again and again. It was his trademark, a salacious preview of what was to come.

I reached between my legs and put my hand on his dick. He grunted. Smiling into the next kiss, I pushed my way around him harder, breath hitching when my clit pressed perfectly on his hardness through the denim.

Jesus, to hell with that denim! I wanted him to grab my waist and rip the jeans off right fucking *now.*

"Brass!" The screen door popped open and banged in its frame.

Mortified, I looked up at Saffron. Brass broke our latest kiss and shot his sister a look that could've cooled the sun. The brunette threw one hand over her mouth and barely stifled the humiliating laughter just in time.

"Well, I was going to ask if you two wanted some dessert...but it looks like you've beat me to the punch."

Red hot blood filled my cheeks. I tried to look away, fighting to wriggle my way off him, but he wouldn't let go. His fingers stayed tight around my ass, painful reminders of sheer sex stopped in its tracks.

"Go back inside, sis. We'll be in after a little while." Anger flowed through his voice. Not a shred of shame. "And yeah, keep something warm for us. Lemme guess – it's that patented brownie a la mode stuff, right?"

Saffron looked right at me and gave a curt nod. Oh, God. I thought I'd be sick right then and there, all my redness turning green now that my shame was complete.

"I'll keep it ready for you two." One more wickedly knowing smile and she went back inside.

I slapped his chest so hard I heard the *thud*. "Let go of me!"

"You fucking kidding, babe?" he growled, tightening his grip until I couldn't move. "We haven't fucked for days. Shelly makes a mean fucking treat in her kitchen, but I'd give up ever tasting it again for one more taste of you. Right here, right now..."

"But Jackie's waiting for us," I moaned, desperate to extinguish the guilty fire roaring inside me.

"She can wait a few more minutes. She's probably stuffing her face with brownie and loving it. Come on. Down by the lake." His eyes narrowed. "Don't bullshit me, baby girl. I know you want this as bad as I do. Things are about to get a lot more fucked up before they get better. We gotta take advantage of these times together, you know?"

I nodded, wondering where he was going. He rocked his rock hard erection into me, raising his hips high enough to lift my whole body, and then I couldn't wonder about anything at all.

I came undone. His dick made me want to jerk and moan like a madwoman, igniting a temporary insanity any courtroom would've approved.

Warm, hot breath poured into my ear. His stubble raked my neck, prickly and masculine. Sexy as hell? Oh, yeah.

Damn! There was that heat again, thawing the glacial shame in my veins, becoming the filthiest kind of lust.

"I'm making sure Fang and his psychos are dead one way or another. Don't know if I'll walk out alive when the big showdown comes." He kissed my neck, right in the middle, giving me a shudder that silenced all the worries his words wanted to stir. "Only one thing's clear: I'm not leaving this fucking planet without having you as much as I can. I don't care if I die tomorrow with lead in my chest, or in my sleep when I'm a decrepit old bastard. We're fucking, babe. Fucking on demand. Fucking day and night. Fucking to remind you you're my old lady, and you're never gonna get claimed half as hard as when I'm between your legs, filling your pussy, no matter what the fuck happens from here. Come on. Live and learn. Let's fuck."

By the time he whispered those last two words, I was a shaking, sweating, sopping wet mess in his hands. My hips were moving on their own, shifting against him again and again, every nerve screaming to be fucked while my stupid head tried to say no.

He wasn't hearing anything without me underneath him anymore. It took me a minute to realize he'd picked me up, and we were heading toward the thick trees near the lake. He carried me in his arms through the cool evening air, into the wilder darkness.

It got a lot cooler when he laid me out on the big flat boulder near the water. It was the perfect height for him to stand between my legs and grind while he sucked and kissed at my throat, like the Earth decided to put it there thousands of years ago just for us.

This is crazy, I thought, shaking my head. *Absolutely fucking —*

Crazy.

No, *crazy* was his tongue, sliding down my shoulder as he pulled at my shirt. He was already tearing at my bra strap by the time it was over my head. My breasts popped out into the cool night air, and my right nipple slid into his mouth.

The temperature couldn't have been much higher than the fifties, but I was burning up each time his tongue circled, bowing and dipping, hungrily lapping at my flesh. My nipples softened in his mouth. God, my hips were still rocking, bucking up and down on any part of him they could find.

"Brass!" I reached for his head and scratched through his hair until he looked up. "I need you inside me. Please."

He looked at me like I'd just granted his deepest, dirtiest wish. Maybe I had. All I knew was I'd never seen anyone undress so fast.

His cut, shirt, jeans, and boxers came off one after another, piling on the ground beneath us. His dark tattoos glistened beneath the moonlight, and it looked like the ferocious bear snarling on his chest was doing an angry dance when he moved for my bottoms.

"Pick your sweet ass up, babe. These are coming right the fuck off."

He wasn't kidding. The instant my butt was up, the jeans were gone, and he tore away my panties in a fistful.

"Oh, God." I whispered to the moon and the stars, a prayer, all I could do to keep sane in the dark calm before he fucked me deep, skin-on-skin for the first time.

Coolness bathed the drenched ache between my legs.

My heartbeat echoed in every extremity, beating its want into my brain. The thud crashed harder inside me when he slid his cock against my folds, and I thought I'd pass out.

"You got any fucking clue how bad I've wanted this? How long I've been waiting to feel you like this?" He rocked his hips.

My pussy coated his dick in cream, and he smeared it toward my clit. My slit couldn't have been hotter, tighter, wetter.

"Just fuck me," I whimpered. The plea in my voice caught me by surprise, but it was honest.

I needed this. I needed him, inside me. Now.

My legs curled around his hips and pinched tight. Brass let out a long growl like a mountain lion zeroing in on something irresistible.

"Just fuck you, Missy? You mean like this?" He shifted his hips, and then slammed forward, steadily pushing his swollen cock into me.

"Yes!"

It was the sweetest shock of my life. Having him inside me with rubber between us was nothing – nothing! – compared to this. My hands scratched at the stone beneath us, too used to having sheets to claw at.

Here, there was nothing between us and nature, nothing between our blood and skin.

"Fuck!" His muscular body shook when he reached prime depth, unable to go an inch more. He filled me completely. "Fuck. Babe, if you were any fucking tighter, we wouldn't even fit."

I pushed against him, hard, clenching my teeth. The pleasure was almost painful because there was so much of it, flowing like lava through every nerve. My brain struggled to process everything.

"That'd be a real...a real shame." It was hard to talk.

Brass grunted, pulling back and slamming himself into me, harder this time. I moaned. More current raced through my skin. My ankles burned just holding onto him.

No way. He wasn't going to do this. I wasn't in the mood for a slow, sweet loving. I started to buck, panting hot desire through my teeth, adding my feminine growl to his.

Fuck. Me.

The message must've reached him through his dick, because my lips wouldn't work after three more strokes. Nothing but screams came out.

He was like a masculine mountain plowing into me, all muscle, all need, all conquest. I threw my head back and pumped my hips, desperate to keep pace.

"Come, babe. Come and scream as loud as you want. Nobody's gonna hear it but me."

Like I could do anything else! He quickened his thrusts, filling me harder and faster, relentlessly forcing me over the edge, until I exploded.

Pleasure gurgled through me and cut off my breath. I couldn't feel anything except the raw heat of my pussy clenching his cock, gushing on his skin, tightening while he drove into me. My head snapped back and I let it all out.

I screamed through the orgasm. I wasn't so sure about

nobody else hearing us, but I didn't fucking care. My brain and body were total slaves to the ecstasy he created, the claiming fire roasting me within every time he slammed deep.

He fucked me straight through it and still kept going. I pushed my way up, keeping my legs wide for him, throwing my hands around his neck.

The first climax took a lot out of me. I needed every limb to hold myself to him now, even as my fingers and ankles dug tighter to his skin. He fucked like an animal, a runaway train powering through my legs, grunting for breath and cursing in my ear when he leaned in to sniff my hair.

"I'm gonna fucking bust, babe. You want it inside you, yeah?"

I nodded and whimpered. Thinking about him flooding my pussy with his molten heat sent me hurling toward a fresh orgasm. I tried not to scratch his neck raw, but it was really hard not to.

I couldn't deny it: I was losing my mind in this sex, losing it to him the same he'd already taken my heart.

"Do it, Brass. I love you."

"Good. Wouldn't dream of wasting this come anywhere else. Love you, babe. Come with me. Wanna feel you milk my balls dry." His breath hitched. "Come on! Fuck!"

He crashed against me, burying himself to the hilt. His hips thrashed against my skin, even when he was all the way in, kindling a wicked heat on my clit with his pubic bone.

I shot straight to heaven, and then I went somewhere higher when I felt his teeth on my neck. He bit me right there, marking me with one hell of a hickey. His erection swelled inside me and exploded.

The heat was intense, a firestorm all over, burning away everything except the feeling of my pussy being filled with fire. He pulsed again and again, pumping magma jets deep in my womb. My pussy clenched so tight I screamed, desperately sucking at his cock, knowing what I wanted.

I was thankful I'd never let any other man come inside me. This was all his, and God willing, we'd never use condoms again.

I came like a mad woman enjoying her strongest hit, and crashed back to earth knowing I'd never settle for anything less. I was addicted to every inch of him, from the tattooed back I'd just scratched to pieces down to the hard perfection still emptying itself inside me.

He came hard. Long. After an eternity, his body shuddered and he released me, gently settling my sore hips on the rock.

My turn to collapse. Brass held me, stroking my hair. We enjoyed the sudden quiet, the beautiful coolness with nothing except our lungs catching mountain air.

"My sis did pretty fucking well. I gotta give her props. This place isn't half bad," he mused.

"Yeah? A girl could really settle down here if she wanted. It's so beautiful." It was strange sitting up buck naked and staring at the dark hills beyond the lake, but I meant every word.

It certainly went beyond the landscape. Everything tonight was beautiful, a starry mountain heaven in the eye of hell.

"Do you think we'll be able to stay in Redding if everything goes right?" I asked, straightening my hair with my fingers.

He nodded. "That's home, as far as we're concerned. This place is Devils' territory. I sure as shit don't belong here. But if I can save my club, maybe coming to Prairie Pussy land with my colors for a visit will be as easy as driving over the state line. You know what else I think?"

"Hmmm?"

He reached down and grabbed my clothes, throwing them onto my lap. "Our sisters are gonna have all that sweet shit eaten if we don't hurry our asses up."

I laughed. We dressed quickly. Just in time too because the cold was starting to make my nipples hard again in a way that wasn't so sexy.

"Dessert? Really? You're still hung up on that?" I stepped into his embrace, running my hand over his jaw stubble.

"I'm hung up on making sure you get the sugar rush you need for tonight." He grinned. "Soon as everybody's asleep, I'm fucking your brains out 'til dawn, babe. Being my old lady's a full time job. So's taking this dick. Get used to it."

He playfully swatted my ass. I jumped, and let him lead me back up the path through the trees, toward the cozy cabin with the glowing lights.

"Good thing I've always been a night owl," I said, already wondering how I'd have to gag myself to stay quiet while he ravished me.

The next few days were beautiful. Mountain walks, good comfort food made by Saffron, and nights I'd never forget. Brass had to take off every day and take care of business with the Devils, but he always came back before nightfall.

Even Jackie seemed a lot more relaxed breathing the magic Missoula air. Up here, the wolves lost our scent. They couldn't follow. Or so I told myself.

But if we ever wanted to go home, or feel safe again, it all came down to Brass and his new partners removing the cancer at the top.

I tried to be supportive. It wasn't hard when he came to me every night like a storm, fucking me with his hand clapped over my mouth, leaving me to scream and bite and thrash when I came on his cock. Coming this hard obliterated all the worries.

Granted, I should've paid more attention to them. But it was such a relief here. Until we came north, I'd forgotten what it felt like to be truly safe.

Heaven never lasts forever, especially when it's lodged in hell's cyclone.

I was laying next to him late one evening, my head resting on his powerful chest. We'd just gotten through another round, leaving us both blissfully drained and sweaty, exposed to the cool peace that always settled after sex with this man.

I'd gotten to scream my lungs out tonight. Saffron took Jackie into town for some ice cream, and also to take a look at the local high school in case we were forced to stay here a lot longer than we intended.

Having the place to ourselves should've been perfect. It certainly started out that way. Then his phone chirped on the floor, still tucked in his jeans, a jarring ring intruding on our post-fuck serenity.

Brass groaned, gently pushed me off, and reached down. I saw his face tighten when he flicked the screen on.

"Yeah?"

"We got a serious fucking problem, son." I overheard Blackjack's gravelly voice on the other line. "The first copies of that tape just hit the other charters today. The mole we've still got in the clubhouse says Fang's mad as hell. He's swearing up and down he didn't kill the guy, promising the other clubs he's gonna get a confession out of whoever did."

Brass gave me a dark look and pulled the phone away from me, hoping I wouldn't hear. He got up and stepped into the hall. I strained to listen.

"Yeah? What fucking leverage has he got? Sounds like the damned thing did exactly what we hoped for."

I couldn't hear what Blackjack said. I reached for the heap of my clothes on the ground, pulling on my panties and a long t-shirt. I stepped up to the door frame and waited, hoping he wouldn't notice I was right behind him.

"Okay, whatever," Brass said. "Send it my way. Better I see this shit for myself..."

There was a long pause. The call ended. Then his phone dinged again, and he tapped the screen to bring up a video.

The short redhead on his screen was beaten bloody. Her eyes were swollen shut, and she jumped each time the demon's hands moved behind her, his fingers flexing rough on her shoulders before he leaned down and showed his monstrous face.

It can't be. Jesus. No.

My face wanted to fall to the ground, but my eyes were glued to the sideshow on Brass' phone. I knew her. It was Jackie's tutor, Christa, and she'd been left behind while we fought our way out.

"You fucking rats are too cowardly to fight man-to-man, face-to-face," Fang rumbled through the glowing glass. "Now, you see what happens." He bared his teeth in a sick, angry smile.

"I'm gonna give you seventy-two hours to show yourselves at the clubhouse and bring every copy of that bullshit you sent far and wide. You'll admit that fucking abortion was a forgery on tape, and then we'll see what happens. I'm done making any promises about anyone's safety except hers."

His fingers tightened on the woman's shoulders. "This bitch dies piece by fucking piece if you don't show yourselves. I know the Prairie Pussies are in on this. They're gonna get the first hand I lop off in the mail, assuming I don't start with these pretty tits first."

He grabbed her breasts and squeezed. Hard. Painful. Christa jerked in his arms, but she was too bad off to

235

fight. He'd broken her resistance awhile ago – maybe days.

Tears burned my eyes. My heart crashed against my ribs like a hummingbird trying to beat its way out of my chest.

"Seventy-two hours, assholes, 'til I carve my first piece. Then it'll be every fucking hour you cocksuckers don't show. Not a minute more. Don't disappoint me. I didn't claw my way to the top of this goddamned club passing out mercy. Looks like some people have forgotten that lately, and they're about to find out I'll do everything in my power to hang onto what's mine. Don't underestimate anything."

The screen went dead. Brass' arms trembled, and for a second I thought he was going to hurl the phone down the staircase next to him, smash it into a million pieces the same way my heart was splitting apart.

I couldn't hold in the anguished squeal. He spun, tucking the cell back into his pocket. He was on me in an instant, had me pressed snug against the wall.

"Jesus, Brass. If only I'd known! I didn't know he had her...thought they just knocked her out when they got Jackie. I thought they left here there. We can't let him do –"

"Babe, I need you to get a grip right fucking now. If you have a stroke or a heart attack right here over this, there's no way I'm gonna be able to get her out. I'll be too busy saving your sweet ass to deal with hers."

I wanted to wipe away the hot tears sliding down my cheeks, but Brass' big arms blocked the way.

"Can you?" I shot him a skeptical look, and it hurt to

doubt him. "I mean, can you save her without killing or hurting yourself or any of your guys?"

His lips twitched. "Yes. Have some faith, babe. There's no fucking way I'm gonna let him spill more innocent blood. Not when it's all for clinging to power and fucking up my club."

His fingers tightened on my arm. Hard. I let out a whimper.

"Shit. I'm sorry." He ripped himself away and stepped back. "Go back to bed, Missy. I gotta grab my clothes and go. Blaze and his crew need to be in on this. They'll help me figure out the logistics..."

I slumped against the wall. My knees wouldn't work, and I kept sliding down, down, toppled by a dark gravity, slowly losing my mind.

That terrible fog that chewed at my brain while I was bound, watching Serial menace Jackie, returned. I shook my head, fighting it.

Brass gave me a look on his way out like he wanted so bad to stay, to help me up. But he was right – viciously right. I couldn't hold him back. Every second he spent dealing with me was one more second of this poor woman's life melting away, bringing her closer to the gruesome end. Everything the demented bastard promised.

I listened to my man's boots thud down the stairs, and then he was out the door. His truck started a second later, and he gunned it, pulling out of the rocky driveway.

It was like taking a huge splash of glacial water in the

face. Or maybe it was pure acid.

I barely knew Christa, but she was innocent. Irony surfaced, raking her cruel nails across my face.

Jesus, dad's desperate mistakes had gotten us dragged into all this, and I'd dragged Jackie in because I'd been too stupid to throw the cash away and run for the hills.

Now, my blackness had spread, eating someone else alive. If it wasn't for dad's sins, we'd have never gotten ourselves captured. I'd never have dragged in Brass and sunken deeper than anything I imagined. My sister wouldn't have needed a tutor, and the girl wouldn't have wound up stuck in this insane biker war.

My temples throbbed. It was hard to stand up, but I managed. I dressed quickly, listening as a vehicle growled into the driveway.

I tensed up, thinking maybe it was Brass. But Jackie and Saffron's laughter at some joke as they came through the door told me otherwise. They'd gotten home just in time. I washed my face in the bathroom across the hall. Must've waited in the darkness for a good half hour before anyone came up to check on me.

"Missy? I've got some chili going downstairs if you're ready to eat." Saffron paused. "Where the hell's my brother?"

I got up and walked toward her, refusing to turn on the light. I couldn't let her see the crazy turmoil scrawled on my face.

"I need to borrow your car."

"Huh? We just got back. But I guess if there's

something you need in town, I'd be happy to drive you –"

"No!" It came out like a bullet. Sharp. Forceful. "I *need* to borrow it. There's shit going on with the club...with Brass...I promise I'll get it back to you in one piece. Help me."

I sounded like a lunatic. Damn, what was one more lie on top of everything else I'd told myself to stay sane during all this?

"Lady, you'd better take a big deep breath and tell me what the fuck is going on before I call up Blaze and find out." It was the first time I'd heard her angry, and she definitely had the fire in her voices that told me she'd been through some crap.

Still, it didn't soften me one bit. "If I say anything else, you won't even think about handing me the keys. Look, I'm going to find myself a ride one way or another...but I'd prefer to have something reliable to get me where I'm going. Preferably a loaner from somebody I can trust to keep their mouth shut."

Saffron reached for my hand and I spun her around. We were both about the same size, but I was way more worked up. She hit the bed with a muffed yelp. Annoyance foamed in her throat as she struggled up on her knees and looked at me.

"This is insane. I'm calling –"

"Don't." We locked eyes in the darkness, and I refused to let go, no matter what she did next. "If you call him, all hell's going to break loose, and I'll never save her in time. Brass can't do it. Neither can the Devils. They talk too much. They're too slow."

Saffron shook her head, frustrated. "Save *who?*"

"Is Jackie taking a shower?" I asked.

Saffron nodded, just as confused as I expected.

Good. You don't have to make a scene and upset Jackie. You've got to go. Now.

"Take care of her for me," I said. "I know I can count on you to do that. One day, I'll find some way to repay it."

I couldn't ignore the shrill voice in my head. I took off and slammed the bedroom door shut behind me, flying down the stairs, leveraging surprise as much as I could.

It worked. Saffron was only halfway down the staircase, screaming after me, when I pulled her purse off the kitchen table. Crap spilled out all over on my way out to her SUV, and I had the keys in my hand just in time.

I popped the door and slid in. There was no time for my seat belt. The vehicle started quick, smooth, and I was backing out as she ran after me. I felt bad watching her pound the hood. She got off one beat, and I kept going. I didn't stop, tearing toward the road through the mountains, leading to the main highway.

My hands went numb gripping the wheel. I didn't relax until I was all the way through town, constantly checking my mirrors for trucks and motorcycles behind me, trying to close in and stop what I had to do.

When Brass and the Devils found out, they'd be furious. Just one more consequence I had to face. Nobody ever said doing the right thing was easy.

This time, it was going to be an absolute bitch.

I drove all night, heading toward Redding, following the dark cold highways as best as I could. I'd never driven this kind of distance. Adrenaline, anxiety, and guilt rode with me.

The sickness swirling in my blood wouldn't let me break. Not until I ran my tank down and had to get gas. I stopped when I needed to for snacks and fuel, refusing to linger a second too long.

For all I knew, Brass and the others were hot on my trail right now. I'd pissed off my old man and probably the Devils too by hijacking Saffron's vehicle. I wasn't sure what was worse.

It didn't really matter. It all paled next to the greater calamity, letting Fang follow through on his savage promises and tear her to ribbons. Christa seemed like such a sweet, soft spoken woman. I couldn't let her suffer like this. I couldn't let her die screaming because of *me*.

I believed Brass would try his damnedest to get her out. Maybe I'd get lucky and Fang would be dead by the time I got into town, the teacher with the dark red hair freed by Blackjack and his men. Maybe.

But I couldn't depend on it. I couldn't depend on anything except showing up and throwing myself at Satan's mercy, hoping he'd let her go – or at least spare her – by taking revenge on a bitch he had good reason to hate.

It wasn't all about freeing Christa either. I swore I'd keep lying, anything to buy time. I'd promise him the video and the entire fucking moon if it helped lead him one step closer to the grave Brass was digging.

The journey was long, and I got lost several times, losing a couple hours. If I ever got out of this, I swore I'd learn to drive like nobody's business. Maybe I'd even figure out how to ride a Harley without being strapped to my old man on the back.

My old man. It hurt to think about him. I'd stabbed him in the back and heaped more chaos on his life, and I seriously wondered if he'd want me if I got out of this alive.

No. You can't think about that.

I nodded, agreeing with the only comfort I had in my head. I had to stay focused. I had to put emotion aside, even if I was screaming down the road like a crazy girl, throwing myself to hell on a whim.

I crossed three states I'd never been to before the trip up. My eyes felt like they were going to fall out by the time the sun came up. But I kept going, crazed and determined to show my face in Redding, to face the consequences.

Someone had to pay for all this. And since daddy was gone, it had to be me.

I was ready to pay the very high price. Anything for a chance at keeping her safe. No one else needed to die for my father's mistakes. If there was suffering, then it was earmarked for me. I'd see myself crucified before Christa or my poor sweet sister.

It was almost noon when I finally got into town. My body got a second wind as I drove toward the clubhouse on the outskirts, ready to floor it at any sign of cops or bikers.

Nothing was going to stop me from seeing the demon face to face. Nothing.

The place certainly didn't look like a war zone when I pulled up. It was just like I remembered. A hard faced man with Grizzlies patches came wandering up to the gate. It was Crack, the foul tempered VP, with two other greasy long haired men behind him.

I got out and stepped up to the gate, leaving the vehicle running.

His gun was out and pointed at me before I said a word. "What the fuck are you doing here, bitch?"

"I need to see Fang. It's about the video that's hurting your Prez, and the woman you dickheads are holding against her will."

Crack's fat nose twitched, his nostrils flaring. He nodded to the two big men next to him.

"Open the fucking gate. Pat her ass down before she goes inside." He looked at the SUV behind me. "Somebody get that fucking thing in here too. We can use another rig after losing two to the cartel last week..."

I'm sorry, Saffron, I whispered in my head.

The thick iron bars slid open. Rough hands grabbed me and forced me behind the gate. They threw me to the wall and slid over me, rugged and unwelcome, taking much longer than they really needed to feel for weapons in my pockets.

I didn't have any, of course.

No, they were enjoying this.

I'd tucked my wallet into my jeans at the last stop for gas. Had to hold my breath when the mean looking man pulled it out and bent it in half. One wrong angle, and they'd find what I had there for Plan B, in case Fang didn't want to cooperate and free the redhead.

I held my breath as his hands passed over it. He missed. Bastard was too busy feeling my ass instead.

Sloppy. Typical. Perfect.

"Get your ass inside," Crack ordered. "I'll take you to the Prez myself."

The familiar stink of the clubhouse burned my nose. All the cleaning I'd done when I was first captured hadn't done a damned thing. It smelled like fucking, blood, and alcohol, all mixed together, worse than the feral stink of death.

Crack marched me down a different hallway, one I'd never seen before, past the office and the big room Fang reserved for himself. An old metal storage door at the end waited. He tore it open in one fist, grabbing me with his free hand and shoving me inside.

My knees hit cement. The door slammed behind me.

"Oh my God." I struggled to stand, shaking my head when I saw her.

Appropriately enough, the room looked like a dungeon. It was bare, spartan, eerily cleaner than the rest of the clubhouse. Nothing inside except a few dirty rags in the corner, and the poor woman slumped in the chair in front of me.

Christa looked worse in person than she did on video.

My heart sank to my knees, and I walked toward her cautiously, wondering if she was even conscious.

"Christa? Can you hear me? It's Missy Thomas. I hired you." The last sentence stuffed a lump in my throat.

She didn't move until I touched her shoulder. She jerked awake, her dirty red hair flopping. Her eyes darted around and she moaned, scared out of her pale skin. And who could blame her?

"What? Missy? What're you doing here?"

I ran my fingers through her hair, trying to be reassuring. "I've come to get you out. I'm taking your place."

"You're crazy!" she sputtered. Her swollen lips were bad – it sounded like she was talking with food in her mouth. "They'll kill you. Kill us both."

"No. You have to trust me. Just stay quiet, wait until tonight. I've got a plan."

Sure. Now, I did. I'd thrown it together at the gas station near the California border, the same place where I tucked the little goodie I picked up at the general store across the street. I hoped like hell I remembered how to pick locks the way daddy taught me.

I refused to say more. There was no point upsetting her, or getting her hopes up. It was hard to judge her mental state too. I had to stay quiet, wait for the devil to come calling, hoping he'd gloat and then walk away until tomorrow.

It must've been an hour or two before the thick door opened. Fang glowered in the hallway, entering alone and leaving his demonic posse behind him.

Christa flinched and whimpered when he walked past. I was sitting in an empty corner, and I stood up. My heart raced on pure instinct, but I wasn't afraid. My focus was all there, and it guided me, let me look the monster right in his black eyes.

"I'm not sure who's stupider," he growled, pacing me like a lion. "You or the rat I should've killed in front of you before he took out my men. I'm human. I made my mistakes. I handed shit off I should've handled personally to lazy fucks who took their sweet time. They cut their own throats and let you take off with him, you and that kid."

He sneered when he talked about Jackie. My heart pulsed in triumph. I liked remembering she was somewhere he could never reach her.

"Cut the crap," I snapped. "You want the video Brass is using to blackmail you and ruin your reputation with your guys, or what?"

He stopped pacing and gave me a hard look. "Of course. I just can't believe they'd send a cunt like you to negotiate."

"I'm here on my own. A free agent. I went behind my man's back." It was strange to tell the truth, and it twisted like a sharp knife in my heart. "I wasn't sure if he'd follow through for her."

I motioned to Christa. "But I can guarantee he'll do it for me. He'll show up, hand it over. And if he doesn't, then I'll make the confession. I'll give you whatever you want on tape, tell you everything I know about how he forged it."

Fang snorted, shaking his head. "And then what? You think I should just let this pretty red haired thing walk out of here alive so she can tell the cops? You think it's really that easy?"

"You really think she'll talk? I still haven't. I just wanted to take my sister and get on with my life. So does she. That's not something you'll have to worry about for a long, long time."

He laughed. It was a low, grinding, evil sound.

"Man, you're one fucked up girl. The only reason you never squawked is because your mouth is so full of rat dick you can't say shit. I'm really surprised about the kid, though." He looked thoughtful. "Don't tell me she's sucking him off too? Seems a little young for that, but that junkie fuck never sat right with me long before he turned rat. Can't put anything past him. Fuck, what I would've given to let him burn back in Montana with the other traitors..."

Fang showed his teeth. I wasn't scared, I was too busy being pissed instead.

Raged curdled my veins. I couldn't believe what he was saying – what he was accusing Brass of being.

It took everything I could manage not to throw myself at his face and gouge out his eyeballs with my fingernails. Fang stepped back, taking a good, long, leering look at me. I barely stopped the cold shiver dancing up my spine before it took over.

"Nothing to say to that?" He asked. "Smart girl. I give you a lucky little star for doing one thing right. As for the rest of this shit, coming here and thinking I'd give you a damned thing..."

He crossed the room to the middle, stopping behind Christa. In a flash, he pulled his knife from his belt, tugging her hair while he held it to her throat.

"No! You fucking promised! Seventy-two hours aren't up. Me coming here shouldn't change that..."

He looked back at me and winked. The redhead groaned, shaking underneath his knife, her eyes spinning wildly. I could practically see her life flashing in the wide black pupils.

There was a long, tense moment where I thought he was going to do it. I thought he'd cut her throat, ruin everything I came here to do, driving me insane as a nice little bonus. I held my breath, all I could do to stop the anger from throwing me at him like a human bullet.

"You know what? Fuck it." He stepped back, leaving Christa to fall back on her chair of misery. "It'll be a lot more fun dismembering this bitch in front of you. I'll be sure the Pussies and your old man get it all on tape. It'll be a sweet fucking preview of what's coming to you if they don't get their asses here in – what? – we must be down to about fifty hours. Okay, whore. We'll stick to the original deadline. I'm a man of my word."

Hot, angry, stale oxygen pumped in my lungs. I watched him give me a nasty grin and then grab the door, joining his men outside.

I walked over to Christa and held her until she stopped fretting. It took a long time. Feeling her calm and soften in my arms helped me keep time, a long count of minutes and hours. It was the longest I'd ever kept count in my head, keeping it going long past what had to be midnight.

Just hold on, Christa. Hold on. You'll be free before dawn, or I'll die trying.

I felt bad for slapping her. But it was all I could do to get her up, make sure she was able to stand. I made Christa walk back and forth, wall-to-wall, several times. If they'd fucked up her legs some way, then everything would go to shit.

No, she could walk. The woman was just tired, dizzy, broken. I'd lead her out, slow and steady, as soon as I got the door open.

It was finally time. I pulled the locksmith kit out of my pocket, one of those cheap Houdini things. The thick storage door was definitely going to be tougher than the crappy little room they'd held me in, but I had to try.

It slid into the lock and sank deep. I twisted it, pressing on the handle, praying it wouldn't make too much noise and attract unwanted attention.

Christa watched behind me. Having her eyes on me was like feeling God watching, or maybe daddy eyeing me from above, desperate to see if I pulled this off.

Shit, shit. It was much harder than anything I expected. No matter how I pushed, jiggled, or swept it around in there, I couldn't seem to –

Click.

The thunk echoed loudly. I tested the handle and almost jumped up and shouted with joy when I felt it slide all the way, forcing the door to give way and creak open. There was no time for celebration.

I grabbed Christa and led her out, dragging her toward the back exit as quickly as I could. Running into one evil faced bastard could ruin us, but I'd done my part. Everything came down to luck now, and I prayed as we stepped outside, working our way around the huge garages, toward the gate.

If there was a separate exit that wasn't fenced off, I didn't know it. I had to work fast on what little I knew about this place. Christa groaned a few times when I tried to make her move faster, but she handled it better than I expected – better than a woman who'd just been damaged should.

I thought the lights on the clubhouse were motion detectors, but they never came on. Luck smiled at us in the darkness, urging us closer, straight toward the manual switch embedded in cement several feet away from the big gate. This one was more primitive than what the Devils had at their place – I'd watched men simply tap the big button on several occasions. There was no code to exit.

It was my turn to do the same. Christa stood in front of the bars, just like I told her, staring at me in the darkness as I tapped the dirty plastic key.

The gate chugged open.

She hit the pavement as soon as the gate gave her

enough room. Joy pulsed through me watching her survival instinct kick in, the hellish urge to run like nothing else. I stood there stupidly for a couple seconds, and then it was my turn. I ran toward the open gate and slowed when I saw my shadow.

What the hell was it doing there in the night? Crap!

The floodlights were on. I got two steps outside before I heard boots thundering behind me. Christa was halfway across the road. She looked back and screamed, right as several men tackled me to the ground.

"Go! Don't fucking stop!" I yelled. "Keep going! Keep —"

A brute hand grabbed the back of my head and slammed me into the pavement, face first. I tasted blood and I couldn't speak. I looked up, seeing headlights. A vehicle was slowing next to Christa and I thought it was them.

But the man inside driving looked like Rabid. Someone screamed *go, go, go* before the gunshots exploded over my head.

The truck took off, roaring into the night. She was gone . I wasn't sure whether to be relieved or horrified, but I'd done my job. Christa escaped.

I closed my eyes and let them lay into me. I didn't bother wasting energy fighting as they held my arms and legs, carrying me inside like a sick animal. I closed my eyes just as the gate growled shut in the distance. Before I opened them, the stink of the clubhouse interior hit me again.

"You're dead now, bitch. Dead! Do you fucking understand?" A man roared in my face and pushed his cruel fingers around my chin.

It hurt. But I didn't look at him until they hurled me back inside the room. I crashed right into the chair where Christa had been, rolling over my tender new bruises until the wall stopped me.

The door slammed shut like a tomb. I felt for my wallet and the lockpick I'd shoved into my pocket on the way out with Christa. It was gone in the mess. The assholes holding me were as sloppy as they were savage. Even they wouldn't fuck up twice.

It didn't bother me that it was gone. If I still had it, they'd never leave that door unattended again. Not before somebody on one side or the other was dead.

The killer who screamed in my face was probably right. The relief I expected from helping Christa refused to relax my chest, replaced with another sadness.

I didn't care about dying if that was the price of helping her go free. But when I thought about how Jackie or Brass would react to my dead body if they saw it, the pain drove deep, a new dagger I had no way to pull out.

God! God damn it.

If only I hadn't frozen, if I'd been a few seconds faster...

The crappy room finally felt like a prison for the first time. The realization bit harsh, bitter, and merciless, gnawing on my head and my heart.

There was no getting out of this. No peace until death.

If they killed me quicker and easier than Christa – and I knew they wouldn't – Brass would burn. So would my poor sister.

Yes, I'd saved the teacher. But now I'd damned myself and everybody stupid enough to ever love me.

X: Nuclear (Brass)

Hours Earlier

"Hold him down, dammit! Just don't break his fucking wrists."

The whole world went red the instant Shelly told me what happened over the phone. I flipped my shit at the Devils' clubhouse, hopped in my truck, and tried to plow right through their gate. The bastards caught up to me when I wouldn't tell them why I was ready to go, why I had to blow town right that fucking instant.

Missy. My Missy.

My woman, losing her fucking mind and heading to Redding alone. Scared. Determined. And definitely no match for Fang, the fuck I swore I'd kill with my own bare hands.

He was gonna die, that much was sure, long before we even headed up to Devils' territory. But now the only question was whether I'd get my hands on his fat neck before he seriously fucked up my old lady.

It took all three senior officers in their club to drag me back inside. I was about to ram my truck right through their fucking gate, but they were quick. Shot out my tires and ran to my door, ripping it open, pulling me out, throwing me to the ground.

I fought them all, kicking and screaming like a mad man. Even colossal Tank strained to hold me down, pushing me to the ground with all his might, snarling like a wolverine as he kneed me in the spine and grabbed at my hands.

Fuck. The asshole finally managed to get a strong hold on me and I couldn't move. Stinger and one-eyed Moose stepped away cautiously, leaving me face-to-face with Blaze. The Devils' Prez grabbed me by the forehead and turned my head up, forcing me to look at him.

"Saffron just spilled the fucking beans," he growled. "My old lady got her goddamned truck jacked by yours, but you don't see me going nuclear. Damn it, boy, settle the fuck down."

My muscles were shaking. I forced myself to relax – the only damned way I was getting out of this. Blaze looked me up and down, then nodded to Tank, who gave a reluctant grunt and released me.

I stood up, brushing the dirt off my cut. All four Devils looked like they wanted to cut my ass to pieces every time they saw my colors on their home turf. Too fucking bad, because this wasn't coming off except when I stripped down and showered, or fucked my girl senseless.

And now, because I hadn't stayed with her, I might never get to fuck her again. *Fuck!*

I spun and clocked Tank right in the jaw. The giant's head snapped back, and I pushed through them before any of the others could grab me, heading for my truck's open door.

"Jesus Christ!" Blaze roared. "After his stupid ass!"

I had one foot in the driver's seat before Tank caught up to me. I knew I was screwed before the giant's fist found the back of my skull.

One deafening blow and the blackness swallowed me, turning everything jagged and red to smooth, dark shadows.

"Brass." Someone snapped his fingers next to my ear. "Wake your ass up!"

"Blaze..." A woman's voice said

I opened my eyes and saw him standing over me. At his side, some blondie in scrubs, probably the one named Emma I'd heard about. She was Tank's old lady and the club medic. Behind her, standing against the wall, there was a dark haired beauty and my sis.

They looked at me like I was a fucking ghost. I sat up, and instantly felt the straps binding my arms.

"Hey! What the fuck!?"

This was not what I needed. Shit, how many precious hours had I lost being laid out here in their infirmary? All while that sick sonofabitch had my girl at the clubhouse, doing God knows what?

"We'll let you go when we know you can be a good boy," Tank growled behind me, out of my line of vision. "You want me to give him the medicine, boss?"

Blaze nodded. Something strong in a glass pushed its

way to my lips and I fucking choked. Tank held my mouth shut like a dog, making me swallow it. I thrashed, thinking I'd been poisoned.

No, not poison. It was just Jack. Sweet, smooth, strong whiskey, something I thought I might never taste again.

"Fuck," I grunted between my teeth.

"We're giving you a shot to calm your ass down," Blaze said. "We're damned lucky Blackjack's a chiller dude than you. I gave him a call, and he's gonna work like hell to get your girl away from Fang. We're all on the same page, so you can stop worrying we're gonna hold you down and slit your throat. Tempting as that would be."

"Get her away? Fuck, you need to stop her, Blaze. Tell Blackjack to sit by the highway, make her pull over before she gets into town..."

Stinger stepped up next to Blaze and grinned. "You've been out all fucking day, asshole. One of your brothers down there saw her drive in, but he couldn't do shit about it by himself. It was too late to stop her from rolling right into the bear's den."

His harsh words almost set me off again. Almost. The whiskey definitely helped soothe the radioactive fire bristling in my blood, throbbing in my chest, ready to beat its way out of me.

Save it, you fucking fool, I told myself. *Save it for the fucks who really deserve it. Not these Prairie Pussies.*

"Just let me up," I said, resisting the urge to bolt up and punch every one of those fucks in their smug jaws the instant I could.

Blondie looked at Blaze. "I think it's time. We can't keep him strapped down here forever, Blaze."

The Devils' Prez looked down at me and nodded. Tank hovered over me, undoing the straps on my arms.

"You're a prick, but you gave as good as you got, Brass. Good hook. Hard fist. I can respect that shit." The giant motioned to the bruise I'd left on his face.

I grunted, halfway amused. He was right there to knock me out again if I did anything stupid. I sat up, fighting to let go of the anger. I looked at Blaze.

"They've got my old lady. We need to ride tonight."

"Already working on it. You think I've been standing here jacking off while you were dreaming?" Cocky as ever, he gave me a fierce wink. "Unfortunately, there's no chance in hell we'll have time to pick up any guys from Dakota to help us out. It's just us, plus all the men you've got playing freedom fighter in Redding."

My heart tightened. Steep odds. Blackjack told me about a third of the local guys deserted after our mutiny, but Fang still had numbers on his side. Possibly huge fucking numbers if the charters all along the west coast decided to stay loyal and send in reinforcements.

Whatever. Shit odds were nothing new to me. Having a woman on the line was, and not just any, but the one I cared for more than anything else in this fucked up world.

I slid off the table, standing. "When do we leave?"

"A couple more hours. Just need to get a few more things ready," Blaze said. "You'll ride with Stinger and Moose. Gotta make sure you've worked all that piss outta your system, and you're not gonna do anything stupid."

That was fair. Didn't change the fact that they were fuckers. I nodded.

Blaze stepped out, giving Shelly a quick hug and a kiss on his way out. The other guys hung back, tucking into their old ladies. Seeing Tank press the tiny blonde into his immense frame and plant his lips on her made lava seethe in my veins.

Then I saw Stinger, his arms wrapped around the dark haired girl, whispering to her. "I promise I'll be back before you know it, baby. Stay sexy and help Saffron with the girl while we're gone. Love you, Alice."

"You know I will," she purred.

They kissed. Fuck. Panic burbled deep in my brain, the horrible possibility I might never see my girl again. Let alone hold her like that, suck her bottom lip, whisper all the thousands of sweet and filthy words pent up in my head.

No. She's coming home in one piece. Same beautiful package I'd rip my fucking heart out for.

You can't fucking lose her like you've already lost your mind.

Hold on, babe. Your old man's coming.

"Brass." Shelly grabbed me on my way out. "Bring everybody home safe, and that means you too."

I managed a thin smile. "Thanks, sis. Uh, sorry about the truck. I hope like fuck nothing's happened to it. I'll bring it home too, if I can."

"You know I don't give a shit about the wheels. It's just one more thing to deal with." She rolled her eyes. "The girl was upset. Crazy. I haven't even told her little sister yet..."

"You work on that," I said. "With any luck, I'll have her home with your ride so you don't have to tell Jackie how fucked up things are. She's been through too fucking much for a fourteen year old."

"I know." She looked at the ground sadly. "And I remember what it was like for us at that age. You've got to be honest to keep them from going off the rails. Mom tried to hide how bad off she was until it drove you away and locked me down."

"Yeah." There was nothing more to say about it. She'd forgiven me for falling in with the fucks who'd slaughtered our disabled mother. The guilt still weighed heavy on my black heart, and saying shit about the bitter past would only feed it.

"You turned yourself around, Brass," she said, throwing her arms around me. "I'm so damned proud of you for that. I know you can fix this too. Go get the bastards who did this."

Yes. Fuck yes. I couldn't do anything less than tear their throats out like the angry wolf I was, but this only sealed the deal.

I pressed her tight to my chest and then I was gone, following the Devils out to the garages. The guns just needed to be loaded into their rides, waiting for the battle to come.

My bones ached on the trip down, and not just from the fight. Crossing a good quarter of the continent in a week without much rest took its toll. Fuck if I was gonna let it slow me down.

I was wide awake. The pain stiffened my resolve. The Devils and I didn't say much to each other – they understood what was on the line, and that was enough. The men glowered, half as intense as me, big bearded Moose looking into the darkness like a one-eyed biking sailing toward Valhalla.

We took turns driving, following the convoy of bikes all the way to Redding. We finally veered off toward a remote spot near Shasta Lake, just north of town. Blackjack and the boys were using an old lake cabin as a base.

Everybody took a breather for a few minutes after the long drive, and then filed in. Shit, and here I thought the tension between the Devils and I was thick. In the little makeshift cabin, it was fucking suffocating.

Devils and Grizzlies eyeballed each other like warriors from separate worlds. One wrong move was all it'd take to make bullets or knives start flying, murdering the uneasy alliance we both needed.

Rabid came up and slapped my back. "Welcome home, brother. I'm sorry as shit I couldn't get her out in time like Christa back there."

He pointed to the little bedroom. Fucking typical Rabid. If there was any pretty redhead who needed comforting, he was always the man for the job. Though I wasn't so sure how pretty she'd be after the brutal number Fang and his crew did on her.

"There's still time," I growled. "It's not over 'til Missy's outta that fucking dump and we've turned this club around for good."

A loud whistle silenced us before we could say anything else. Blackjack and Blaze were gathered at the little wooden table. All twenty guys from the two clubs coalesced in a circle.

"Make a little room for Brass," Blackjack growled. "He needs to see this."

Fuck. See what?

I pushed my way through a couple big Grizzlies, taking my place next to the de facto Prez. Blackjack was holding a phone, his dark eyes glued to the screen.

"Sorry, son. This just came in a few minutes ago."

He held it up for everyone to see, especially me.

They had Missy in the dank fucking storage room, parked on the same rickety chair where they'd tortured Christa. Fang was behind her, his sharp knife with the custom bear claw handle at her throat.

Don't fucking do it, don't fucking do it, don't...

My vision started to blur to red again. My fists shook at my sides. For a second, it felt like the whole fucking universe was compressing into a tiny hot ball around me.

Smaller, darker, and deader. My soul prepared to rocket outta my body and swing straight down to hell, screaming and killing anything that got in its way.

The knife fell back. Not even a trickle of blood on her throat.

Thank God.

"You know the drill by now, assholes." Fang's voice was

more irritated than I'd ever heard it. "Different girl. Same terms. Except you've just cut your remaining time in half. You're down to five hours to comply. I expect the tape, the confession, and the rats by o-sixteen-hundred or I'll be carving two pieces off this cunt for being so troublesome. Starting with those pretty tits."

The video went blank, but not before I had a perfect shot of Missy's face. She looked eerily calm, numb, like her heart and mind had shut down to survive the world of pain coming her way.

He was fucking hurting her, even if he hadn't laid a scratch on her yet. My fists burned, hungry to punch, choke, break, and kill.

Just seeing Fang's rotten carcass wasn't enough for me anymore. I had to beat everybody else to the punch and kill him myself, or I'd never sleep again. Fuck.

"Brass?" Blackjack, Blaze, and half the room stared at me.

I swallowed my rage, saving it for later, nursing the swollen fireball in my stomach. "What's the plan?"

"Direct assault," Blaze pipped up. "It's the only fucking way. We gotta go for their throat, quick as we can, and hope we tear it out before we got a hundred fucking bears nipping at our legs."

Angry eyes fixed on the Devils' President. "No offense," he added, diffusing tensions by half a degree. "Tank?"

"No disagreement, boss. We don't have too many options, and waiting sure as fuck won't help."

"Wait." Everybody looked at me, but I didn't meet their

eyes.

I was too busy staring through the small crowd, back towards the sad redhead in the bedroom. The door was open, and she was standing. Her back was turned to us and she was gazing out the window.

"We know the video wasn't full proof," I said. "Fang's guaranteed to have numbers on his side. Doubt half the charters believed it, especially since it came from the Devils."

"I don't see where you're going with this," Blackjack said, furrowing his brow. "What the fuck, Brass?"

I walked around the table and leaned into his ear. "Step in the back with me. I want her to hear it too."

Blaze followed, and I didn't stop him. He had every right to know what the fuck was up with his men on the line and two Grizzlies whispering to each other.

The other men waited while we stepped into the room and closed the door behind us. Christa turned around. Her face was bad, scratched and puffy as shit. She'd been a pretty girl, and our former brothers had definitely fucked her up.

Almost felt guilty for the shit I was about to propose, but it was the only thing that might save all our asses from getting slaughtered, plus Missy too.

"Brass? What the fuck is this?" Blaze was getting impatient.

I spilled it. Both their jaws hit the fucking floor when I laid it out. Christa listened silently.

When I was finished, Blaze spun, slammed his fists on

the wall. He turned back to face me, shaking his head. "You're outta your fucking mind. I know it's your old lady and nobody can think right when something like that's on the line. But, fuck, man, you're asking us to take one helluva risk with some chick who's already been through the grinder."

"I've got to agree with Blaze," Blackjack said. "This is..."

His face tightened. *Fucking nuts,* he was about to say, or something like it. He hesitated, trying to soften the blow for my sake.

"Sorry, Brass," he said. "Direct assault's the only way to clean this mess up and get your girl out. You know it."

"Stop," Christa spoke, soft but determined. "I'll do it."

A couple hours later, everything was ready. Less than three hours to spare before the demon in our clubhouse started laying into my woman. Just enough time.

Blackjack had every copy of the tape the Devils brought, and all the men were ready to ride.

Rabid was still milling around the beat up redhead. I walked over, more than a little nervous he was about to talk some sense into her. Fuck, I couldn't force her to do shit if she pulled out, but if she did...we'd be fucked so bad there was nothing left to do but ride into a massacre.

"You're sure you wanna do this?" Rabid watched her nod as I approached. "Fuck. You're a brave, brave girl. I'm gonna be right there with you, baby. No fucking way am I gonna let anybody drag you back where you don't belong. Those fucks will *never* get their paws on you again."

I laid a hand on his shoulder. "Where is it?"

Rabid looked at me, smiled and pointed at the Harley several feet away. "She's all there. Got her out right in the nick of time, before Fang and company stole her, right before everything went to shit at the warehouse."

"Thank fuck. I'd have to skin all their greedy asses for sitting on my baby."

Rabid stayed with the redhead while I walked to my bike. Jesus, it had only been about a week, but it felt like half a fucking lifetime. The only thing sweeter than sliding onto my Harley again would be having Missy in my arms, and I was dead set on it.

I swore to heaven and hell I'd put *everything* in my life back where it belonged.

I couldn't wait to get my woman back, even more than I wanted to put a bullet in Fang's head for what he'd done. Love's a powerful fucking thing when it tames rage, tames hate, and everything else in between. There was a lot to snarl at in all this, but mostly, I just wanted her home.

She'd never get off my bike or outta my bed after this. Never. The first thing I was gonna do when I had her again was squeeze her so fucking tight she'd never dream about walking into harm's way for the rest of her life. Later, I'd spank her pretty ass raw for doing this.

What I really missed was those lips. Their taste, their softness, their sweet flutter on mine like honest-to-fuck pixie wings.

I'd been too soft, too distracted with club business. The realization hit me right between the eyes like a hot sword boring into my skull. Now, my entire soul bled for her, bled dirty red blood from a scalding wound that wouldn't close 'til I had what was mine pressed up against me again.

There was no other cure. Nothing else would undo the damage I'd taken, my failure to keep what was mine close as my own gun.

"Two hours!" Blackjack's voice howled near the front of the column. "Let's fucking go, boys."

A dozen engines growled, igniting as one, joined by a few stragglers at the end. I strapped on my helmet and felt the comforting purr of my Harley beneath me. She'd always been a fine war horse, and now I needed her to carry me to my girl.

Blackjack pulled out first. We all hit the highway and rode down toward Redding. I was near the front with Rabid and the redhead on his bike, only separated by Blackjack and Blaze by Tank. It was a weird, motley platoon of sworn enemies riding toward hell, joined together in a fucked up marriage all about saving all the asses in the leather seats today. Motorcycles rumbled behind me, at least ten of them, and then a couple trucks from both clubs bringing up the rear.

Blackjack agreed to meet Fang near a hilly wilderness outside town. We'd promised him everything, but we knew he'd be on alert for us fucking him over. Hoped like hell the ruse I had planned would be such a shock he wouldn't see it coming.

It all came down to conscience. Fang didn't have one – some devil had ripped it outta him and chewed it up ages ago – but did the rest of the club? We were about to find out.

The column slowed when we roared onto the unpaved road, heading for the forest clearing. They were parked by the trees. Legions waiting for us.

Even my eyes bugged out when I saw how many Grizzlies Fang brought to cover his ass. Fuck, he must've had half the Tacoma and Portland charters, plus more brothers from Idaho. Basically, every able bodied man who wasn't busy getting killed down south by the cartel's raiders.

Shit. There must've been a hundred guys to our fifteen, possibly more, and he was fully surrounded. Protected.

Blaze and Blackjack stopped a few feet away, undaunted by the huge army facing them. I pulled up next to them and Rabid did too. My brother looked nervous as shit, keeping his hands on the redhead 'til she pulled away forcefully.

My eyes scanned the guys next to Fang and Crack. Fuck, they were supposed to do the exchange here!

Where the fuck was she? Where'd he put my girl? My heart forced adrenaline loaded waves into my blood. I shook, sweated, rubbed the nine millimeter in my belt.

Easy, I told myself. *They'll see that shit and hit you between the eyes before you take a single step forward if you make a dumb move.*

She's gotta be here somewhere. He wouldn't have left her at the clubhouse with nobody there on guard duty.

I counted all the bastards who'd stuck with him from my club. Rough, Gnaw, Pitbull, Chubb...five more prospects past them. No, they were all there. That meant Missy had to be with them, tucked back in the crowd, maybe bound up in one of their fucking trucks.

Blackjack looked at me and nodded. I walked with him and Blaze. Christa moved up several steps behind me. Rabid had to hang back, or else there'd be more guys on the other side coming to meet us besides Fang and Crack.

Nobody wanted that shit. More brothers eyeball-to-eyeball meant more danger.

"What the hell's this?" Fang grunted, stopping in the middle. "I asked for the video, the rats, and a confession. Didn't ask to see this fucking bitch again."

He spat at the ground. Blaze grabbed the small black package underneath one arm and threw it on the ground.

"Here, asshole. Five copies. There's the master, plus the fucking camera it was shot on. That's everything."

Fang reached down and picked it up, grinning on his way up. He looked at me, and then at Blackjack.

"Okay. Let's go, boys. We've got a nice trial ready out back with all your brothers. Promise we'll make it quick, just as soon as one of you fucks tells us straight up where that video came from."

Trial. Right. Never heard the shallow graves he probably had waiting in the woods called that before.

I looked him in the eye and reached for the redhead, grabbing her hand. "I shot that fucking video," I said loudly, making sure everybody could hear.

"You never ordered the hit. The bastard was just a fucking freak trying to fuck my old lady's little sis. I killed him. I framed you. I fucked up."

Fang let out an angry laugh. "Damned right you did, kid! Hmmm, I suppose that's confession enough, but I'm still gonna want it on camera before we decide how to end this. Didn't think you'd give it up so easy."

He licked his lips. Fucker had murder written all over them.

I smiled. "That's because I thought this was all harder and more complicated than it really is. I didn't see all the evidence of the shit you've done right underneath my nose."

"What fucking evidence?"

I reached behind me and grabbed her, holding her in front of my chest. Christa flinched once, but then stood still, staring at the monster through her swollen eyes.

"*This*. Take a good, long look, everybody. This is why we turned on national! This is why we'll never follow this motherfucker, as long as he's Prez!" I was screaming.

Crack looked at me in a stupor, and Fang's eyes darkened. Didn't think it was possible for him to beam more hate, but he sure as fuck did. My hands loosened near her belly, holding on tight, ready to throw her down as soon as he let the demon inside him off its chain.

"This is what our Prez does. He rips innocent girls to pieces. He kills anybody who disagrees with that shit, frames 'em as rats. He's too fucking busy fattening his own wallet off the blood this club's spilled to inspire us, and that's exactly why the cartel's running over our bodies. We beat 'em by being better than vermin. Right now, this club's just as brutal. Just as fucked up. Is that what you wanted for the Grizzlies MC when you put on that patch?"

Silence. A long, tense, fiery quiet.

The surprise on Fang's face shrank, slow and vicious, turning into volcanic anger. His hand flew to his hip, surprisingly spry for a man his age. I had exactly one second to throw Christa to the ground and keep her there while he fired.

The gunshot echoed loud over the horizon. I waited for more, holding my breath, wondering if we were all about to die.

"Shit!" Blaze cursed.

I rolled, looked up, and saw the hole in Blackjack's thigh. He hit the ground, clenching his leg, blood pooling between his fingers. Fuck! Fang missed us, and hit the only man worth serving in this fucking club instead.

One 'shit' spoken, and about a thousand more to go. Only way to describe the situation.

Blackjack clenched his leg harder, a sinister smile on his face. Blaze crouched with his gun, and everybody in our crew behind us locked and loaded. I was reaching for my own sidearm, ready to blow Crack's fucking head off.

Except I didn't have to. The bastard's skull exploded before he could draw on me, and it came from behind him.

Fang spun, stunned silence twisting the sneer on his face. The huge throng of Grizzlies serving him had their guns drawn on each other. Another shot exploded. Another guy went down, one of Fang's men.

Total fucking chaos.

The guys who'd decided they didn't want any part of serving the asshole hit the dirt. Some ran toward us, only to be mowed down by the bastards staying loyal. They were brutal fucks, men like Serial, who loved everything Fang did to drive this club into the ground, hungry for more of it to satisfy their sadistic urges.

I struggled to stay down, protecting Christa, but I had to see what the fuck was going on. All that mattered to us was numbers. If enough of them mutinied, especially in this storm, we had a chance.

Looking to my other side, I saw Blackjack keeping focus, pressing both hands tight to his wound. Blaze had his gun trained on Fang, who was high-tailing it back to the guys he had left.

Shit! The Devils' Prez emptied his clip and one hit the bastard in the leg. Fang dropped, grunted, and started to crawl. He was on the ground, roughing his way forward, when several goons ran toward him and picked him up.

Our guys were pouring past me now. Rabid leaned down to me, reaching for the woman's hand.

"Let her go, bro. I got her. Need to get her to the rear."

I nodded. Good. Now, I was free to go, following the long push toward the woods, where lots of vehicles were abandoned in all the commotion.

"Missy! Missy!" I screamed her name when I got closer, looking all over for anything bigger than a bike, or maybe a pit where they'd thrown her for the exchange.

Nothing. More shots rang out around me, and several

brothers wrestled on the ground, Grizzlies and the odd Devil doing close combat.

A dead eyed fuck popped out of the trees and lunged with his dagger drawn. I blew his head off and went forward, forward, heading for the place where I'd seen them dragging Fang.

No fucking way was he getting away alive. Not today.

Someone tugged on the back of my cut. I spun, pressed my gun to his head, and felt my heart stick in my throat when I saw it was Blackjack, struggling to upright.

"Christ! You should've stayed back. What the fuck's going on?"

"Keep going, son," he growled. "Don't fucking worry about me. I can't rest until I see him dead. We have to find him."

I nodded. The gunfire was dying down around us, and I was relieved to see mutineers and Devils standing around prisoners, gathering the fucks together who'd thrown down their arms.

Blackjack hung close to me. We walked through the trees, and I cleared a path for him through the brush. Almost tripped on a dead man with a hole through his chest. Shit, it was one of the bastards who'd grabbed Fang. He had to be somewhere.

I heard him before we caught up through the brush. He'd rolled through the weeds toward a shitty little pond, and he was holding his leg, screaming at the asshole who'd gone with him.

"Come on! Keep fucking moving. We can't stop. We've

gotta get outta here."

The man groaned. I saw he was bleeding out from a hole in his stomach, barely even conscious. The soon-to-be-dead Prez was still berating the poor bastard. Suddenly, Fang pulled his gun, pressed it to the man's temple, and fired.

"Fucking useless! All of you! This is what I get for thirty fuckin' years of glory? I *made* this club. It was all me – me! And now you bastards are tearing it to pieces, turning over like snakes and cowards, ruining *everything* I gave you..."

I told Blackjack to hang back and pushed through the weeds first. He fired at the weeds I rustled, and a new emotion I'd never seen entered his eyes: fear.

Arctic terror. And it was goddamned beautiful.

Two bullets buried themselves in the mud, dangerously close to my leg. I kept going. His gun was clicking on empty by the time I stood over him.

Blackjack pushed his way to my side, breathing a little heavier than before. Both our guns were trained on him. I got ready to squeeze the trigger first and take flak later. Blackjack deserved the kill almost as much as me, but no fucking way was I letting someone else hand Fang his one way ticket to hell.

"Don't!" Fang roared, throwing a hand up, as if he still had a choice. "We can figure something out. Take my patch, drain my money, ship my ass to Alaska...you can't fucking kill me. You know I built this thing from my bare hands, Blackjack. I built you!"

"You built yourself a tower of shit, Fang," the old man

said. "There was a time when we needed a man like you in charge. Not anymore. You spilled too much blood, carved too much flesh. It's no wonder we've got wolves at our gates."

"You want to live?" I stepped up, pressing my gun to his temple. He nodded, shifting his evil head against my gun. "Then tell me where you've got her. Where's my old lady?"

Fang licked his lips. "There's a van parked about a mile from here. Nobody in it but her, tied up and gagged in the trunk. I was gonna send my guys to get her if you hadn't fucked me over...but I knew you would. I *knew it*. I keep my fucking word. Always. Do you, Brass?"

I looked at Blackjack. He nodded.

"You do the honors, son."

"No. But I'm gonna say thanks for being honest just once in your life," I growled to Fang.

He was shaking. I pulled the gun back, stuck it in my holster, and brought out my knife. Let him feel a second of misplaced relief before I let him see it. The fear in the ex-Prez's eyes swelled, and then it was just a reflection of murder.

I did everything he threatened to do to my girl, piece by fucking piece. Blackjack watched for five grisly minutes before I finally slammed my blade into Fang's skull.

When it was over, I cut away his patch, and threw one arm over the old man, helping him struggle back through the brush.

"Put me down," he said, as soon as we saw the Devils and our crew again. "They'll take it from here. Go. Go find your woman."

I didn't need to be told twice.

I found the worn blue van parked off a little service road, right where the asshole indicated. All my muscles tensed up as I approached the trunk.

A man never knows what he'll find in the back of a car in this world. If the lying bastard hurt her, killed her, then I'd run right back into the woods and dismember his ass all over again. What little was left to slice and dice, anyway. Shit, if he'd lied to me, I'd learn the darkest black magic I could to make sure his soul suffered worse in Satan's care than it already deserved.

I shook my head, pushing away the fucked up thoughts. The glass was dirty and I couldn't see inside. There was no sign of anyone screaming or banging within.

My hand caught the handle and pulled. It was unlocked, and it popped open with a *whoosh*.

Fuck. There she was. Gagged, red eyed, balled up in the tiny space next to some old oil bottles, her hands and feet bound. But she was alive.

Missy tried to scream through the dirty rag in her mouth when she saw me. I threw myself in, pulling her into my arms, reaching for the same knife I'd just used to send Fang to justice. I cut her bindings first, then sliced carefully past her hair, ripping away the shitty cloth blocking her sweet lips.

"Baby girl." I said it softly, just as she sucked in a huge breath and started to cry.

I flattened her on my chest, stroking the soft brown hair I was damned lucky to feel once again. I wondered how the hell it always stayed magnificent, sexy, even when she'd just been on a round trip through Hades.

"The asshole's dead. So are all the shits who did this to you. It's over, babe. There's nothing left for you to fear."

"Brass." She croaked my name and I helped pivot her face up to mine. "I'm sorry, I'm sorry. I'm so fucking sorry. I had to do the right thing. I didn't realize saving her and putting myself on the line would hurt you, hurt Jackie."

She shuddered. Her face scrunched up and I thought the waterworks were gonna keep flowing, but she caught herself at the last second, drawing in a deep breath.

"I'm a screwed up mess. I thought I was strong, but I cracked in there." She gestured to the van. "They left me bound up, and then I heard the gunshots...look at me. I'm a fucking mess."

"Quiet, babe," I growled, a little more angrily than I intended. She blinked. "It's okay to scream and scratch the ground when some fuck keeps you under the gun. You're doing what comes natural. But I want you to listen real fucking close and get this through your head."

She tensed up in my arms. I clenched her tighter. No fucking way was letting her slip away before I drilled it into her pretty skull.

"You're *my* fucking mess. You're my old lady. I own you, babe, now 'til the last day I'm alive and breathing on this rock. If you think freaking out or showing me you're scared and hurt's gonna drive me away, think again. Open up your head and make sure you're thinking at all, if that's what's running through your sweet head." I paused, inhaling her delicious scent, pressing my forehead to hers. "I love you, Missy. I don't say that shit easy – I never fucking said it to anyone 'til you came along. Not even Shelly. My love's a wrecking ball and it only swings one way once it gets going. You got it? You're mine, babe, mine to love and only mine, whether you're howling underneath me in bed or walking into mine fields to save some chick."

When I pulled my face away from her, she was trembling a little, but I knew it wasn't fear. She was fucking overwhelmed. And that was okay. Long as she was full of the same crazy thing I had ticking for her in my chest, I didn't give a damn.

I was about to start walking her back when she pinched her hands around me, feeling me up right there in the forest, raking her nails down my back like she couldn't believe I was real. Fuck me if I didn't get goosebumps singeing my skin while my dick swelled in my dirty pants.

"Babe, we need to get the fuck –"

She flung her face forward, crushing her lips against mine before I could say another word. And I mean *really* pressed them tight in the hungriest kiss I'd ever had with a chick in my entire life. It sucked all the hot air right outta my lungs, shocked me through my skull, lit my fucking blood on fire.

Then I couldn't think about anything at all except this incredible kiss. My brain knew it was better than sex, though my cock would've protested that with all his might.

We kissed for what felt like an hour out there in the wilderness, the wind blowing small wafts of burned flesh and blood toward us every so often. Shit, the club was gonna be cleaning up this mess for days, hopefully before any badges figured out who left a small battlefield behind.

None of that mattered. It was as distant as the damned moon. I just focused on her taste, her smell, swirling my tongue around hers.

Didn't matter how many times I took what was mine. It never got old, and it never would. She was like a perfect fruit that stayed ripe, waiting for my mouth, waiting for me to own her flesh the best way I knew how.

"I love you, Jordan," she said, after a small eternity locking lips. "You know I'm not going anywhere as long as you keep giving me chances. I can't promise I won't screw up again...my life's got a lot of work left to straighten it out. And Jackie – God! Where is she?"

I smiled. "Shelly's bringing her down with a rental as soon as we sound the all clear. Should be here tomorrow now that we've cleaned house. The Devils won't be hanging too long. They'll be itching to get home as fast as they can, rather than clean up our fucking mess."

"Wow. You've really thought of everything, haven't you?" She quirked an eyebrow.

"No way, babe. I've got a lot of shit on my plate. I've still gotta find a place for us to settle down. Maybe book a nice long getaway to Vegas or Reno. We've all got a lot to clear outta our heads. Best way I know how is drinking, fucking, and gambling." She cocked her head, looking at me like the crazy bastard I was. "All right. We can throw in a mud bath massage thing or two at the spa. Whatever you girls like."

"Jerk." She punched my arm playfully, wiping the last salty remnants outta her eyes.

I shrugged, starting to walk her toward my bike. Had to take the furthest loop possible to keep her away from the savage scene left near the woods.

"It's what I do. And I'm gonna keep jerking your sweet ass around, every way that's good for you, as long as you call me your old man."

"I guess I'd better get used to it," she mused. "This is what I got myself into. And there's no way I'd ever want out."

I grinned. Next thing on the list after settling club business was getting her a proper brand. Fuck, she'd look hot as hell wearing my name on her back in leather, and somewhere on her skin to boot.

The whole ride into town, with her wrapped around me, I couldn't believe we'd built ourselves something so real outta playing pretend.

Several Days Later

We were packed in like sardines at the clubhouse. There were so many brothers from all the charters up and down the coast Blackjack had to get the Grizzlies MC table dragged out into the bar, using the main stretch for this mega-church session.

The tension was thick. But it was an anxious, uncertain fog in the air, not the same scared-for-our-lives shit buzzing around under Fang.

I sat at the head of the table next to Blackjack, Rabid, and a couple other guys. The old man lifted the infamous bear claw off the bandage on his thigh, where he'd kept it resting until he was ready.

Everything about this shit was weird. Everything, from the throngs of Grizzlies in front of us, to seeing him with an energy in his eyes like nothing else. Then there was the brand new VP patch on my cut, something I never thought I'd be wearing 'til after I hit thirty.

"Brothers!" Blackjack smashed the bear's foot on the wood.

The commotion started to die down, with the local Prezes helping quiet their men. All the eyes focused on us. Good thing I didn't have any issue being the center of attention.

Wasn't sure I could say the same about Rabid. He looked a little freaked out. But maybe he was just trying to figure out how the fuck he was going to explain going after his new redheaded fixation to his favorite redheaded whore. He kept showing up at Christa's doorstep, ostensibly to keep tabs on her and make sure she stayed quiet after the shit that went down, but it seemed like he was going outta his way to do more than that.

"This is a brand new day for the Grizzlies MC," Blackjack said, as soon as it was quiet, except for restless boots scraping the floor. "There's no need to sit here on my perch and recount the turmoil we've been through the past few months. Suffering under a tyrant, fighting the cartel off our throats, working with an MC we've spilled blood with..."

Several brothers in the audience growled. I wasn't gonna start loving Prairie Pussies anytime soon, but I didn't feel the old aching need to slam daggers into the backs of the sorry bastards who'd bailed our asses out either.

"Hold onto those memories. Then take your best blade, dig them out of your skull, and set them on fire." Blackjack paused, letting his words sink in. "They're all done. Nothing but ashes now. Once upon a time, the Grizzlies MC was great. We had the tightest brotherhood from Billings to San Diego. No other club fucked with us west of the Mississippi because they'd get swarmed before they even thought about drawing our blood."

I looked through the crowd. The tired, worn out men with gray in their hair and beards knew those days. It was no surprise a lot of the old timers had deserted Fang first.

"With me heading national now, we're bringing those days back, brothers. There's plenty of shit ahead left to sort out – rogue charters, Mexican hit men, the cash flow situation – but we'll do it. We always do. The blood of every brother who's fallen for this club flows in your veins. Guard it the same way you guard your colors, and remember what it means. If you do that, boys, you're already halfway there."

Men stood and applauded. I looked at Blackjack and gave him a stern nod. Had to assert my authority, after all.

The man had a gift for gab, though, nobody in the room could deny it.

The meeting was way too big to be anything but a ceremony for crowning the new leadership. The real business would come later, filtering down the charters from border to border, dangerous and glorious as it always was, and always would be with a man in charge who deserved to be called Prez.

A couple minutes later, the bear claw came down with a resounding clack. "Church dismissed. Now, go rock the fucking roof off."

What would the biggest gathering of the club in years be without a sendoff party? I hung around and had a couple beers, shooting the shit with Rabid and a couple other guys. The whores rolled in about an hour later.

I passed Twinkie in the crowd a couple times, and she gave me a longing look. I turned my back and showed her the bear patch without hesitation. No fucking way was my dick going in any pussy that wasn't attached to my old lady from now on.

No other pussy compared.

Maybe it meant I was growing up, or else I'd just lost my damned mind. Regardless, I was dead set on doing right by my woman and my club. Taking the VP patch seriously meant the days of getting stinking drunk and fucking random sluts was behind me. They faded into smoke, almost as distant and unworldly as the ones I'd lived pushing shit into my veins.

"Brass."

A hand fell on my shoulder and I turned, setting my empty beer glass on the bar. Blackjack stood behind me, decked out with a few more patches on his old cut.

"I've got something I need to give you, son. Come with me."

I followed him down the long hall, passing several brothers with girls against the wall, their hands dipping between the bitches' legs. Loud rock drowned out almost all the sound, blasting through the clubhouse's sound system.

We stopped in front of the storage room. I gave him a dark look as he opened the huge door. The thing was slowly turning into a real storage room, changing from the dank and brutal dungeon it had been under Fang.

He walked me back to the end of two new shelves, and then grabbed a big black bag. "Right where I left it. Take it and get the hell out of here."

It was awfully familiar. Heavy too. I looked inside and did a double take when I saw all the cash stuffed in there.

"What the fuck? This is Missy's old inheritance." I looked up, meeting his eyes. "I thought this shit belonged to the club's coffers now?"

"Not anymore. A million in cash is what your girls deserve for their pain and suffering through all this." He reached into his pocket, plucked out a cigarette, and gave it a light. "This club's got to get its sins right. I'd give you the rest, but it's already been deposited and spent, laundered through our legit operations."

"It's plenty."

"There'll be more for her if she wants to work the club's books. We need an accountant who can keep her mouth shut. Barrel decided to go down with Fang's ship, and I'm not sure about any other brothers keeping watch," he said, talking about our old club treasurer. "Fucker had been skimming money off left and right for years. So did Fang. Fat lot of good it did them in the end."

I nodded. Blackjack looked at me and waved his hand.

"Go on, Brass. Get lost. You deserve a little fun before we come home to our war tomorrow, and I know you won't find it here."

"Thanks, Prez. You're the fucking best."

I really meant it. I tucked the money carefully into my saddlebag and rode, fast and hard, taking off to the hotel where I had the girls while we waited to find something more permanent.

"Is Jackie home?" I asked, as soon as I pushed my way into the kitchen. I tucked the bag in the closet near the door, just out of view.

Missy ran toward me and gave me a kiss. My cock jerked fierce. Damn that woman had a gift for making me jump, no matter how tired or preoccupied I was with other shit. As soon as her lips landed on mine, there was one thing on my mind. It was hard as fuck to put sex on hold, but I needed to do this.

"She's doing homework. Why?"

"Get her in here right now. I got something for you girls. Both of you."

She gave me an odd look, and then moved to the door joining our two rooms. I'd rented double, knowing we'd be here for at least a week or two.

One knock and the kid opened up. She came out, and both of them sat at the little table in the corner. I ripped the closet open and pulled it out.

It took my girl several seconds to realize what was coming down in front of her. Then her hand trembled, reaching for it cautiously.

"Present from Blackjack. The shit you were owed all along from your dad. It's not everything...but I think you'll agree it's plenty."

Missy unzipped it and pushed her hands through crisp, fat stacks of cash. Jackie let out a squeal and jumped out of her chair, looking like she'd just run face first into one of those gawky boys she loved to listen to, signing about broken hearts or some shit.

"Use it wisely, girls, I know you will."

Missy dropped the two wads of money she was holding back into the bag. It was her turn to freak out, jump into my arms, and wrap her legs around me. Big fucking mistake.

I couldn't resist kissing her hard, all while her little sis laughed and made a face.

"Thank you," she whispered. "You don't even know what this means..."

"Yeah, babe, actually I do," I said. "Means you're gonna send the kid to college and finish school yourself. Then you're gonna do whatever the fuck you want with that money. It only took a drive through hell to bring it back where it belongs, right?"

"Right," she agreed, pushing her smiling face into mine.

We'd spilled a lot of blood and suffered to turn everything upside down rightside up again. And now, it was all worth it, clear as the sun and laughter lighting up the room.

XI: Room to Love (Missy)

One Month Later

The Nevada sun was high and hot, but I wore it anyway. Ever since I put on the jacket with PROPERTY OF BRASS sewn on its leather back a couple days ago, I felt totally naked without its smooth, comforting embrace on my skin.

I sat beneath a sunbeam at the massive casino hotel, looking down over the pool where Jackie spent the majority of the last two days when she wasn't with us. My little sis was definitely making the most of her Memorial Day – stretching out in the warm water, trying to catch a tan. Some gawky looking boy kept coming around, making her flush and giggle.

"Shit. Is that kid sniffing around the girl again?" I turned and saw Brass standing there with my afternoon coffee and a beer for himself.

"Oh, leave her alone," I said with a smile. "She's having fun here. I'm sure she likes having somebody besides us for company."

"Says the big sis who doesn't notice all the friends she's

been having over lately." Brass narrowed his eyes, still looking out the window. "Girlfriends are one thing. I'm keeping my eye on that fucking punk, though. She's too young to know a good man."

I laughed and rolled my eyes. "I hope we have a daughter someday. You're going to make one hell of a dad."

That got his attention. He stepped away from the huge window and pulled me up, tugging me into his arms. "Fuck, babe. Any kid you give me's gonna come out so perfect I'll have it easy. But right now, I'm too damned horny to worry about changing diapers or waving a shotgun in some scrappy boy's face when he comes by for prom."

"Oh." I looked down and noticed the lump in his pants. "Sounds like we'd better go take care of that. You never know when Jackie might get sick of her company and come knocking for another night on the Vegas strip."

"Plenty of time for everything, Missy." He leaned closer as we walked toward our room. "I'm gonna fuck you hard enough 'til we can get back to it around midnight. You're gonna feel it when you slip your heels on and hit the town tonight. I'm not ashamed to leave you sore."

No, he wasn't. The instant we pushed into our room and he kicked the door shut, he ripped the coffee cup out of my hand and set it on the bathroom counter.

"Save that shit for later. You'll need a pick me up when we're through."

Rough hands pushed me to the wall and he sank down,

tasting my lips, kissing his way across my throat while he groped my breasts through my shirt. Jesus, the leather wrapped around me was really sweltering hot now.

I tried to push it off, but Brass grabbed me by the shoulders and shook me. "You lose everything but that. Leave it on, old lady. I wanna see my name on you when we fuck."

"Brass!"

He tugged at my jeans, and then my panties. They came off fast and he allowed me to step out of them. Then he grabbed my legs, pushed them to the wall, keeping my thighs splayed apart for his face.

"Shit! That feels so good..."

And that was only the first lick. It was somewhere beyond amazing by the third or fourth time his tongue pushed into my wet pussy, lapping cream and readying me for the ecstasy he promised. I tensed, pivoting my fingernails on his scalp for support, the only thing that would keep me from toppling over while his tongue worked quickened.

My heartbeat spiked with the rising pleasure. My knees started to shake around him, but he only tightened his grip, looking up at me with hungry eyes. His tongue smothered my clit and rolled, circular and delicious, its energy shooting straight to my very heavy head.

You'd better fucking come for me, babe, his eyes said. Keep fucking my tongue. Don't stop 'til you squirt. Have you forgotten who's this pussy is?

I heard the answer throttling in my head just as I squeaked out one last breath, before the fire overwhelmed me.

Mine.

He burned the word into my flesh, wild and wicked as the first time he said it, everything I'd ever be for the rest of my life. My muscles convulsed. I pinched my fingers tighter through his hair and screamed.

My ass climbed the wall several inches before rocking into his insatiable mouth again. Bucking, grinding, fucking the man I'd given myself to, loving his sweet control. It was total, overpowering, and sweet, even when he had his face between my legs.

Hot breaths and the cool rush of air where he'd been woke me out of my stupor. I looked down and saw him wiping his mouth, then he stood and began to loosen his belt.

"Get your pretty ass over to the bed."

I nodded, trying to shake the orgasmic tickle out of my legs as I went. The room was a total luxury with padded beds, decorated like a palace. So was the adjoining one we had for Jackie. I almost felt guilty laying down on the big bed, naked and exposed. It was a far cry from the dirtier, duller places we'd always fucked before.

"How does it come so natural for you here?" I whispered, admiring his naked body.

The bed sank down as he settled between my legs, catching my hair in one fist. "You talking about these digs? Shit, babe. I wouldn't think twice about fucking you in the

Taj Mahal. If you think this place is too good for us, think again. I haven't begun to give you what you deserve."

"Yeah?" I reached between my legs for his dick, already poised dangerously close to my pussy lips. "Show me."

His eyes practically burst into flames and melted out of their sockets. He fucked his way right through my hand and swung his hips down, pushing his way inside me until my fingers couldn't hold him anymore.

"Fuck!" Brass growled, his beautiful tattooed chest swelling as the fire danced lower. "I got no problem handing out reminders when you're this tight and wet. Stop thinking, babe. Turn your head off and fuck me as hard as you can."

He kept his thrusts slow. Hard. Intentionally teasing me with rough, long, steady strokes until I began to buck back, the itch in my womb exploding inside me.

Amazing what a little sex could do to clear the mind.

All the worry and doubt eroded, stroke by stroke. Soon, I had my arms and legs wrapped around him tight as he fucked harder, desperately rising to meet his thrusts, every part of me winding up in the sheer need to –

"Come!" Brass growled. "Let it fucking go for me. I wanna feel fireworks around my dick."

His wish, my command. My body couldn't say no to the mad heat roiling my clit, his fullness rocking and thrashing inside me.

I ground my head into the mattress and exploded. Coming with Brass the second time always felt better, longer, sweeter for some reason. I gurgled pure pleasure and rolled my eyes on black and red, sweating and clawing at his back, dying and coming back to life on his dick.

And *coming* was the keyword above all else. I came until it felt like my own soul left my body and then slammed back into these exhausted bones.

Of course, he wasn't done. It was never that easy.

His rough hands tugged at me, rolling me around, setting me on my hands and knees.

"Right there, babe. Let's see how fucking hard this fancy bed shakes when my abs are slapping your ass."

Oh, God. The thought made me horny all over again.

He sank into me, holding me up by the leather shoulders. I couldn't see him behind me, but I knew his eyes were glued to the brand on the back, PROPERTY OF BRASS written in white on black, the light to all the darkness we'd fought through together.

"Fuck," he grunted, thrusting his cock deeper, finding a rougher tempo in his favorite position.

It was quickly becoming mine too. Something about the slap of his balls on my clit really set me off. Soon, the fireworks he wanted flew through my blood again, colorful star bursts becoming screaming meteors.

We fucked hard and fast. The bed shook like it was the middle of a great earthquake, and my hair flopped all over the place. I hoped there'd be time for a shower later to hide the sex hair from Jackie – though my sis knew damned well what was going on almost every night since I'd gotten this jacket.

I was his old lady, and I didn't hide it. I didn't dare

dream of anything else besides screaming his name, loudly and gratefully, an echo for the whole world to absorb.

The leather formed a sweet, sultry cocoon over my flesh. I roasted inside and out, sticky, but not even caring. The greatest heat was still a few more minutes away.

Brass slowed his thrusts just long enough to grab my hair and hold me up, reaching one hand past my naked waist. He pinched and rubbed my clit, vicious little strokes timed to match his new rough thrusts.

"I want you to come with me, babe. I'm not gonna bust 'til I feel your pussy clenched around me. Come on." He quickened his strokes. "Come with me. Let me feel your pulse, your slickness, your heartbeat. Let me feel your love."

The fiery tingle started deep and slow. Strange, given how rough his friction rubbed inside me, rocking me from head to toe, kindling a slow moving firestorm that jerked my hair with him.

God! There was no stopping it when I finally exploded.

My pussy clenched tight around his dick and I barely stopped myself from collapsing on the bed. Brass' rough hands held me up, thrusting at light speed when he felt me start to spasm on his length. He jerked his cock as deep as he could go and all his muscles swelled around me.

"Good girl. Very, very fucking good."

It was the last thing he managed before his voice disappeared into the same orgasmic riptide swallowing me whole. His come burst inside me.

Molten. Deep. Filling.

We rocked and came together, snarling out our pleasure, our eyes rolling in the starry void of our heat. While we were fused, everything we'd done together flashed before me. All our pain and joys, maybe even things yet to come.

"Shit, babe," he said when it was over, pulling out and rolling me onto his chest. "I've never fucked a girl so hard she's seen a ghost."

"Sorry," I whispered, brushing my lips against his. "I was just thinking how much I love you."

He grinned. "Missy, you can look as haunted as you want, long as you're thinking about me. Don't apologize. I'm not sorry for any of this – even the brutal shit – because it led me to right here. It led me to the thing that matters most, as long as I'm alive and breathing. It led me to the fucking best old lady a man could ever ask for."

He thumped his chest, right over his heart, and I laughed. Before I knew it, his lips were heading for mine. We shared another kiss, sunny and warm as the clear Nevada sky.

Thanks!

Want more Nicole Snow? Sign up for my newsletter to hear about new releases, subscriber only goodies, and other fun stuff!

JOIN THE NICOLE SNOW NEWSLETTER! – http://eepurl.com/HwFW1

Thank you so much for buying this book. I hope my romances will brighten your mornings and darken your evenings with total pleasure. Sensuality makes everything more vivid, doesn't it?

If you liked this book, please consider leaving a review and checking out my other erotic romance tales.

Got a comment on my work? Email me at nicolesnowerotica@gmail.com. I love hearing from my fans!

Kisses,
Nicole Snow

More Erotic Romance by Nicole Snow

KEPT WOMEN: TWO FERTILE SUBMISSIVE STORIES

SUBMISSIVE'S FOLLY (SEDUCED AND RAVAGED)

SUBMISSIVE'S EDUCATION

SUBMISSIVE'S HARD DISCOVERY

HER STRICT NEIGHBOR

SOLDIER'S STRICT ORDERS

COWBOY'S STRICT COMMANDS

RUSTLING UP A BRIDE: RANCHER'S PREGNANT CURVES

FIGHT FOR HER HEART

BIG BAD DARE: TATTOOS AND SUBMISSION

MERCILESS LOVE: A DARK ROMANCE

LOVE SCARS: BAD BOY'S BRIDE (Borrow on Kindle Unlimited!)

Outlaw Love/Prairie Devils MC Books

OUTLAW KIND OF LOVE

NOMAD KIND OF LOVE

SAVAGE KIND OF LOVE

WICKED KIND OF LOVE

BITTER KIND OF LOVE

SEXY SAMPLES: <u>BITTER KIND OF LOVE</u>

I: Shades of Betrayal (Alice)

When I felt the knife against my throat, I knew I'd fucked up bad.

Stinger wasn't coming to pull me feet from the fire either. Not this time, not when I'd run away from him and his club like the terrified girl I was.

He'd offered me the world, and I'd forsaken him. Now, I was going to pay the price.

"I'll ask you again, little bitch. *Where. Is. It?*" My interrogator's eyes were pitch black.

God, how many times had I seen eyes like that before? They were as black and dead as the last few months of this new life, lost to the world, abandoned in the deep cold darkness.

"I...I can't remember. I already told you that. I'm not lying!" I spat at the floor and looked up, trying not to shake.

My eyes passed over the patches on his cut: NERO, PRESIDENT, 1%, WRECKING CREW, SLINGERS MC. Skulls wearing cowboy hats and smoking pistols menaced their way out of the leather. Above it all, his black eyes devoured me, darkness set in a bald head and cheeks pocked with scars.

Sick irony twisted my stomach. I'd fled to Idaho to get away from biker gangs intruding on my life, only to have a truly feral MC threatening to make sure I never had to worry about intrusions ever again. And all because I couldn't give him something I didn't know I had, that fucking map my father hid before they murdered him.

"Bullshit!" Nero lowered the knife and gave me a good shove against the wall.

Behind him, another man laughed, giggling like a hyena while he scratched his arm. Nero's head whipped back and he gave the psycho an evil eye.

"Shut the fuck up, Hatter." He drew in a heavy breath before turning back to me, bathing me in those inverted spotlights he had for eyes. "Your amnesia act's not pulling the fucking wool over my eyes, girl. Maybe it worked before, getting every fool from here to Missoula to swallow your shit, but I'm not biting. I know the Rams kept you for days in that shitty clubhouse after we killed your old man and ripped through his fucking truck. Don't tell me the Feds took it. I won't believe that shit for a second."

I looked up at him, hatred swirling in my veins. My fiercest look didn't faze him. All it got me was the knife at my throat again, cold and threatening as ever.

"Who the fuck took it, slut? Did you bring it out here when you decided to move West and shake your pussy on stage? Should I rip apart this whole fucking house looking for it?" Nero looked up at his men and snapped his fingers.

His crew moved behind us, stomping into my tiny kitchen. Crashes blasted my ears as they turned over the table and started to open every drawer and cabinet they could find, hurling out the contents, killing the grim silence with a ferocious clatter.

Shit. He knew damned well I wasn't hiding anything in plates and cups, didn't he?

Maybe it was a new, sick form of torture. I didn't give a damn that they were destroying what little I had. It was the noise that got to me, the thunderous explosion of dishes, silverware, glass, and food hitting every surface within striking distance.

The one called Hatter added his high, insane laugh to the chaos too, a soulless cackle that drummed into my bones.

"Okay! You fucking win! I'll tell you everything I know. Just please...make them *stop*," I screamed, jumping in his arms, wishing I could get his gross hands away.

I nicked my neck on the knife while I was thrashing around. Nero tucked it away, satisfied with my surrender, but not before I felt a warm trickle of angry blood pooling in my cleavage. He blinked, his eyes wide, allowing me to hold one hand to the wound while he clapped his hands and yelled at his men.

"All right, boys! Keep your peckers down and stop ripping shit to kingdom come. Our little raven's gonna sing..."

He smiled, reaching up to run the back of his hand through my black hair. I twisted away, stopping just short of slapping his stupid hand. Jesus, it was tempting, but I knew I'd get pure hell if I laid a finger on him.

The crashing stopped, replaced with wintry silence.

Hatter's sick laughter faded into their heavy, excited breaths. They came tromping back to their boss, surrounding us in a cruel circle that would've made the biggest badass in the world sweat bullets.

My memory gathered itself while I stared into Nero's cold eyes, collating all the terrible things I'd forgotten for months. Everything I'd tried to escape forever.

I was an idiot to think I could run from it. Evil things always caught up with me, no different than this pack of vicious murderers.

"I watched Dad die in their clubhouse. The Rams kept me prisoner," I said, remembering the worst days of my life. "I couldn't have been there more than a few days..."

"You gotta do better than that, little lamb. That shit's the first thing I learned through the Grizzlies grape vine, and it's fucking useless!" His last word exploded in my face like a bomb. "I want those fucking routes. I need your old man's map. Don't give a shit hearing about the Rams' escapades while you were chained down like a bitch."

Don't shake. Don't cry. Don't give him anything except stark, bitter truth.

"The Prairie Devils picked me up. I was with them for...damn, it must've been several weeks. They held onto me while their drama with the Rams dragged on. This man, Stinger –"

It hurt to say his name.

Stinger repulsed me, fascinated me, and stirred more conflicting emotions than any man I'd ever met in my life. I couldn't handle him. I ran, as fast and as far as a bus ticket and a little cash could get me, hoping I'd never have to say his name again.

Nero held up a hand, hissing through his teeth. "I already told you, bitch, I don't need to hear all these little details. I don't give a fuck about hearing how many times they used your tight ass. If you don't spit out something useful in the next two minutes, Hatter and Wasp here are gonna use your holes instead. And I can guarantee they'll give you a pounding a whole lot harder than anything those Prairie Pussies gave you..." He turned the blade in his hands, bored beneath his rage.

I shouldn't have said his name. I'm not worthy to even think it.

My heart sank, thinking about the only man who gave a single crap about me since these demons killed Dad.

Stinger was a total angel, a guardian, handsome as he was strong, determined to keep the brutal world off my back. He protected me, the total opposite of what these idiots thought about the Devils, and I repaid him by fucking off without even saying goodbye.

"It doesn't matter," I whispered, the worst lie I'd told all night. "I didn't see much. The Devils had their own crap going on – one of their brothers almost went to prison. They barely told me anything about their business. Just asked me a bunch of questions until the Rams hit them that night."

"Yeah, yeah. Poison," Nero grunted. "I know all about what those sloppy motherfuckers did. Didn't off a single Prairie Pussy, did they?"

I shook my head, remembering my last night with the

club, nearly all the men laid up and suffering. The tainted whiskey did a number on their stomachs.

But it wasn't the club that mattered. It was *him*, and I was right by his side, holding his hand while he writhed in pain, then laying next to him – repaying the same favor he'd done me the first night I left hell.

Then there was the kiss the next morning, when he was still delirious...

I closed my eyes. It was too damned much.

I was an idiot, and the world didn't offer second chances.

"You're right. None of them died," I said, reluctantly forcing my eyes open.

"Fucking amateurs," Nero growled. "So, what, then? The Pussies cut a deal with the Feds, I know that much. How did the Rams die? That fucking thing had to be at their clubhouse. I know they fucked us over. And I know the Feds didn't tear them a new asshole. Their dicks are too limp these days for massacres and media spectacles. Who killed them?"

I swallowed the painful lump in my throat. Nero stepped closer again, catching the glint in my eye that told him I was holding back.

"You coming clean, or what? Fucking tell me, bitch! You got one chance, and you're losing it by the second." He grabbed my shoulders and pressed me to the wall, hot breath spilling onto my face, carrying the faint and sickly stink of whiskey. "We're not gonna do this same old song and dance all night, girlie."

My feet dangled off the floor as he lifted me higher, hanging my face just a few inches over his repulsive mug. No matter how hard I tried, I couldn't look away, knowing if he wrung out the next bit, it would seriously fuck over the people who'd saved me.

And Stinger too – especially Stinger!

I'd already stabbed him in the back by running. I couldn't twist the knife by fucking over his club – could I?

"I get it." His voice went cold, the anger doused to smoky rage. "Cutting up that pretty skin or having a dick inside you doesn't rustle your panties too much. Hell, you're probably already fucking guys in your off hours at the strip joint, yeah? You got a body worth a few dimes, bitch, and having us steal what you're selling doesn't get you in a fucking twist."

I refused to answer. I had to keep my lips sealed, had to stay quiet. No, my memory wasn't perfect, but I'd be damned if I let it go.

"Let me tell you something." He let my shoes drop to the floor with a shove. "You've never fucked the way we do. You see my bro, Hatter, over there?"

He grabbed my face and twisted it in the right direction. I was forced to look at the skinny, nasty freak behind him, the man who couldn't stop twitching and giggling like a lunatic.

"Show her your goods, brother!" Nero ordered.

Hatter laughed louder as he rolled his leather cut down his arms and pulled up his shirt. I gasped.

Crazy emblems lined his body like every biker, but they

weren't tattoos. They were deep red scars, gouges in his skin. Several long lines of flame were deep red, nearly bleeding. The smoking gun on his chest was lined with thousands of little cuts designed to look like thorns.

The other two men laughed. I felt the blood draining from my face.

"This is what he does for fun," Nero said. "Likes to carve shit up like it's Thanksgiving dinner three hundred and sixty five fuckin' days a year. Not just his own skin neither. Fuck, you oughta take a good look at his dick...this man's the only bastard I've known in all my years who takes razors to his pisser."

The demon grinned and reached for his jeans, squeezing his crotch. Then he reached into the holsters near his waist and pulled out two matching daggers, holding them across the lump in his pants, giving me a smile straight from the darkest corner of hell.

Nero knew what he was doing. The bastard *knew* I'd take damage to keep my secrets, but not *this*. I couldn't fight the monster leering at me with his knives and manic evil, drool slipping down his chin.

No, no, Jesus Christ, no.

I couldn't let this sick animal have his way with me. I wouldn't survive.

Right then and there, I broke. My cowardly mind spun, ready to cough up anything to get me out of this. Anything to take away the pure fucking evil circling me in this room.

Hatter reached up, began to unzip his fly. I couldn't even stand to see it. Terror hit me like lightning, and I flinched in Nero's hands.

"Stop it. Stop. Call him off," I whimpered. "I know where the stupid map is."

"Okay," he said softly. "I'm gonna give you one more chance, bitch, and only one. *Who* killed the Rams? Who the fuck was there before the Feds rolled in? Who took it?"

"The Devils. The whole club combed the place over good before they gave it up to the cops. If anyone's got my Dad's stuff, it's them. The map's at their clubhouse, stuffed up in some office. Now, please...let me go."

Nero never smiled. He just nodded and did as I asked, letting me fall to the floor. He coughed once, watching me collapse in a sobbing heap on the ground.

Cold. Satisfied. Happy, maybe.

And why shouldn't he be? The bastard just watched me sell my soul.

"Come on, Shark," he said to the larger man in the corner. "Bitch finally gave us a gold nugget we can use. We'll call it in to the rest of the club and figure out the best plan of attack."

The man with the VP tag and the silver teeth nodded, and began to follow him out. I looked up, staring through my tears, wishing I could see through the walls, straight to the dense gray winter sky.

I'm sorry, Stinger. I'm sorry.

God, I'm so fucking sorry!

I saw it in my mind already. These assholes weren't going to waste much time. They'd show up not long after Christmas if they had to, a sneak attack. Nero and his men would burst in with guns blazing, brandishing their blades. They'll kill, torture, and burn anyone they had to for that damned map.

The Missoula boys would never see it coming. Blaze, Tank, Moose...Stinger.

They'd all fight like mad until their last breath. But it wouldn't be enough. They'd be flattened on the ground with holes in their chests.

I'd watched the club nearly get slaughtered in one ambush while I was there, and the Slingers promised hot lead instead of half-assed poison.

I thought about Stinger's strong face, lifeless and pale, a neat dark hole through his head.

Fuck. This couldn't be happening!

I couldn't let him or any of his guys die because of my screw up.

My hands stretched across my face and just kept going, pulling on my skin. I wanted it to hurt. My surrender was going to get a lot of good men killed, and probably their old ladies too. I might as well have put a gun to Stinger's temple and pulled the trigger myself.

I stopped stretching my face to total hell and looked up. The other two demons, Hatter and Wasp, lingered. I wanted them gone like yesterday. I wasn't sure there would ever be a way to bleach their evil presence out of my rental.

After this, I had to leave. I had to get out and go far, far away.

Maybe I could leave the Devils an anonymous tip, a

letter or a call to tell them what was coming...but first, I needed these killers *gone*.

Shit, why weren't they moving, following their nasty leader out the door?

"Hey!" I screamed, my life returning. Nero stopped with his VP at my front door and turned. "We're done here, aren't we? Take your guys and go. I gave you what I promised."

At last, I saw his smile, evil and crooked as the rest of him. "There's a special place in hell for traitors and cunts who can't keep their lips sealed. Don't worry, baby, your friends from the Prairie Pussies will be joining you down there soon. Daddy's waiting too. Old Mickey's paying for some seriously fucked up sins on Satan's bench right now, I'd wager..."

My eyes bulged. My lungs felt like they'd been filled with cement. I couldn't even shake my head or ask him what the hell he was talking about. It was all there in his savage face.

"I'm gonna give you boys an hour with this bitch. Have your fun and then clean up the mess. We'll dump her body off on the way to Montana."

Nero was out the door, his VP behind him. I took one look at the two smiling assholes closing in on me fast, trying not to let my knees turn into mud.

Run. Get away. Fight.

I hurled myself downstairs, heading for the basement, listening to their heavy boots clomping behind me. The last thing I thought before my screams pierced the darkness was Stinger.

I hurled my frenzied wishes, my prayers, my everything high into the cold, indifferent winter sky. I would've given anything for a miracle, anything for him to hear it and come for me.

Yes, I prayed, even when I saw what a total, undeserving bitch I'd become, the last girl in the world who deserved a rescue by the man who haunted her dreams.

But I wasn't stupid. The universe never, ever worked like that. I didn't believe in coincidence or miracles, and I definitely didn't deserve one after what I'd done.

Shit! It was so fucking dark down here, and I didn't dare turn on the lights and give them an easier time. I ran into the washing machine, its cold metal slapping my hands. When I looked up, the bikers' dark shadows blocked the hall, boxing me in.

When Hatter lunged, pulling at my hair, I lost it.

The screams, the prayers, and everything else went numb. He whirled me around, slapping me against the wall before I lost my balance and began to fall. Nothing broke it. Nothing caught me. Nothing except brutal regret as I hit the floor and they started tearing at my clothes.

That thing they say about your whole damned life flashing before your eyes right before you die? I thought it was crap – until it happened.

I remember everything, past and present flashing like strobe lights, colliding jigsaws in my head. Every piece of Stinger, I tried to cling onto, but I couldn't. It was all coming in a blizzard, churning too fast, the few good pieces always out of reach.

I'd lived on a merciless ledge, and I was an idiot to think there'd be anything different at my life's sudden dead end.

One second, I caught a fragment. Just one.

I remembered Stinger's warmth, his strength, his powerful arms wrapped around me, so real my heart stopped shaking to tatters in my ribs. And then it was gone in a wink, replaced with the savage wolves behind me, grabbing me by the ankles and ripping at my clothes...

Look for Bitter Kind of Love at your favorite retailer!

Printed in Great Britain
by Amazon